The
Water Dancers

wm

WILLIAM MORROW

An Imprint of HarperCollins*Publishers*

The Water Dancers

TERRY GAMBLE

HarperCollins books may be purchased for educational, business, or sales promotional use. For information please write: Special Markets Department, HarperCollins Publishers Inc., 10 East 53rd Street, New York, NY 10022.

FIRST EDITION

Designed by Claire Naylon Vaccaro

Printed on acid-free paper

Library of Congress Cataloging-in-Publication Data
Gamble, Terry.
The water dancers : a novel / Terry Gamble.— 1st ed.
p.   cm.
ISBN 0-06-054266-7
1. World War, 1939–1945—Veterans—Fiction.   2.
Michigan, Lake, Region—Fiction.   3. Women domestics—
Fiction.   4. Summer resorts—Fiction.   5. Social classes—
Fiction.   6. Rich people—Fiction.   7. Amputees—Fiction.
I. Title.
PS3607.A434 W3   2003
813'.6—dc21   2002043245

03   04   05   06   07   WBC/BVG   10   9   8   7   6   5   4   3   2

TO PATSY

Jesus answered,

"I tell you, if my disciples keep silence,

the stones will shout aloud."

LUKE 19:40

Ah, could we but once more return to our forest glade and tread as formerly upon the
soil with proud and happy heart! On the hills with bended bow, while nature's flowers
bloomed all around the habitation of nature's child, our brothers once abounded, free
as the mountain air, and their glad shouts resounded from vale to vale, as they chased
o'er the hills, the mountains, rowed and followed in the otter's track.

Oh, return, return! Ah, never again shall this time return.

It is gone, and gone forever like a spirit passed.

MAC-KE-TE-BE-NESSY

(Andrew J. Blackbird from *History of
the Ottawa and Chippewa Indians of Michigan*,
the Ypsilanti Job Printing House, 1887)

ge-oph-a-gy, *n.* *Pathol.* The practice of eating earthy matter, esp. clay or chalk.
Often assoc. with malnutrition or religious ceremonies.

lith-oph-a-gy, *n.* The eating of stones.

C ONTENTS

A C K N O W L E D G M E N T S

First, my deepest gratitude to my agent, Carole Bidnick, for her tenacious, undaunted belief in me. You said I could, you said I could . . .

Second, to my writers' church, sisters bound by more than words, without whom I would not have kept going: Elissa Alford, Sheri Cooper Bounds, Phyllis Florin, Suzanne Lewis, Mary Beth McLure-Marra, Alison Walsh Sackett.

Third, to my fine and clearheaded editor at William Morrow, Jennifer Brehl, who wanted this book, and to her assistant, Kelly O'Connor, for seeing the possibilities.

Fourth, to my generous teachers: Donna Levin and Adair Lara for their faith; Lynn Freed for her wisdom.

Fifth, to my early-on editor, Alan Rinzler, and my later-on editor, Linda Schlossberg, for their tough love and kindness.

Sixth, to my father, James Gamble, who shared with me his love for Michigan.

And to all of the angels who helped me along: Peggy Knickerbocker, Mark Coggins, Monica Mapa, Susan Pinkwater, Mike Padilla, George DeWitt, Liz Willner, Mary Jean Dominguez, Sheryl Cotleur, Marty Krasney, Winnay Wemigwase, and especially, Patsy Ketterer.

And lastly, to Peter, who has done everything possible to support me, and to Chapin and Anna, who know their mother is a writer. All my love.

P R O L O G U E

1942

Rachel Winnapee's grandmother was dying. Her chest rattled like stones. The girl had found stones in stranger places—a pocket, a cup, even her mouth. Perhaps her grandmother *had* swallowed stones?

Dusk came late in the Michigan summers, the sun not setting till nearly ten. Down by Horseshoe Lake, fires crackled, cooking something hunted or stolen—like the shingles Aunt Minnie had hidden beneath her porch—found or stolen, she wouldn't say. Not that it mattered. The Horseshoe Band of the Odawa were squatters to begin with, and even the lake, the beach, the woods belonged to someone else.

By nightfall, her grandmother's breath had become like the wind that shuddered through the pipe in winter. A high, thin note—in and out. The girl counted the breaths, listened as they slowed, watched as her grandmother's feet and hands became rocks, faintly blue.

A pale band of moonlight drew shadows along the walls as Rachel moved about the shack, opening boxes, looking for stones she would need to anchor her grandmother when her spirit rose to the *Gitchi-manitou*, became sky.

When she had collected three of them, she laid them on her grandmother's chest.

"Grandmother," Rachel said, shaking her on the bed they shared. "Grandmother."

But her grandmother's skin was drawn back, her teeth grown big in her head. The girl waited, watching her throat, but there were no more breaths. Setting one last stone on her grandmother's chest, the girl crawled in next to her, wore her like skin.

The next morning, when her Uncle Jedda came, Rachel screamed at him to leave. *My home,* she said. *My body.* Two days later, Rachel hurled one of the stones from her grandmother's chest at the door where her Aunt Minnie stood.

"There's no corn in that husk, Rachel. Let her be."

"Get out!"

"Taw," said Minnie, backing away on the porch. "The stink!"

Outside, the sizzling cadence of heat bugs, the sullen slop of waves. The chanting had started. In the shack down the beach, Uncle Jedda was drinking. To keep herself from wailing, Rachel held her ears.

By the time the nun came from the convent, all the Indians had complained, saying that the old woman stank too bad to bury her right, with paint, song, and drums. Mother gone, uncle drunk, and her Aunt Minnie was no better. Best that the child be taken to town to live in the convent with the other girls who had been abandoned like junked cars in a yard.

"Burn the shack," someone said.

Before the nun could stop them, they pried Rachel from her grandmother, dragged her out. Soon, the cabin became a pyre. The wood kindled, snapped, combusted, but as it burned, the smoky outline of a woman rose from the flames like a *manitou* and sped into the sky.

"Look!" Rachel screamed.

"Sweet Jesus," said the nun, grabbing the child, holding fast.

Later, they would say it was only a trick of light, a singed flickering of sweet grass, but Rachel knew it was her grandmother's spirit that went up in fire, the ashes falling about her like rain.

Part One

Chapter One

1945

For six weeks, Rachel had been working at the Marches'
house—six weeks of lining drawers, airing closets, carrying
laundry, and she still couldn't keep the back stairs straight. One
flight led from the kitchen to the dining room, the other up two floors to the
bedrooms. Even the hallways confused her, twisting or stopping altogether.
Wings and porches splayed out. Doors banged into each other. Twelve bedrooms and no one to use them but an old woman, the hope of one son, the ghost
of another, and a girl who had died in infancy.

Even Mr. March would only come toward the end of August, if he came at
all. It was a house of women. Since the beginning of the war, women had prepared the food, cleaned the floors, kept the books, given the orders, folded the
sheets, scraped the dough off butcher's block. Then there was the ironing.
Rachel had scorched three damask napkins before she got it right. The Kelvina-
tor in the pantry made her crazy with its humming. The oven smelled of gas.
Something was always boiling, fueling the humidity. When she had left the
convent that morning to come to work, the air was so close, the dormitory
where the girls slept had grown ripe with sweat.

"Sister told us you could iron," said the cook, Ella Mae.

Her old, black eyes rested on Rachel's braids as though there might be bugs in there or worse.

"Remember," Ella Mae went on, shaking a finger, their dark eyes meeting, "the Marches have took you in for charity."

Charity. Even Sister Marie had made that clear from the start. *Our campanile, our statue of Mary—all gifts from Lydia March. You may think she has everything, but fortune is a two-edged sword. The Marches have given God a son and a baby girl. They will pay you four dollars a week.*

The Marches' house smelled of must, camphor, lilacs, and decayed fish that wafted up from the beach at night. Located on the very tip of a crooked finger of land, it had the best view of all the houses on Beck's Point. Who Beck had been, no one seemed to remember, but one of the girls at the convent told Rachel it used to be a holy place where spirits dwelled and no one dared to live. Now it was chock full of summer houses, all white and lined up like pearls on a necklace.

Across the harbor, the town of Moss Village sat at the base of limestone bluffs, residue from an ancient, salty sea. Then came the glacier, molding and carving Lake Michigan like a totem of land, the Indians at the bottom, then the French, a smattering of Polish farmers, the priests, fur traders, fishermen, lumberjacks, and, later, the summer people.

And always the church. Even after the first one burned, the Jesuits built a second, then a third, its steeple rising above everything else. Next to it—a large lump of a brick building full of girls, some small, some older, all dark. All sent or left or brought by the nuns to learn American ways and to forget all things Indian. No more dancing to spirits with suspicious, tongue-twisting names. No more clothes of deerskin. Put the girls to work, and when they were big enough, some summer family—preferably Catholic—would take them.

Beyond the tip of the point, the water widened into a bay, the trees and hills

beyond the town of Chibawassee faint upon the opposite shore. From the
southern edge, the bay extended west toward the horizon. To the north of
Beck's Point was the harbor—docks and trimmed lawns, raked beaches,
moored boats—the best port between Grand Traverse and Mackinaw. From
every window, Rachel could see water, hear water, smell it, taste it. Not like
Horseshoe Lake, which was small, tranquil, almost a pond.

"So much water," Rachel said to Ella Mae's daughter, who was helping her
with the fruit.

"Like the flood itself," said Mandy, who could not swim. "Gives me the
heebie-jeebies." A girl had drowned once, she told Rachel. Years before. A girl
from the convent.

"I know how to swim," said Rachel.

Today, they were helping Ella Mae make cherry pie. Ella Mae worked the
flour into butter until her thick, brown arms were gloved with white. Rachel
pitted the fruit. It was July, and the cherries brought up from Traverse City
were at their best. The juice ran down her arms. Whenever Ella Mae looked
away, the girl hungrily licked them. She was always hungry, even when her
stomach was full. As a child, she had licked stones and dirt, ravenous for their
minerals, as if she could consume the earth itself.

Mandy was watching her. "How old are you?"

"Sixteen," Rachel said, running her tongue around her lips. She was never
quite sure.

"Sixteen? I thought you and me's the same age."

"How old are you?"

"*Seventeen,*" said Mandy.

The air filled with sugar, butter, cherry. Because of the war, it had been hard
to get butter these last few years. That and gasoline. Stockings. Things Rachel
hadn't even known to miss.

"Chocolate," said Ella Mae, listing the rationed items. "Try to find *that*."

Ella Mae had taught Rachel to roll the chilled dough out thin and cut it so as to waste little. Rachel wadded up doughy crumbs and put them in her pocket to eat later. She wondered if Ella Mae would taste like chocolate if Rachel licked her. Same with Mandy and Jonah, Ella Mae's husband. Their skin was darker than hers, which was the color of milky cocoa.

Outside, Mrs. March, her gray hair coiled on top of her head, pointed to the empty fishpond. Victor, the gardener followed her finger, shrugged. After the war, he seemed to be saying. After the war we will fill the pond with fish, the lake with boats, the house with laughter.

A guest was arriving that afternoon. "Before the war, we filled all five guest rooms," Ella Mae said. "The senator from Ohio stayed a week."

Mandy dipped into the bowl and swiped a cherry. Rachel almost reached out and touched Mandy's lips, they were so big and wide and black. Where'd you get those lips? she was about to ask, but Mandy spoke first, fingering Rachel's thick, black braids. "Where'd you get that *hair?*" she said. "I could make it better."

Rachel touched her hair. Unbraided, it curled down her spine and spoke of something not Indian. French, perhaps. The fur trader who had taken her grandmother as his common-law wife.

"You're plain," Mandy said. "That nose of yours. Where'd you get that nose?"

Even Rachel had to admit her nose was different, not flat and squished like most Odawa's, but longer and beaked like a bird of prey.

"And your cheeks!" said Mandy. She blew out her own until they were rounder than the girl's.

Rachel looked at Mandy's head—twenty tiny braids to her own thick two. It had been so long since someone had touched her, combed her hair. In the churchyard there was a statue of Mary holding the baby Jesus. Sometimes, the girl wanted to crawl right into Mary's arms, her face so sad like she knew she'd have to give her baby up.

Jesus died for your sins, the nuns told Rachel.

The Marches' daughter had died in the great influenza. There was an empty crib in one of the bedrooms, the curtains perpetually drawn. Had the Virgin Mary known her own sweet-faced son would die? Perhaps her own grief deafened her to Rachel's pleas to send her home to Horseshoe Lake.

"I wouldn't mind," Rachel said, letting Mandy touch her hair. Rachel's hands had grown sticky with cherries. Jesus bleeds for me, she thought as she picked up a towel, reddened it with her palms.

The Buick idled in the driveway as Jonah and Victor hauled up the fiancée's luggage. One trunk, two suitcases, three other handled boxes for hats and bottles and shoes. The boats on the harbor clanged in the breeze as Rachel and Mandy unpacked clothes, sorting piles for putting away or pressing.

"Girl," said Mandy, "you're going to be ironing till next Tuesday."

"Truly," Rachel replied. From the window, she could look across the harbor to Moss Village with its piers and brick buildings, the spire of the Catholic church. She wanted to ask Mandy how the one son had been killed and when the other would be home. Two flags hung in the parlor window, each with a star— blue for the son still fighting in the Pacific, gold for the one lost in Belgium. She held a cashmere sweater up to her chest and stroked it.

"You'll catch hell if she sees you," said Mandy.

Church bells rang across the water where the Odawa had once lived, their villages spreading for miles up the shore. Before the fur traders came, before the priests.

Mandy started to say something else, but the door flew open and the fiancée walked in. She was older than they were, closer to twenty and yellow-haired. Her name was Miss Elizabeth.

"Has either of you seen my bathing suit?"

Hair like butter. Rachel wanted to run her fingers through it, sniff it to see if it was real. She pointed to the bureau. "In there."

"Thank you." Miss Elizabeth's nails were shiny and red. She opened the drawer, plucked out the suit, started from the room. Over her shoulder, she called back to Rachel, "That sweater you're holding? It snags if you so much as look at it."

"Hmph," said Mandy after Miss Elizabeth had gone. "Like she knows. That girl's got more clothes than Bathsheba."

"What's he like?"

"Who?"

"The one she's marrying."

Mandy started to hum. "A fool since he met her. She come up one summer with Miss Serena Boyd and beelined straight for Mr. Woody. Not that the Marches objected. She's one of the St. Louis Parkers. My mama said she's determined as a mule in heat."

"A *mule?*" Rachel laughed and shook her head. "She's too pretty to be a mule."

Mandy, laughing, too, reached out and tugged one of her braids. "And what do *you* know about pretty?"

The kitchen had new linoleum, blue as the lake, but the floor sagged and one of the windows was cracked. They sat on the kitchen floor, Rachel leaning against Mandy's legs. The comb running across her scalp felt like the cool hands of Jesus himself. Ella Mae was baking something with layers of chocolate shallow as puddles. At midmorning, the house filled with the smell of chocolate, loam-rich and bittersweet.

Mandy raked up a tuft of hair. "I've never seen such nappy hair in my life 'cept on a colored girl. You colored?"

"Indian. Part."

"What's the other part?"

Her grandmother's Frenchman. The German lumberjack her mother had met in a bar. "Mixed," she said.

Mandy divided Rachel's scalp into eighths, braided and looped it with pieces of yarn and rubber bands, weaving hair the way her grandmother had woven sweet grass into baskets.

Over the sink, the buzzer sounded. All eyes turned to see what number had popped up. "Miss Elizabeth's awake," said Mandy. "You're done."

Miss Elizabeth had been there for almost two weeks. Every morning, Rachel brought her tea and a muffin while she stayed curled under her covers, a few strands of yellow hair escaping the sheets. Some days, Rachel would hear her laughing with Mrs. March. Their laughter warmed the house as they discussed linen and china and waited for the son to come home. Miss Elizabeth's golden hair was pulled back from her face like wings. She must be an angel, the girl thought—a beautiful, messy angel who scattered her jewelry everywhere, left cigarettes burning in ashtrays, dropped her clothes on the floor. Rachel would pick them up and fold them, trying not to covet. Even so, she had tried on a ring with a green stone surrounded by tiny pearls.

All across the bureau, Miss Elizabeth had set out photographs. In one, her head turned at an angle, her eyes gazing upward. Her lashes and brows were dark, her eyes gray, her hair a white cloud against a smudged sky. Mandy told her it was Miss Elizabeth's engagement picture. Rachel thought it was beautiful.

As she set the tray down on the bureau, a snapshot stuck in the mirror frame caught the girl's attention. In it, a young man sat on the dock, happily kicking the water. Spray rose in the air. Beyond him, boats were moored, just as now. The man's eyes were pale, possibly blue or green. Rachel thought, *It is* his *harbor. It belongs to him.* He was smiling into the camera, but Rachel was almost certain he was smiling into her. She felt the spray as he kicked it.

This is not stealing, she told herself as she peeled the snapshot from the mirror—quickly, stealthily, before Miss Elizabeth woke. *This is borrowing,* the way one borrows a cup of sugar or butter that has been rationed.

She slipped the photograph into her pocket. Pushing back the curtains with triumphant energy, Rachel wanted to point to the harbor and say to Miss Elizabeth, Isn't it beautiful? It will all be yours!

But Miss Elizabeth only groaned.

The room smelled of cigarettes and last evening's perfume, a half-empty glass of bourbon. Rachel picked up a sweater from the floor and laid it on the chair. "Your tea's ready."

Miss Elizabeth's hands peeked out like turtles' heads. They pushed down the blanket until two eyes, puffy and closed, appeared on the horizon of the sheet. The wings of her hair fell loosely about the pillow. Last night, Rachel had seen Miss Elizabeth coming home from the club on the arm of a young man, not the Marches' son. The man was laughing at a joke he'd made, and Miss Elizabeth, too, was laughing, but to Rachel, Miss Elizabeth's laughter was like the hollow cones of tin on a jingle dress. Miss Elizabeth had tripped and nearly fallen, stumbled past Rachel, but didn't seem to see her.

Now Miss Elizabeth slowly opened her eyes, squinted at Rachel. She didn't say a word. Then she laughed. "Well, if I had a do like that, I'd be the *hit* of the parade!"

Rachel turned to the mirror. She cocked her head, examined herself with solemn regard. Her eyebrows were black and thick as a man's over too-big eyes. Her hair, braided by Mandy, was as complicated as the quill baskets her grandmother used to make. She wondered if she looked pretty, thought of asking, but Miss Elizabeth had sunk back into the bed and pulled the covers up.

Ella Mae asked Rachel to get out the big pots for dinner. "Not those!" she said, shaking her head at the pots the girl pulled from the cupboard. "They's for corn. The *big* pots. The ones we use for lobsters."

Miss Elizabeth's laughter still burning in her ear, Rachel banged the pots onto the stove top. "Cone, cone," she said, imitating Ella Mae's voice. "They's fo' cone."

"What's got into *you?*"

Rachel slid onto a stool across from Mandy, twisted off a rubber band, and started undoing the braids.

Mandy yelped. "Took me an hour to braid that hair!"

Rachel clawed at the tangled braids. One by one, eight rubber bands hit the floor, her hair raveling like rope. She ran her fingers through snarls of black. Undone, her hair was wild, kinked from braiding.

Mandy shot her a glance. "Looks even worse than before!"

Rachel threw down a rubber band and screamed, *"Then fix it!"*

Mandy laughed. Rachel lunged at her, but Ella Mae came between them, her teeth, gum, lips in the girl's face. Ella Mae held her while Rachel tried to bite. Ella Mae said, "Stop this sass."

The doorbell sounded. Ella Mae did not let go. Her chest was soft and deep. "Child," she said, "child. You are *charity*."

Rachel pulled away. Through the window, they could see the Western Union van. As Jonah went to answer the door, Ella Mae strained her ears. Even Mandy and Rachel stopped glaring and listened. Except for the radio, all was quiet. Ella Mae flicked it off, said *hush* to no one in particular, waited for Jonah to come back downstairs. Low voices. A resigned creak. A slam and a wail as Miss Elizabeth ran through the house.

Jonah pushed through the kitchen door, leaned against the radio, wouldn't look at anyone.

Ella Mae laid her hand on his arm. "Dead?"

Jonah squinted up at the buzzer like there were answers in numbers. "Missing."

"Missing?"

"In the Philippine Sea," Jonah said. Something about a plane. Something about an explosion.

"A plane?" said Ella Mae. "But he was on a *boat*."

The air had turned briny. A wave rushed over Rachel, caused her to shudder. She touched her forehead, her chest, her shoulders. She fingered the snapshot in her pocket.

All afternoon, Ella Mae prepared the leg of lamb. Rationing had made meat scarce, so the butcher sold chances to buy it at a nickel apiece, profiting from the scarcity. This week, Mrs. March had been lucky. By evening the air was succulent with the smell of fat and flesh. Mandy eyed the wine goblets as Rachel lined them up.

"My daddy says drinking's from the devil," Mandy said. Her voice was brisk and happy. "These Marches are going to hell."

Rachel repositioned a tall-stemmed glass, replying if that were true, then half the people she knew growing up were going to burn, and faster than the Marches, who at least used glasses.

But Mandy thought all Catholics were sinners. The pope, she said, was the anti-Christ. Rome—the Great Harlot.

Rachel didn't know about the pope or Rome. She only knew that the *Gitchi-manitou* was the great spirit whose eyes were the sun by day, the moon by night, and that Jesus bled for her.

Mandy looked at her with pity. "It's the priest, you know. Every Thursday, it's the priest who comes to dinner."

Rachel shrugged and headed back to the kitchen. Both Mandy and Mrs. March seemed sure God was on their side, but Mandy hedged her bets with "the Bible this" and "the Bible that" while Mrs. March prayed her rosary. At the stove, Ella Mae was laying slices of lamb in pools of mint sauce. Fussing over the plates, she set out plump, honey-colored biscuits the way Rachel's Aunt Minnie would have set out stones for the dead.

At dinner, Miss Elizabeth's face was swollen, her hair pulled tightly back. Father Tom said grace, praying for the safe return of the Marches' son.

"Amen," said Mrs. March.

"Amen," said Rachel and Mandy as they served the soup. Rachel saw Miss Elizabeth's fingers open and close around a knife, saw the knife still shaking when she let it go. Mrs. March stared into her soup as if she could read lentils like tea leaves. Rachel could not read tea leaves, but she knew one thing. The boy in the photograph could *not* be dead. She knew it sure as she knew there'd be rain by morning or that the geese were heading south.

Mrs. March's hand was steady as she sipped the soup, but on the table all around her, spoons, forks, knives vibrated. Looking over her shoulder, Rachel saw Miss Elizabeth try to be strong, to hold her head high like Mrs. March. Mrs. March reminded Rachel of a statue, the way she would sit at her desk, writing letters, drafting checks, her spine rigid and straight. Over her bed hung a crucified Jesus, but Rachel couldn't imagine Mrs. March kneeling before anyone.

Later, as Rachel and Mandy cleared the bowls away and put out plates for the lamb, Mrs. March turned to Father Tom. "Victor refuses to fill the pond. 'What's the point?' he asked me."

The priest was weak-chinned, pale-eyed.

"Did you tell him to get more fish?"

"He says there aren't any."

"Still," said Father Tom, stroking his nonexistent chin, "the pond looks better filled."

With a shaking hand, Miss Elizabeth poured another glass of wine and drank it, casting Mrs. March a thin, watery glance. Drops of red wine stained the tablecloth. She bunched a napkin in her fist. "Do you think . . . ?" she started. Her hand flew to her mouth.

"Perhaps, dear," said Mrs. March, "you would be happier upstairs."

Miss Elizabeth nodded, pushed away from the table, rose to leave. The priest rose with her, but she lifted her hand. "Please don't."

Rachel looked down at the lamb still heaped on Miss Elizabeth's plate. Mrs. March smiled at her. In a spent, dry voice, she said, "Rachel." It was the first time Mrs. March had said her name. For an instant, their eyes met and stitched together.

Rachel could barely contain herself. She would tell Mrs. March her son was alive. Injured, yes, but living. An explosion, Jonah had said. Rachel could imagine it all. Halfway around the world, past plains and mountains, across oceans, a man arced through the sky in a burst of flame. Oh, the drumming! Oh, the keening wails of chants! Her heart beat harder as she started to say "Mrs. March," but before she could speak, Mrs. March's face seemed to freeze into a mask, her skin peeling back to bone. A cloud like a giant mushroom rose from her head and settled as Rachel's words evaporated. The priest was saying something about a boat race as Rachel squeezed her eyes against the vision.

When she opened them, Rachel saw there was nothing. No smoke. No screams. No rain of fire.

"Are you all right?" said Mrs. March.

Her head still filled with drumming on some half-forgotten lake, the girl recalled a burning hut, a spirit rising, someone's hand upon her arm.

"Yes," she whispered.

Mrs. March gave Rachel a long, appraising look. "Please be so kind," she said, "as to take out Miss Elizabeth's plates. And Rachel? Please tell Ella Mae you are welcome to the leftovers."

Rachel sat in the kitchen eating cold meat and the dregs of soup. From now on, she would taste charity in the cracked bones of lamb.

Later, after the dishes were done and the house lay quiet, she walked back to the convent along the harbor. In the distance, heat lightning flickered. Every other house on Beck's Point sat dark, waiting for the sons to come home. In the bars of Moss Village, there was no laughter, just the hoarse rememberings of old men happy to get a drink. A loon wailed, split the water, and Rachel stopped to listen, suddenly alert as if to a sign.

The blue lights at the ends of the docks pulsed steady as heartbeats in the August night. Rachel shuddered, wished she had a sweater. She hoped she could smooth out her hair. Tonight she would pray over a stolen snapshot, tomorrow she would confess her sins. She would go to Father Tom, say forgive me. She would say, He bleeds for me.

CHAPTER TWO

1946

The train rocked inexorably north. Woody's left side hurt all the way from his abdomen through his hips, his thigh, the place below the knee where the rest of his leg should have been. The changing of trains in Chicago had been a jostling, awkward affair—the nurse and the porters, his father directing everyone. Woody had tried to get out of the wheelchair but couldn't manage the steps. People had stared. Someone had actually saluted—saluted! It had been six months since he'd given a sharp salute to the officer who'd discharged him from the hospital. Now all Woody could muster was a limp wave back.

The club car smelled of cigars and diesel, the leather on the armrests was worn from the palms of travelers. They had crossed into Michigan after Gary, Indiana. Three summers had passed without his coming to Beck's Point. The last had been '42. He remembered the dance at the club, both he and his brother, Lip, in their officers' uniforms, Elizabeth whispering into Woody's ear how his hat made him look too grown up, then throwing back her head and laughing. They had thought it all would be over soon. They knew exactly how it would turn out. Lipscott Evans March, who was made for medals, would be the decorated hero, returning victorious to run the family's bank. Woody, on the other hand, would find some less demanding pastime. Bonds, perhaps.

But Lip had not come back. And now Woody was preempted, seated across from his father in a club car hurtling north past the factories of southern Michigan. Twice Elizabeth had come to see him in the hospital in California. She had held his hand, her eyes tracing down his leg. We thought you were dead, she kept telling him, and slowly it occurred to him that she had already mourned. She denied it vehemently, but he insisted it was so. Even when he arrived back in St. Louis at the end of winter to black, leafless trees and relentless brick. *God*, he had said to Elizabeth, *I can't even walk.*

He fingered the rosary his mother had given him. The dome of his father's head rose above the *Journal.* The paper rustled, his father glanced at the rosary. That *thing*, his father would have called it. And Woody might have agreed. Whatever it had symbolized was lost to him. He had seen crosses on a field marking the dead beneath them. But the dead stayed dead, and still he fingered the cross. It was something to hold in his palm, numb from the fusion of flesh to metal. They'd actually seen the plane coming toward them. It was so small, it looked as though it could be batted away like an insect. He hadn't believed what he was hearing—the shouts, the gunners strafing the water. When the explosion came, he had turned to the man next to him to say, Did you see that? But the man was overboard, and Woody was clutching a rail that had turned exquisitely hot.

"You need a drink?" said his father. "I can call the man."

"No need," said Woody, turning away, palming the rosary back into his pocket. Shame had always been associated with his mother's faith. His grandparents had even made his father wait a year before marrying Lydia Forrester, as if her papist bent rendered her unsuitable for their refined, Protestant blood.

A gutter religion, Woody's paternal grandmother had called the Roman Catholic Church, insisting that he and Lip be brought up Presbyterian. But his mother's Catholicism persisted, even after she became the banker's wife. It seeped into their prayers at night, along with the quick, furtive crossings. *Mother forgive me,* thought Woody.

Now his parents slept apart, their marriage cold as ash. His father still showed up at dinners in tweed and an ascot, at weddings and funerals in pin-striped suits. When Lip had died, his father had cried in a separate room, if he had cried at all.

We thought you had died, Elizabeth kept saying, and Woody had responded, *Yes.*

Yes, what?

He had died.

And so she broke it off. Woody couldn't blame her, really. He rested his head against the window, waiting for that first glimpse of lake. He and his father had barely spoken since St. Louis. His father's skin was dappled with liver spots—the skin of some Scotsman five generations back. Woody wanted to say, I know you wouldn't have chosen me to succeed you. But it seemed too obvious for words. A plane had born down, and he had clutched the rail, letting go only when the piece of metal had pierced his leg, flinging him into the sea. They'd given him up for dead.

Lip would have done it differently. He would have seen the plane and been on the guns. The kind of man you'd want at the boardroom table. Not like Woody, always questioning.

"The lake," Woody said, nodding at the sliver of blue that appeared beyond the hills.

His father took out his watch, held it away from his face. "Four more hours," he said. "Hope Jonah remembers the ice."

Woody stared at his father, wondered if the old man had felt the same sort of dread about returning to Beck's Point that he was feeling now. His father—Charles to his mother, Mr. March to his employees, Sir to the servants—had stopped spending summers with his wife years ago, using the bank as an excuse to limit the occasional one-week visit to a week—just long enough to take out his boat a few times. The *Blue Heron* seemed to be the only thing his father cared about. Stay the course, he would tell Woody. Steer straight.

Woody closed his eyes. Four more hours. The hot stinging had started again in his left knee. Nerves, the doctor told him. It would take some time for them to settle down.

"Nurse!" said Woody.

Soon she would come. Woody would tell her what he needed. His father would take refuge behind his paper as the nurse filled the hypodermic, pushed up Woody's sleeve. *My dear,* his mother would call out from the porch while Jonah helped him from the car. She would come down the steps, touch her lips to his cheek. She wouldn't mention the war—just pat his hand and say, *You're home.*

Touch made him physically ill. Woody never liked it, even as a child. Fortunately, there was little of it then. Now it seemed constant. Ever since the first hospital in Manila, hands had traversed his flesh. Hands of strangers—lifting, moving, thumbing up his lids, pressing his chest, dabbing, cutting. Hands had taken away his leg. Or did he dream that?

Now he was stretched out on the bed of his childhood summers, one leg useless, the other mostly gone. Lying back against the pillow Woody thought the fingers of the hand sponging his belly were cold, but he could no longer be sure. Certain kinds of touch registered as heat that were nothing of the sort. Ice in his mouth produced blisters, the cool hands of an orderly had caused him to cry out. At the moment, he could only be certain that the nurse smelled of gin.

"Your summers?" said the nurse. "You always spent them here?"

She pushed up his left buttock to reach the small of his back, and Woody glanced down, disgusted to see his erection.

"Sorry," he said.

The nurse moved the sponge to the other side. "It's a reflex. You can't control it."

But what *could* he control? Choices were chimeras, the mere impression of will. He was to have been married by now, moved into one of the bayside rooms. Had it been his choice or Elizabeth's prudence to postpone the marriage until after the war?

"In the navy, weren't you?" said the nurse.

Through the window he could see the Chris-Craft motorboat berthed at the dock, the *Blue Heron* hanging from its mooring. A vision came of sailing with his father, the *Blue Heron* plunging into troughs, smashing through peaks of white. Woody was twelve, his brother fourteen. Lip was belly-down on the bow, readying the foredeck for the spinnaker. Woody was mesmerized by the way his brother attached the shackles to the sail while the bow bucked like a stallion. They tacked, rounded the mark. He was pelted by spray, and his father was yelling, *Let it out! Let it out!* Woody needed to do something with the line, but his father's voice was too loud, too confusing.

Up ahead—the rocky shoal. His father was heading between it and the shore when the wind suddenly gusted, catching the sail. The line ran through Woody's clenched hand, burning, cutting—almost to the bone.

Screaming, *Forget your hand! Pull it in, pull it in, pull it in . . . !*

And then that smell of burning flesh.

Woody roused himself. "Pardon me?"

"Is that how you became a sailor?" the nurse asked again.

Unclenching his hand, Woody said, "Yes."

The radiator began to hiss and clang. Downstairs, Ella Mae was frying bacon. The comfort of the familiar gave way to dread.

The nurse had tied up his left pant leg so he wouldn't trip. His toes seemed to hurt, but it was only the ghosts of toes. Outside, the light was golden green, the summer light he had dreamed of when all he saw for days was water and the occasional island whose name he could not pronounce.

His room was brighter than he remembered. There were books on the shelf. Verne, Kipling, Steinbeck. The osteopath had come and gone, leaving instructions to work the muscles in the right leg and toughen up that stump. He had worked Woody deep and hard, worked him till he cried out.

The nurse rolled Woody onto the brand-new lift. His mother had demonstrated it the day before, extolling the virtues of the widened doors, the wonders of the funicular. It took up half the stairs and allowed him access to the main floor and the bedrooms, but until he could walk better, he'd have to be carried down to the sidewalk. *It won't be long,* his mother said.

The nurse pushed a button, and he lurched down the stairs to the dining room. From the servants' stairs, Woody heard the low voice of a girl. He wondered whom it belonged to, but the pills had left him fuzzy.

"I'm going to take a shower," said the nurse, propelling him toward the dining room table.

"Fine," he said, knowing she was going for a drink. "Have one for me."

"Mr. Woody, you going to eat your sausage, or do I got to cut it up like when you was a boy?"

"My hands hurt."

"Let me see."

He had been gripping the rail when the plane hit. Red sky, steaming water, the fusion of hands to metal.

"Mmmm, mmm," said Ella Mae. She knew how to read palms, but there were no lines to read on Woody's—no lines for love or children. None for life. She set down his hand and patted it, picked up a knife.

"Thank you," he said as she cut the sausage.

When had everything become so ridiculous? A china cup shaped and painted like a chicken held his egg. A piece of driftwood was fashioned into a lamp.

"Learn how to handle a tiller," his father had told him, "and you've learned half of life's lessons." Steer straight. Don't waver. Know your course. The commander of Woody's ship did all these things, and still a plane plunged into it.

Ella Mae had made a nice little pile of sausage. The sight of the egg in the chicken-shaped cup, both familiar and alien, moved Woody unexpectedly. He turned into her broad hips. The seersucker of her apron pressed into him. "Ella Mae," he said, "I don't know what to do."

Ella Mae leaned into his face, her hands on his shoulders. "For starters, eat your breakfast. Mrs. March says you'll be walking soon."

"And if I can't?"

"If you can't," Ella Mae said, "she'll do it for you."

Woody had wheeled himself out to the porch and was looking at the lake. That vast prairie of blue was the first thing he saw each summer when the train crested the hill at Pont du Lac. His friends didn't understand the boundlessness of Lake Michigan until they saw for themselves how it went on past the horizon, how it threw up waves that could break ships in half. But Woody knew. He had seen it chop up with whitecaps, turning green before dusk, streaked with silver after a squall or draining of color, flattening to white when the wind died. Mad lake. Crazy lake. Each summer, his pulse quickened when he saw it.

There would be swimming, of course. The gratuitous laps back and forth, the races to the end of the dock. But that was on the harbor side, nestled safely between ropes and buoys, intruded upon only by the wake of a ski boat, the submerged eruption of an artesian well.

The bay was the wild card. Fickle shoals, uncertain shorelines, its approach rocky and precarious. It was the bay that sent him running to his nurse or Ella Mae, afraid of the waves, afraid of the drop-offs. They said a girl drowned there. One of the Indians employed from the convent. But Woody had been too young to remember, could remember only his brother, Lip, teasing him, saying it wasn't so bad, that the water was warmer on the bay side anyway, and there was treasure beneath those rocks.

Come on! Stop being such a girl!

Lip dipped and emerged like a seal, holding up an ancient fossil.

Woody, you priss! Get in here!

Woody shrugged, waved him off. He could still see his brother's broad, sure strokes as he swam away from the shore, growing smaller, arms flailing, shouts—nothing alarming at first, then the growing panic, the realization that something was wrong, the pain of bare feet as he stumbled across the rocks and dove to save his brother. He had swum hard and fast, his arms never graceful but driven, this time, by need.

Of course it was all a joke. Lip was waiting for him on the rocks, almost choking with laughter when he saw Woody's pale terror. *Jesus,* Woody had said. But it was the farthest he had ever swum. Sitting with his brother in the shallows of the shoals, he had looked with amazement back at the shore.

27

All his life Woody had come back to this spit of land, this summer home with its white-columned porch. Twenty steps below him, the lawn rolled down to the dock with its berths for five boats, its pavilion on the end. Ella Mae had taken him fishing when his father wouldn't, sitting for hours on the edge of that dock—a small white boy next to a great dark woman, a cluster of dark people around them. It had been the coloreds' day off. All the next day, the house smelled of perch.

On the bay, a fleet of sloops danced and ducked, beating to the windward mark. One by one, they rounded the buoy, spinnakers exploding like scarves from a magician's sleeve. Gazing at it, Woody recalled the Philippine Sea. They had left Manila, the smell of fried bananas and girls with the voices of children squealing, *Mr. Sailor! Mr. Sailor!* By Okinawa, the sounds of the planes should have been horrible, but there had been beauty in their menace. He had looked up one night to see the moon break through black clouds. The ocean was ablaze with firepower. Men were scrambling across the deck, shouting orders while all around them sirens had wailed above the bellow of guns, the roar of water, bloodied and wrecked. And through it all—the moon.

Below him, the path to the beach was becoming overgrown with blackberry and pine. Picking her way along it was a girl. She froze when she saw Woody. Wary as a fawn, she seemed to disappear into the foliage, but Woody couldn't look away from her shawl of wet hair. For a moment, he thought she might be another of Ella Mae's daughters, but she seemed more Indian than Negro. Her eyes were almost oriental. He had known a woman in Manila—one of the girls who came to the docks. He had paid her—not enough, he decided later. Her heart had beat so fast when he touched her throat, it was as if he held a hummingbird.

Woody started to ask this girl if she was the one he had heard that morning, but she had moved past the porch to the back of the house without even a nod, silent as moonrise.

It was early evening, still light when Jonah wheeled out the cocktail cart.

"Drink, Mistuh Woody?"

"Sure, Jonah. Martini. Dry."

"You got it." Jonah opened bottles of gin and vermouth, poured them into a pitcher.

"Malcolm McGee," said Woody, lowering himself onto the glider.

"Pardon?"

"Malcolm McGee made the best martinis in our group. You remember Malcolm, Jonah?"

"Sure, Mistuh Woody, indeed I do. He a frienda yours. How is Mistuh Malcolm?"

Woody didn't answer. Malcolm had died early. Went and joined the RCAF. Reckless fellow, Malcolm. The bay had never bothered *him*.

Woody watched Jonah's long, dark fingers pour the drink, add an olive, hand him the glass. As the butler started to leave, Woody said, "Stay a minute."

Jonah's hooded eyes turned to him, waiting for instructions.

But Woody had no instructions. He was suddenly interested in the butler's life. Did Jonah remember the maid who drowned? How Lip used to joke? How long had Jonah and Ella Mae been married? And had their marriage been a happy one? Before the war, Woody wouldn't have cared.

"It's nothing," Woody said.

His leg ached. He needed a shot or a pill. Alone, Woody took a sip of his martini, but the smell of lake had infected everything. With his right leg, he propelled himself back and forth. The glider's course was soothing, as passively rocking as the lurch of a ship. Wonderful invention, Woody thought. Part couch, part cradle.

The martini sat half drunk, the sun bled from the sky. When his mother joined him, he was studying a bright point, wondering if it was Venus.

His mother sat beside him on the glider. "So," she asked, rocking, "what do you think of the nurse?"

"I would prefer a pretty one."

"She was recommended by the Hewetts."

"She drinks."

His mother stroked his fine, dark hair. "It's good to be home, isn't it?"

Woody, enduring her touch, tried to answer, but what could he say? Was home this vast shingled house with so many windows? This glimpse of lake?

"We should thin out those trees," his mother said. "They block the view."

"I like the trees."

"Don't you want to see the lake?"

"It's all I see."

Together, they moved the glider back and forth in silence. His mother sighed and rose, told him his father was waiting for dinner to begin.

"Life goes on, Woody."

The nurse had given Woody a shot. He lay there quietly, thinking about the nature of fear—its metallic taste, his lungs constricting, the sad, sorry sense of caving in. He had felt it for as long as he could remember, before he was in uniform, before his graduation, before his engagement, his adult life. It dogged him, this fear. Why had his brother felt none of it?

He closed his eyes and lay back on the pillow. A door opened, closed. Again, that memory of Lip on the sandbar. He could swim out there now, Woody told himself. Swim *past* it even. Swim until there was no turning back.

Lying on the bed, he waited for his pulse to slow, for the cedar walls to close in on him. He could hear music across the lake, wondered if he was dreaming. If there was a party, he should get up, pull on a fresh shirt and a blazer. He should head down to the club, find Bud or Malcolm, cut in on whomever was dancing with the prettiest girl. They'd had that band up from Kalamazoo. Pretty good, except for the drummer. The horn player had passed off a so-so Dorsey, and Lip would have been out there, swinging with Serena Boyd or one of the Miller sisters.

You couldn't cut in on Lip. Woody had tried once, and like quicksilver, Lip had turned the tables, and Woody found himself dancing with his own brother, Serena Boyd standing on the sidelines, laughing.

"Kind of a short guy, aren't you?" said Lip, even though Woody was nearly six feet tall. He could still see the amusement in Lip's eyes as Woody, embarrassed and flustered, had broken away.

That had been a good night. August 1941. Woody had kissed Serena Boyd who was maudlin over Lip. Serena had sighed, saying Woody smelled like his brother, but didn't kiss as good. Not as handsome, either. Did it make him mad when she said that? Or had he laughed at her, saying, You're only sixteen, what do *you* know? Those were the girls he'd grown up with. Girls like Serena Boyd and Elizabeth Parker, girls who had cotillions and pearl necklaces and trusts set up for their children. He hadn't known there were other girls till they'd put in at Guadalcanal and Manila.

Adrift in morphine, he could see Malcolm dancing in the shadows, but it was only the wind, the faintest thread of "Star Dust." Can't cut in, Woody thought. I'm getting married. Besides, Malcolm had been shot down over Brighton.

Through his window, the harbor reflected a sliver of a moon. In a half-dream, Woody stepped from a boat and began to run in its silvery path. Faster and faster he ran. There was no turning back. With every stride, he cracked the surface, shards of moonlight in his wake.

C H A P T E R   T H R E E

Every afternoon, Rachel went down the pine-needled path to the bayside beach. From there, she headed west, away from the tip of Beck's Point, passing beneath the houses, not stopping till she had passed the NO TRESPASSING sign and come to a stretch of dunes and weeds and untracked sand. Today, she was late. Hurriedly, she took off her clothes, walked in up to her waist, braced herself for the shock of cold, and dove in. The lake washed away the smell of onions and Borax as she swam, taking her back to a time when her skin smelled mostly of clay. The water deepened. Soon she couldn't touch bottom, could barely see the boulders far below the surface. Ahead of her, little waves marked the shoals. Since she was strong-armed from swimming each summer as a child, her strokes cut fast and straight. Minutes passed. Reaching the rocks and breathing hard, she climbed up, the water not quite to her knees. Even in the solitude, she wondered if anyone could see her—a naked girl who seemed to walk on water.

Back on the beach, she lay nestled on a dune, waving off flies as the sun warmed her skin, listened to the rocks rattling as the waves rolled out. Soon, the lap of waves became breaths, slow and deep, her eyes suddenly heavy with the drone of insects. She could imagine she was someplace else. The sun arced over her as she slid into sleep, dreaming of dark, watery places where only fish could live.

When she awoke, the shadows had lengthened, the sand had grown cool and powdery. Not even bothering to brush the sand from her skin, Rachel pulled her dress over her head and started to run.

"The table?" she said as she burst into the kitchen to the sound of china clattering.

"Table's set," said Ella Mae.

"The napkins and the silver?"

"Done, done, done." Ella Mae blew up her cheeks till they were big and round as buns. She nodded at the potatoes. "If it *ain't* too much trouble, girl, you could clean those up. That is, if it suits you."

Pulling a stool up to the sink, Rachel began roughly scrubbing dirt off red-skinned potatoes no bigger than golf balls. When Mandy, looking righteous, came over to fill a bucket, the girl felt her neck grow hot. "What are *you* looking at?"

"What do you think of him?" Mandy asked as the water clanged into the pail.

"Who?"

"The son."

Rachel sighed. She'd found him ugly, a disappointment bearing no likeness to the boy in the snapshot. Three days since he'd gotten out of the car, so thin and sickly looking, Rachel knew something was wrong—the way he watched her from the porch, the way he struggled with his food. It was more than his leg. His eyes were bluer than she had expected, almost on fire. Last night, when she was closing the windows, she had passed by his room and peered in.

"I've only seen him once or twice," she said to Mandy, adding that she'd seen crucified Jesuses that looked better. With her nail, she dug a brown spot out of the potato and flicked it into the sink.

"Did you see his *eyes?*" said Mandy, hoisting the bucket. "Apostle's eyes, I swear."

Two cottages down, a baby was crying. There would be dinner that night for three. The mother, the father, and the son. Miss Elizabeth, word had it, was staying in St. Louis. Rachel, who had no use for apostles, licked the dirt from her finger and spit.

Removing Mr. March's half-finished bowl of soup, Rachel noticed the raw roll of flesh resting on his collar. He seemed a cheerful man, pink-jowled, slightly bald, but he had never smiled at her.

"The Addisons always pick inconvenient times to die," he said as she replaced his spoon.

"Is it so important," Mrs. March asked, "that you have to be in St. Louis? Binnie would love to see you."

"Binnie saw me last summer. She won't know the difference."

"You *never* stay."

"I told you . . . the Addisons' probate. I'm the executor."

"It's just that . . . nothing's the same, is it?"

Mr. March waved for Jonah to fill his glass. "Looks the same to me, eh, Jonah? Same houses, same flowers, same boats. Same bawling babies to replace last year's batch."

"There's always plenty of those, Mistuh March."

Mrs. March's eyes slid to the son's empty seat. "We would be blessed to have some babies in this house."

Mrs. March was just like the nuns, thought Rachel. The way she prayed her rosary twice a day, the way she fingered her crucifix.

Mrs. March beckoned her over. "Rachel, please tell Ella Mae to keep this soup warm for Mr. Woody."

Ella Mae was garnishing the roast beef when Rachel returned with the soup. Glaring at the bowl in the girl's hand, Ella Mae said, "Is something wrong?"

"It's the son's."

"You mean he's not *eating*?"

"Can't if he's not at the table."

Ella Mae clicked her tongue, pointed at the back stairs. "You get up there and see what's happening with that nurse."

Rachel expected she would find the son asleep, but when she reached his room, he was seated on the bed, his wheelchair beyond his reach. A glass had overturned. Water puddled on the floor. He was dressed, but his shirt was buttoned wrong.

"Where's the nurse?" said Rachel, not moving from the door.

The son's blue eyes regarded her. Apostle's eyes, indeed! His hair was darker than she'd thought—more brown than gold. The boy in the picture, the one kicking the water, had looked healthy and whole. Now his body looked thin, weightless as a *manitou's*.

"The nurse is doing what she does best," he said.

Rachel moved across the room, peered through the door into the adjoining room. The smell of alcohol, the snoring nurse told the story.

"Leave her and come here."

Rachel moved toward the bed and waited.

"This is embarrassing," Woody March said, "but I need your help." He nodded at the wheelchair.

"Is she always like this?"

"Mostly." He cleared his throat. "I need for you to bend down."

Rachel hesitated, then stooped and offered her shoulder.

"Crook your arm, please."

She did as he said. He rose up, and she realized he was taller than he seemed in the wheelchair. His hand slipped to her waist. For a moment, they teetered, the son hopping to balance on his right leg. He grabbed the chair with his left hand, stabilized, then lowered himself. Once in the chair, he breathed exhaustedly.

"Are you all right?" Rachel asked, her own breath coming harder.

He nodded, still gasping. "I'm sorry, what's your name?"

She didn't answer. She stared, instead, at his face. For a whole year, she had fingered that face in a photograph. Now the thought occurred to her that perhaps a candle was more beautiful once the wax had melted and dripped.

"You have one, don't you?"

She started. His father had never asked her name. "Rachel."

He studied her, looking more amused than curious. "What's your function, Rachel?"

"Excuse me?"

"You a nurse? A physical therapist? What?"

Rachel tugged at her braid. She felt he was mocking her, but he looked like a wounded hawk—desperate and fierce.

"I'm a maid."

"Ah," he said. "Since when?"

"Since last summer."

He paused, as if he was calculating the years. "I missed that summer," he said finally, his hand playing across his thigh.

His cheeks were gaunt as a martyr's. Rachel eyed his stump. "Are you in pain?"

"Always."

There was a lamp made from a piece of driftwood. Books on a shelf. Everything dusted and readied for the return of a boy.

He crossed his arms and stared at her. "Do you know how to give shots?"

Rachel shook her head.

"In the top drawer of the nurse's bureau, you'll find some little bottles. Take one and the syringe and bring them here."

Rachel hesitated. It had made her sick when her uncle's diabetes had gotten bad and he'd had to use the needle.

Impatiently, Woody said, "The nurse would, but she's blotto."

"I'll get Ella Mae."

"Don't. Besides," he said, his hawk eyes peering intently at her, "*you're* the one who's here."

The nurse's snore was jagged. In her drawer, the bottles gleamed in their little compartments. Rachel plucked one, held it up to the light.

When she returned to his room, the son had already pushed up his sleeve. The pale flesh of his arm was tracked with puncture marks. Rachel caught her breath.

"You don't approve?"

The veins were like estuaries. "I believe this stuff is bad for you."

He looked away, but kept his arm extended. "I believe *you* are the maid."

Fine, thought Rachel. Who was she to argue? She broke the top off the bottle, filled the syringe as her told her. He flinched when she touched his hand, but as she pressed the drug into him, she felt him soften, shift, grow wings.

"Is that better?" she asked him.

But he had already taken flight.

CHAPTER FOUR

Only 10 A.M., and already the air was thick as butter. Rachel sat at the kitchen table, sewing a button on a blouse the way she had once stitched bark. *It's like this,* her grandmother had told her, showing with old woman's fingers the way to embroider birch bark with flowers, eagles, trees. *You need tough hands to push the quills like so.*

Yet every time Rachel would try to pierce the bark, the needles punctured her skin. *It's no use!* she would say. *And who cares about these things anyway?*

Ella Mae struck a match, held it to the burner. When the match blew out, she swore under her breath.

"Mama!" said Mandy, shocked.

When Rachel had arrived from the convent at dawn, Ella Mae told her Woody March had tried to walk and fallen. Now he was ill, half out of his mind. Throughout the morning, the phone rang, voices were hushed and hurried. The doctor showed up and, later, the priest. Even Mr. March had put off his departure.

Holding the cloth close, Rachel aimed the needle, pulled it through. She was sure they'd think it was her fault when they found out about the shot. *You can't trust an Indian,* they'd be saying. But Rachel pitied the son with his sawed-off leg, his pink-palmed hands. What else could she have done?

"I tell you," said Ella Mae, "the whole house is gonna blow up someday."

Rachel set down the sewing and fanned herself.

"Open a window!" said Mandy.

With a loud, rushing sound, the burner lit. Someone knocked at the door, and Rachel looked up, expecting to see the delivery boy from the pharmacy, but she couldn't make out the man on the other side of the screen.

"May we *help* you?" Mandy said, exaggerating each word.

The man on the other side of the screen mumbled something.

"Say again?" said Mandy.

"I got your wood."

"You know where it's stacked," said Ella Mae, shooing him off.

But the man didn't move. "It's *her* I want to talk to."

Ella Mae turned to her. "Rachel?"

Embarrassed, Rachel went to the door. Through the screen, she took in the ruddy skin, the blunt brow, the coarse black hair. "Honda?" she said.

She hadn't seen him or anyone since she left the lake. Four whole years. Still, she remembered Honda Jackson. He was one of the boys who had pulled her from the cabin. *You can't trust a Jackson,* her grandmother had said, but Rachel never knew why. Maybe it was the way they were always selling something. Maybe it was their being part Sioux.

"Au-ne-pesh au-ʒe-gwa ke-gi-aw-ya?" he said to her.

Rachel didn't answer. She could feel Mandy watching her, knew she was thinking, Ignorant Indians. Well, Rachel wasn't going to tell him where she'd been all this time. Surely he knew. It was bad enough she was about to lose her job, and here was this Jackson staring at her uniform. Rachel raised her head and said, "I'm sorry. I don't understand."

"What are you doing here?"

Who was *he* to talk? At least she had a job, wasn't some scavenger selling wood. There had been miles of forest around the lake. Birch, beech, oak. Plenty of wood for burning. Plenty to sell.

She touched the screen door. He leaned in closer. "Tell me," she whispered in a voice meant only for a priest's ear, "how are my Uncle Jedda and Aunt Minnie?"

Honda cleared his throat. "Your uncle's gone drinking again," he said. "Broke his leg last winter on the ice."

But Jedda was always drinking. With a quick look over her shoulder, Rachel added, "And Minnie?"

Ella Mae, who had gone to answer the buzzer from Mrs. March's room, came rattling down the stairs. Honda touched his hand to Rachel's with only the screen between them.

"Forget that chatter, girl," Ella Mae said, catching her breath, her eyes snapping at Honda. "Mrs. March wants to see you."

The windows in Mrs. March's room were layered with gauzy casement that all but hid the lake. Sitting at her dressing table, Mrs. March glanced in the mirror at Rachel. Above the big iron headboard, Jesus hung from his cross. Down the hall in his own slender bed, Mr. March was still asleep. *Mr. March wouldn't be caught dead sleeping under no crucifix,* Mandy had said to Rachel, but Rachel, having seen the cool way he looked at his wife at dinner, knew there was more than religious difference.

"You've heard about my son?"

Rachel had seen Mrs. March praying her rosary, her lips mutely moving. She might have been as old as Rachel's grandmother. It was hard to tell. Everything about her was tidy—her hair, her clothes, the diamond pin she always wore at her neck.

Rachel dropped her eyes and nodded.

"Tell me, Rachel," said Mrs. March, "are you happy here?"

From the bathroom came the drip of sweating pipes. There had been haloes of rust in the toilet bowls that spring when Rachel scrubbed them out. A dead mouse found in a drawer.

"This used to be a happy house," Mrs. March went on when Rachel didn't respond. "You must find it dull. How old are you?"

More strange than dull, thought Rachel, with its stale odor of ancestors. Rachel studied the pictures on Mrs. March's dressing table. A boy on a sailboat. A younger Mrs. March in 1920s clothing posed with her husband.

"Seventeen," said Rachel. When would the woman get to the point?

Suddenly, Mrs. March picked up a bottle, dabbed some scent on her wrist, held it out to Rachel. "Smell this."

Rachel hesitated. In the spring, she had cleaned this room when the house was opened for summer. She had smoothed and tucked the bedding the way she was taught—the blanket cover and sheets hospital-tight. She had opened the windows to let in air. Now Mrs. March's prayers swirled around the room like dust balls. They coated the bureau and desk.

"Go on," said Mrs. March, her wrist close to Rachel's nose.

Embarrassed, Rachel closed her eyes, leaned forward, and inhaled something sweeter than lilacs.

Mrs. March then took Rachel's own wrist, streaked it with the perfume. "*I* was seventeen once." She picked up her rosary, set it down. "Have you ever prayed for a miracle?"

Rachel's eyes drifted to a photograph of the son with Miss Elizabeth. Her arms were thrown around him. He looked almost happy.

"At any rate," Mrs. March said, following Rachel's gaze, "he should be better soon."

Rachel stared at the picture. There *was* something about his eyes. She started to tell Mrs. March that her son had begged for the shot, and who was she to say no?

"We all have our callings, Rachel. The nurse is hopeless. I've let her go."

Rachel's eyes drifted to Jesus on the cross, wondered if he was the first thing Mrs. March saw in the mornings when she opened her eyes.

"It won't require much of you," said Mrs. March. "I've already spoken with Sister Marie. Of course, we'll pay you more."

The room grew stuffy. It smelled of cod liver oil and lilacs gone rank. As Mrs. March laid out the details of how Rachel would bathe him, push him out on the porch, give him shots when he absolutely needed them, Rachel thought, Why not Mandy? Why not Ella Mae? Outside, she could hear Honda stacking wood. She wondered how much they paid *him*. Not enough, she decided.

Again, Rachel lifted her wrist to smell the peculiar scent. She remembered going to the post office at Chibawassee with her grandmother to fill out forms for the government. They had stopped to look at a cigar-store Indian when a man came up to Rachel and commented on her braids.

"Hey, honey," said the man, "would you mind posing next to that statue?" He had held up his camera and smiled.

And then Rachel had seen the money. The man was giving her grandmother money, and her grandmother froze and looked at it as though it was an omen. Something that could be used.

The man must have taken her picture, because the next thing Rachel knew she was being pulled down the sidewalk by her grandmother who was muttering in Odawa. "Taw," she said. "These people think everything we got is for sale."

Rachel lowered her wrist, glanced sideways from beneath her lashes at Mrs. March.

"You see," said Mrs. March, "he's in so much pain." She touched one of the pictures on her dressing table. Rachel noticed she was fighting to keep her voice steady. "Do you think you can help?"

There seemed to be more to the question than the giving of shots. A plea, perhaps. An unuttered novena to save her son.

Rachel opened her mouth to say, You're asking the wrong girl. But her wrist, anointed with perfume, burned, and she couldn't find the words.

Ella Mae and the Hewetts' maid from next door were gossiping at the kitchen table, their heads shoved together.

"And not only that," Ella Mae was whispering. "Miss Elizabeth was the one who called it off."

"If that don't beat all!"

Rachel plunged her hands into hot, soapy water, pulled out a pot, attacked it with steel wool.

"She could do worse," Ella Mae sniffed. Rachel banged the pot hard against the counter, threw down her towel.

"Girl," said Ella Mae, "what's got into you?"

"Why can't *Mandy* give him baths?"

Ella Mae looked at Rachel as if she were crazy. "You talking about Mr. Woody?"

"Mrs. March fired the nurse."

"No one told me."

"Mandy could do it."

"*Mandy?*" Ella Mae glanced at the Hewetts' maid, and they both laughed. "Can you see Mandy wiping some boy's heinie?"

The buzzer rang. Ella Mae and Rachel stared each other down. Finally, Ella Mae sniffed. "Besides, if I recall, Mr. Woody asked for *you* specific."

Rachel climbed the stairs.

The son's wheelchair was parked by the window, his face white in the glare. Rachel waited by the door. It was a room of model boats and children's books and bedspreads patterned with anchors.

After a moment, the son said, "Lucky you."

"Can I get you something?"

He rubbed his arms. "Aren't you cold?"

Rachel shook her head.

"Sometimes," he said, "I'm burning up."

His shirt was open. Faint, reddish hairs traced across his chest. Everything about him seemed hollow—his laugh, the skin at the base of his throat. "Tell me your name again."

Such pale skin. His eyes were the color of cornflowers, deep as the lake, blue and wounded, as if he had stared too long at the sun.

"Rachel," she said shortly. She noticed he was shaking. "Can I get you a blanket?"

"Rachel," he said. He held out his hand, looked at her beseechingly.

She moved toward the bed, but the son already had rolled up his sleeve, was holding out his arm.

Rachel ironed and listened. The osteopath had come, and now upstairs— groans of protest. It had gone on for weeks. Again and again, footsteps across the floor—a small hop, a longer drag. The iron hissed as she flicked

it with water. Rachel thought of the needle, the filament of blood that sometimes tendrilled up before she squeezed.

Three weeks, and Rachel knew the son's every vein and ligament. For
years, she had helped her grandmother peel the bark from birch trees, cutting
deep to get a piece thick enough for making boxes, but not so deep as to kill the
tree. Now she knew where the needle must go. Behind the knee. Between the
toes. Into the fleshy part of a thigh.

It was all she could do not to go to him.

The walls of the old house were thin. In minutes, the osteopath would leave.
The sleeves of Rachel's dress were mooned with sweat. She was dizzy with the
heat. It is a poison, she thought. The old woman has poisoned me. Now I am
light-headed and weak. She pressed a cuff embroidered with the initials WFM,
folded back the sleeves, leaned against the ironing board. Almost gasping, she
pulled the plug.

Woody had fallen back on the pillow. Rachel watched as the drug suffused
him, cell by cell, his eyes losing the hot need that had engulfed him only a
moment earlier. She was becoming addicted to the cessation of his pain.

Yesterday, Mrs. March had stopped Rachel in the hall to ask why Woody
was so mercurial.

"Mercurial?"

"Moody," said Mrs. March, impatiently. "Inconstant. I thought he would
have been better by now."

Your mother, Rachel told Woody, knows something's up. "You must cut
back on this stuff."

Woody shrugged it off. "My mother wants me up and cutting a rug by
August."

"And?"

"A broken branch like me?"

Still, he told her, he had phantom pain, the false sensation of a limb like the memory of a much-loved place.

"Only, the place is gone," said Woody. He kicked off the sheet. His right leg was finely muscled, but his stump was scarred as bark.

"Do you believe in ghosts?" he asked her.

"Don't you?"

He laughed quickly and looked away. Surely, she thought, looking at his leg, he must know about ghosts. She had seen them herself, dancing on water, walking in flames. "At the lake where I grew up," she said, "we were always seeing things. Impossible things. I saw my own grandmother's spirit go up in fire. I feel her presence even now."

Woody wouldn't meet her eyes. His palms were turned upward, pink and dry. Fused by burns, they could not sweat.

"You don't believe me?"

"I believe," Woody said, gazing about his room, "that everything has changed."

Rachel looked at him with pity. "Why should that surprise you?"

The room shadowed in the late-day sun. Woody rippled the sheet with his toes. "Your lake," he said. "Is it like here?"

What could she tell him about a place like that? To love it so much you could taste it—that the essence of its soil filled you, leaked from your pores? To him, it would be a pond, a mud hole, even less. To the Horseshoe Band, it was sustenance. "Not *our* lake. McCready's." Still, their band had lived there long enough to forget it wasn't theirs. "It's always changing," she said, "depending on its mood. When it's happy, it's green. Like in summer. Autumn, though, it turns gray. It's not so happy that winter's coming. Then it's covered in white."

"And your house?" he said. "Did you really live in a wigwam?"

A breeze stirred the curtains. Bones ignited. The pop and sputter of flesh.

When Rachel didn't answer, Woody laughed and toed her with his good leg. "I'll be gone in a minute. Just tell me."

Rachel, suddenly angry, remembering hunger, remembering cold, yanked up his blankets. "You ask too many questions."

"Woody," his mother said as the coffee was served, "the doctor says you can start with the prosthesis."

Woody had barely touched his food. The dining room was coated in honey—the cedar walls, the candlelight, the dim chandelier. The drug had made him slow and distant, but he could hear the conversation with uncanny accuracy. Words were color and heat. The words his mother spoke, the unspoken ones of his father.

"And if I *don't*?"

"Don't be ridiculous."

His mother set her coffee cup carefully in its saucer. She was wearing the diamond pin Woody's father had given her for the birth of their first child—Hannah, dead to influenza. Now Lip was gone in the war. Would his father give her jewelry for the dead? Woody noticed her silver knot had been cut off, her hair short and gray for mourning. His father, on the other hand, looked the same, an ascot knotted in at his neck. An affectation, Woody thought. Like the little pin of the family crest stuck in his lapel. Again, Woody recalled that long-ago helm, the stern patrician in the commodore's hat.

A candle sputtered, dripping wax onto the damask cloth. Cupping her hand behind the flame, his mother blew it out. "What about Elizabeth?" she said. "You haven't returned her calls."

"Hmmm," Woody said, watching the smoke curl up from the extinguished flame. Smoke was a fickle stuff, subject to the currents of air—like Elizabeth who was now saying she had changed her mind. *Darling*, she wrote, *I was being silly* . . .

"You could at least answer her letters." His father's words flowed like a river of blue.

His mother reached over and covered Woody's hand. "What about talking to Father Tom?"

"Oh, Jesus."

"This won't do, Woodrow," said his father.

His mother pressed on. "He's wonderful with pain."

Woody laughed. Shades of red. "I *have* something for the pain. I don't need the priest."

Mandy was clearing the dishes. Woody wondered where Rachel was. Dark, weighted with a cat's grace—her words would be pale green and lavender.

"Wouldn't you like to dance again?" his mother said. "Get on your feet?"

Woody liked the feel of Rachel's smooth, brown hands when she rolled up his sleeve and carefully stroked his skin.

"Have some people over for cocktails?"

That morning, she had smelled like the lake.

"The Boyds? You always liked Serena Boyd."

Rachel came back with Mandy to clear the table. She took his plate. A shimmer of pink. He turned to his mother. Woody wanted to tell her he *never* liked Serena Boyd, but his words were black, stuck like tar.

He waited for her on the bayside veranda. The sun beat against the cerulean lake, the blue of his summer memories. A screen door slammed. He peered over the rail to see her head.

"Rachel?"

She stopped, turned.

"Where are you going?"

Her face in the sunshine was younger than he thought, the planes of her cheeks soft as a girl's. Again, Woody recalled the Philippine Sea, a body floating past him. What could Rachel possibly know of life?

"To the beach," she said.

"Mind some company?"

A rogue cloud shadowed her face. In her eyes, he could have read anything. Contempt. Indifference. Love. Yet she came up the stairs, her uniform smelling of bleach, her hair of pine. Leaning into her, he detected a trace of his mother's perfume as they hopped down steps to the path.

Released by the sun—the sweet scent of cedar and honeysuckle. Behind them, the house disappeared behind a blind of trees. Woody's crutches sank into the sand. The lake curved against the sky. Slowly, they made their way to the water. At its edge, Woody realized he had traveled six thousand miles to get here.

The wind blew Rachel's hair across her eyes. A half mile offshore, waves broke on the pale band of shallows. She toed the pebbles at the water's edge, bent down, snatched up a green bit of glass.

Woody caught his breath and pointed to the shoals. "My brother and I used to swim out to that. It was a contest to see who could make it to the sandbar first." He recalled the summer he had found out that Lip was going to run the bank someday. They had been skipping stones on the beach when Lip brought it up. How old had Woody been? Fourteen? *You're the free one, Woody,* Lip had said as they stood beside each other, seeing who could skip the farthest. *You'll get to do as you please.*

"It's not so far," Rachel said.

They started up the beach, Rachel gathering pieces of gull bone, the rib of a fish, a shell, driftwood. She put everything into her pocket. A band of rocks rattled in the waves.

"Most girls I know like jewelry," said Woody.

He scooped up a fistful of tiny stones—reddened by iron, greened by copper, pocked, mottled, glinting with quartz or mica. When he was a boy, he used to scavenge these rocks, looking for shells or bits of fossils, some evidence of Pleistocene life, immortal and petrified, the rubble of the glaciers.

"Look," said Rachel. She took his hand, poked through the gravel, teased out a tiny fossil no bigger than her nail. Woody lifted it carefully with the tip of his finger, held it close till a gust of wind carried it off.

Life goes on, Woody.

But life need not go on, Woody thought as he let Rachel lead him away from the water to a dune where he could lie on the sand, inhale its warmth. Rachel examined the smooth palm of his right hand.

"What was it like?" she asked.

Woody thought for a moment. "Foreign," he said. "Like no place I'd been."

Minutes passed. His bones softened like wax, his skin liquefied, darkened. Reaching up, he touched the tip of her hair, rolled it like silk.

Rachel licked the sand off her fingers, stared at the lake.

What are you thinking about? Woody wanted to ask her. She seemed so different from other girls. That absence of chatter—was it a sign of deeper waters? But he was drifting off, his spirit light as helium, and Rachel was reaching out to shield his eyes from the bright and quickening sun.

After that, they met each cloudless day at three, making their way to the beach as his mother napped. Woody would brace himself on Rachel, feel the outline of her clavicle as, gradually, sensation to his fingertips returned. He could walk with a cane now, but still he leaned on her. Sometimes, she pushed away and ran ahead—a brown-limbed girl, clutching the hem of her dress, knee-deep in water.

Woody followed her down the beach, the print of his right foot alongside a gouge made by the dragged prosthesis. From time to time, he stumbled on the rocks. Rachel looked back quickly, made sure he was all right, moved on.

She was a girl who licked stones. He began to notice how she absentmindedly brought them to her lips. A strange thing, this stone-licking, but when he asked her, she looked away. It was another of her secrets. Perhaps she was ashamed, but he couldn't be sure. That girl at the dock in Manila—she had had no name. He had gone back to give her more money, but he could never find her again.

"What do you taste in these rocks, anyway?" Woody said.

Her gaze seemed to measure him. Even Woody was surprised at his question. "My ancestors," she said.

The sun was still high, but that night there was to be dancing at the club. He had promised his mother. Woody bent over and plucked a reddish rock from the pile at his feet. It tasted dull, metallic. He pocketed it.

That evening, Woody stared into the mirror over the bureau. Looking back was a thin man, his face older than its twenty-six years, his hands scarred, one leg missing, a wooden leg joined to the stump by a leather sleeve. Pants on, no one would spot his disfigurement, though he walked with the jerkiness of a puppet, a wobble and thrust, as if the ground were uneven. Strengthened by food and exercise, he could walk almost a mile with his cane, gaining yard after yard by placing the good leg first, launching the other. The pain of his severed limb still rocked him, but it was the other, deeper pain that morphine quenched. *This will kill you*, Rachel had said the day before, knocking the needle from his hand.

Only then did he realize he had started to care.

Woody buttoned the cotton shirt, fastened the sleeves with monogrammed cuff links. Woodrow Forrester March. He knotted his tie, chevrons of blue and yellow. The evening was as familiar as a recurring dream, one marked by the foreboding of twisted sleep. Now that his father had returned to St. Louis, Woody would escort his mother, sit at a table for two, try to rise when his elders passed by and greeted them.

Don't get up, they would tell him tonight.

He adjusted his tie. It was a boy's tie, worn to prep school dinners. Pain and conscience had collapsed the skin around his eyes, his cheeks.

"Life goes on," Woody said to the mirror. He was older than his brother had been. Lip would be eternally young, the remains of his twenty-four-year-old body buried at Arlington.

"You look better," his mother said as they started down the sidewalk. Woody's leg faltered, but his mother did not reach out. Only when they arrived at the club did she take his arm. The war, it seemed, had not taken place. Two stone fireplaces on either side of the dance floor anchored the room as it ebbed and flowed beneath stars of white lights and the watchful eyes of dead commodores. No more uniforms, no dearth of men. Woody scanned the room for Lip, Bud, or Malcolm—all dead. The silhouettes in the flickering light could have been anyone.

"You are so naughty, Woody March! Six weeks and not a peep!"

Woody turned to see Serena Boyd, her hips thrust out beneath bottle green satin. Her left hand, holding a cigarette, was weighted with a large, square diamond. She wriggled her fingers at Woody. "You look divine!" She turned to his mother. "Doesn't he look divine, Aunt Lydia?"

"Mother," said Woody, his voice suddenly loud, "can I get us a drink?"

Serena touched his shoulder. "Aren't you going to congratulate me?"

Woody scanned the room for the waiter. "I need to sit down."

"Well, *aren't* you?"

"What for?"

"I'm engaged to Max *Bailey*. Where have you *been*?"

"We've been working on Woody," said his mother.

Serena rolled her eyes. "We've *always* had to work on Woody."

"Lucky guy," said Woody, lowering himself into a chair.

Dropping her voice, Serena nodded at his leg. "You can hardly tell, you know." Then she smiled brightly. "Dance later? For old times' sake?"

He mumbled something about being too rusty. What old times was she referring to?

"Everyone's rusty," said Serena. "Believe me."

The waiter took their orders. Before long, their table was surrounded by the concerned faces of friends.

"Such an ordeal," said Mrs. Boyd.

In a booming voice, Mr. Boyd added, "I'm sure Woody'd rather not talk about it."

Woody wished his martini would come. He tried to focus on the dancers spinning past him, the too-stiff men trying to lead the women who coaxed them on with smiles and smacks to the shoulders for a more daring step, a bit of energy in that dip. He recognized the ramrod straightness of his Andover days, the tightness of the male spine. Everyone, he thought, was turning into wood.

"Well?" said his mother.

"Well what?"

"Are you going to dance?"

He looked around the room, saw Serena coming at him with a balding young fellow in tow. "Hell," said Woody.

Max Bailey jerked out his hand, pumped Woody's frantically. "It *must* have been hell, pal. Just hell!"

Before Woody could answer, Serena grabbed his hand. "So, kiddo? You ready?" She swiveled her hips. "Max says he's only a teensy bit jealous."

Woody's stump hurt. He felt the low-belly panic of going before a group, of doing something he detested.

"I'll go easy on you," said Serena. The band was playing Cole Porter.

Max said, "There's no stopping Serena, guy."

Woody could feel his mother looking at him, could see Serena's blank, pretty face. A dim recollection of himself as a boy dressed in knickers and knee-high socks, his father holding up a paperweight, pointing to the ship inside, his own wonder as he took it from his father's hand, his surprise at its heaviness. His father watching him, saying, *Well?* as Woody's fingers slipped, that split second as the glass tumbled to the floor and shattered.

Hoisting himself, he let Serena guide him to the dance floor. She put a hand on his right shoulder, clasped his left hand and started to sway. *"Don't get no kick from champagne!"* she sang sloppily into his ear. Gin had loosened her smile, added weight to her eyelids. Woody lurched into a box step, Serena pulling him along.

"There you go, Woody! You've still got it!" Her words lapped together like waves. "Elizabeth's a lucky girl, I've always said. Even if you're . . . you know." She rested her head on his shoulder. "The March men were always the bestest." She yanked her head up. "So when're you going to do it?"

"Serena, you're pulling me over."

"Tell me, Woody. You ever slept with her?"

"Serena . . ."

"I mean, a lot of guys thought they were going to die, right? The things you boys used to say. 'Just this once, baby. I'm a goner for sure.' You know how many times I heard that? The only one who was good for it was Lip."

"You and *Lip?*"

"Would've with *you* if you'd asked." She screwed her eyes into a meaningful stare. "Only two more weeks till Elizabeth gets here."

Woody suddenly let go of Serena and stopped.

"Oops!" she said. "Guess Aunt Lydia wanted to surprise you."

"I haven't talked to Elizabeth."

"Don't I know it, bad boy. I even told her to drop you. You never go out. Aunt Lydia says you're morose." Serena's face grew sullen. "Well, things aren't as fun as they used to be, that's for certain. Before you know it, we'll have three screaming brats. Not just Max and me. You and Elizabeth, too. Baby puke and pabulum. Can't you just see it?"

Realizing she was on the verge of tears, Woody took Serena's arm and led her back to Max.

"Oh, Max!" Serena said, draping her arms extravagantly around his neck.

"She's all yours, my friend," Woody said. Leaning down, he whispered something to his mother.

"You can't just leave!" she hissed.

"Good night, Mother."

Outside, he gasped in the fresh night air. The door banged shut behind him, muffling the sounds of music and laughter. Everything was receding—his youth, his engagement, the war. Only his childhood memories clung fast, and those—even those—had yellowed like old newspaper.

His veins itched with need. Perhaps he would sit on the porch. Make a very stiff drink, rock back and forth on the glider. The moon—a full one—slid like a coin behind the clouds.

Rachel stood on the wide plank porch. Across the lake, a band played music—not the chanting, beating, wailing of the ceremonies and celebrations of her childhood—but a lively sound, not without rhythm. So what if the music had the same hearty falseness Rachel heard each night around the Marches' dinner table? It was gay and seductive, and it begged her to move. Soon, her hips were swaying side to side, answered by her shoulders, neck, and hair.

A figure was coming down the walk, and from the jerkiness of his gait, she knew it was Woody March. She heard him say her name as he climbed the steps.

"I saw you dancing," he said as he reached the porch. His jacket was off, his tie loose. Breathing hard, he asked, "You like this kind of music?"

Hot patches of color drifted up her neck. "You thought I'd prefer drums?"

She could see he was amused. He probably was thinking, Crazy Indian.

Can't dance either. She wanted to say that she could, too, but the ones she knew weren't like his.

"So," she asked, "was the broken branch able to cut a rug after all?"

Woody lit a cigarette, leaned against the rail. "I've never been much of a dancer."

Glancing at her now-still hips, he told her that when he was a teenager, he and his brother would sneak away from the club to go skinny-dipping in the lake. Lip, he said, was the stronger swimmer, but if he had had enough to drink, Woody would forget his fear and match him stroke for stroke.

"I like to swim," said Rachel.

Woody stubbed out his cigarette, tossed it off the porch. When his eyes met hers, she flinched. "Okay, then," he said, "let's go swimming."

Rachel laughed.

"I'm serious."

Rachel looked away. The lights from town had smudged the lake. "The nuns," she said.

"It's early."

She thought about the convent with its white, barren walls, her thin bed, the other girls' soft snoring, their braided hair.

Flipping her own braids back in a come-what-may fashion, she said almost defiantly, "Okay, why not?"

The path to the beach was all shadows and moonlight. Something scurried beneath the ferns as they laughed, tripped, nearly fell before pushing through the stand of twisted pine and landing on a ghostly beach. Rachel felt him watching her. When he touched her face, she was not surprised.

"Will you help me into the water?" he said.

Frogs called back and forth. Woody took off his tie, unbuttoned his shirt, pulled it off. Sitting on a rock at the edge of the water, he struggled with his pants, then tossed them away. Finally, he undid the canvas strap, the leather sleeve, groaning with pleasure at removing his leg.

"Now you," he said.

The moment opened before her like the first time she had pierced his skin. She had seen his body half-naked when she helped him to his bath, had touched his skin before she pricked it. He had been watching her for days. Now she felt shy to the point of shivering.

He stood up and reached for her while she undid her dress, thumbed her collarbone when it appeared, the beads of her spine. As she stood in her underwear, a large wave broke and rushed about their feet. She shuddered at the shock of it.

"It's rocky," he said. "I'll hold on to you."

They picked their way through the rocks until they were waist deep in water. Slowly, Woody abandoned his footing, cradled first by her hands, then by the lake.

"*Goddamn!*" he yelled as he pulled himself along in a wide breaststroke, his arms made strong from crutches.

"*Now* you're dancing!" she shouted back, staying close.

Far away, an outboard hummed. Woody choked on a wave, sputtered, laughed before she could ask if he was all right. Together, they swam away from the beach, the bay stretching out before them. The water was cold and black. By the time they reached the rocky shoals, they were gasping for air. Waves foamed around them, but it was shallow enough to sit looking back at the gaudy lights of summer homes above the silvery beach.

Once this had been a holy place. Rachel's ancestors had pulled their birchbark canoes onto these beaches to plant corn and burn tobacco, praying to the *Gitchi-manitou* that the water be smooth, the crops fruitful, the furs too numerous to count.

"When I was a kid," said Woody, "this was where we raced our boats. The trick was to judge the rocks."

They'd always owned boats, he told her. Sailing was the test of resolve and purpose. It was a source of family pride.

Rachel thought of her ancestors' canoes gliding effortlessly along the fickle shore. She looked at Woody. "You're shivering."

He seemed to be lost in thought. Side by side, they swam back, staggered onto the rocks, and collapsed. Rachel cried out as her knees hit the stones, but she felt happy as a child.

"I'm exhausted!" She laughed and looked at Woody. "And you?" She picked up a stone, tasted it—an ancient rock, cooled from molten sand, rich with magma and desire.

His eyes silver and alert, Woody reached out and took it from her. Rachel caught her breath. She listened for something, heard only the drumming of waves. His face blocked the moonlight as they lay on the ragged edge of shore, lapped by the lake. Tentatively, his mouth brushed against hers. She became ravenous with the taste of him, was surprised at his weight when he was nothing but hollow flesh and bone. A wave washed over them. When he kissed her again, she opened her mouth, tasted him with her tongue. Searching for a way home, she felt the curve of his hip against her thigh. He overtook her like the lake, his eyes never leaving her face. She took his pain into her, was rent by it. It cleaved her, caused her to buck, to call out his name, but when it was over, he was the one who cried.

Chapter Six

Rachel looked in the mirror to see if she was different. Her face appeared untouched. The same thick brows, the same dark eyes. A cloud of black still surrounded her head.

She examined her teeth, as firm in her gums as the day before. They weren't bad teeth, considering. One was chipped. Another toward the back was missing.

Holding her hand up to the light, she studied the skin between her fingers. Blood streamed through capillaries. She sniffed her wrists, ran her fingers across her jawbone, the nape of her neck, between her breasts, over her belly, across the spray of hair between her legs. She sat on the cot in her dormitory room, looked at the bottoms of her feet. Nothing.

At work that day, she folded sheets into the linen press the way she folded blankets at the convent. Each sheet, lightly starched, was halved and halved again, then twice more. She made blades of their edges, stacked them up just so.

Woody came up behind her, encircled her with his arms, searching, too, for the changes in her bones, her belly, her thighs. She did not turn, but leaned slightly back, allowing his chin to rest on her head. Mandy was sweeping down the hall. Rachel told him to go away, but nothing could keep him from her. He put his finger to her lips, pulled down a folded sheet. She tried to contain the stacks and her laughter, but he pulled sheets down twice as fast as she could push them back. When Mandy came around the corner, they were standing in a rumpled sea of white.

The days blew by, sultry as laundry on a line. He compared her eyes to figs and chestnuts, to amber syrup not yet hard. Lousy metaphors, he admitted, but he liked to tease her till she grew angry so he could compare her eyes to stormy seas.

"Tsss," she said. "You talk too much." But she remembered every word.

They pressed themselves into abandoned rooms full of sheeted furniture, a boat room in the basement, hulls stacked against the walls. They lay on stacks of mildewed sails, the thick-stitched seams leaving ladders in their flesh. Father, forgive me, Rachel thought as they sinned in places redolent of mothballs, fibrous with spiderwebs, in forgotten rooms scattered with mouse droppings. Moving through hallways, they pushed together behind doors, or stumbled down the path to the beach where, naked and dusty with sand, they lay on a blanket in the dunes, rained upon by pine needles, stopping only to swim in the blue, August lake.

"Rachel," Woody said, watching an ant trail up the gooseflesh of her thigh.

Mandy was the first to say something. They were at the kitchen table, shining silver with a polish that looked so much like chocolate pudding, Rachel was tempted to take a bite. Mandy rubbed a spoon with a soft cloth till the polish dried white, then buffed it off with an old diaper. Suddenly, she stopped.

"Rachel!" Mandy said. "Your knees!"

Rachel dropped her eyes to her knees, scabbed and bruised from kneeling on rocks. She took a deep breath, looked up earnestly at Mandy.

"Sometimes," Rachel said, "I pray so hard."

Mandy made a sound like a sneeze. "I'd cover those legs if I was you."

Rachel crossed her legs, let her skirt hitch higher, picked up a fork, ran her tongue along its tines. Mandy pursed her lips, checked her own reflection in the back of a spoon.

The buzzer rang twice. All eyes rose. Ella Mae stopped skimming a pot of stock, tightened her apron, headed up the stairs. Fifteen minutes later, she returned to the kitchen and held out two tortoiseshell clips—finely carved garlands, mounted on silver barrettes. "Mrs. March wanted me to give you these."

"What for?" asked Rachel.

Mandy picked up another spoon and gave Rachel a knowing nod. "She musta found your hair in her soup. Big black curly thing. Girl, you gotta do something with that mess."

"She seems to be pleased with Mr. Woody's progress. Even so," said Ella Mae, "a rubber band would do."

Rachel pulled the sides of her hair into the clips, bent down to see her reflection in the toaster, moved her head from side to side.

Ella Mae folded her arms. "Mrs. March *also* said that the bay-side guest room needs airing. Looks like we're having company."

Rachel's eyes slid away from the toaster. "What kind of company?"

"What's it to you? Ain't your company we're talking about."

That afternoon, Mandy eyed Rachel as they set the table.

"Sister, you got a look about you makes me shiver. Brrr. I ain't seen such demon looks since my cousin took ill from the weed."

Rachel didn't answer, just rearranged the way Mandy had placed the butter plates.

"And where do you come by setting the table different than me?"

"Mrs. March prefers these *over* the dinner plates," said Rachel. "Not to the left." The plates were blue upon blue, painted with scenes of windmills and sailboats.

"Oh, she does, does she?"

Head high, back arched, Mandy strode downstairs to the kitchen, returned with Ella Mae. Ella Mae jabbed her hands into her hips, circled the table slow as Jupiter, eyes pointed.

"Mandy," she said, looking at Rachel, "tells me you got a problem."

Rachel shrugged. "Mrs. March likes the plates this way."

"She tell you that?"

"She moves them herself before company."

Ella Mae's eyebrows shot up. Her voice was daggers. "Anything *else* she likes different? Her egg cooked softer or her tea stronger?"

"Is there a problem?" Mrs. March was standing in the doorway.

Ella Mae began to tap her foot. She didn't look at Mrs. March. "This girl here says you want the butter dishes like so. First I heard about it."

It was Mrs. March's turn to raise her eyebrows. She crossed her arms, moved toward the table, checked on one place, then the next. She turned a butter knife so that its handle was to the right, left the plates where Rachel put them.

"There," Mrs. March said. "Like so."

After Mrs. March left the room, Ella Mae's eyes snapped onto Rachel. "Child," she said, "it don't pay to get too smart."

That night, Rachel and Mandy served dinner. Woody sat across the table from his mother. The Hewetts had joined them. The girls removed the soup, returned from the kitchen with plates of whitefish on beds of potatoes, creamed spinach on the side. Rachel served Woody, looked down on his dark head, the crescent of lashes lowered away from her. He murmured as she took away plates, put down new ones. Too embarrassed to thank her, he spoke to her hands.

Mrs. March said, "Thank you, Rachel." Then she spoke to the Hewetts. "Isn't it grand to see Woody looking so well?"

They both agreed that it was.

Once Rachel thought Woody glanced up at her. She quickly looked away to keep from laughing. It became a game of not meeting eyes. I dare you. I dare you. Break your mother's back. I dare you.

The conversation drifted to paint and how often it needed redoing in these old houses.

"The winters!" said Mrs. Hewett.

Mrs. March shook her head. "Charles says they don't prime. I'm always telling the gardener to make sure they prime."

"He hires his cousins," Mrs. Hewett said. "They spend the winter hunting and do the work five minutes before we get here."

Rachel refilled the goblets with water. Ice clinked into them. A large chunk spilled into Woody's, splashing the tablecloth.

"It's okay," said Woody, mopping up the puddle. "I've got a napkin." He bundled the cloth tightly into Rachel's hand, raised his eyes to hers. His cheeks colored. Now she knew his mother's back would break.

In the kitchen, she unfolded it to find some tiny stones, a hunk of sea glass, grains of sand. Over the weeks, Woody had given her a Petoskey stone, its surface fossilized into tiny suns. A rusted train engine smaller than her palm appeared in the bottom of a soup bowl. She had found a crab claw in her pocket, a snipping of his hair. Even a map became a gift—latitudes, longitudes, islands with names she could not read.

Ella Mae clicked her teeth. "Does Mrs. March know you've been walking on the beach with her son?"

The napkin was cool and wet. Rachel held it to her neck. "He's a grown man. Why should she care?"

Besides, Mrs. March had given her the hair combs and a hand-me-down sweater just like Miss Elizabeth's. Perhaps it *had* been Miss Elizabeth's! A button was missing, the lace on the collar was frayed, but the sweater itself felt like the downy breast of a finch.

"Huh," said Ella Mae. "Grown man or not."

The next morning, Woody's mother called him to her room. She had taken it upon herself to invite Elizabeth. "She needs to talk to you. She may have changed her mind." When Woody stared at her, unable to find words, his mother added, "Aren't you pleased?"

Beyond the window, the lake glittered fiercely.

Woody met Rachel in the hall. She was carrying sheets, two sets of twins. Face-to-face, she told him they were for his "guest," as if the word was pill-bitter upon her tongue.

Woody wanted to dash the sheets from her hands. "My mother asks me nothing."

He looked at Rachel's fingers. Slightly rough, cuticles ragged. Long feet, the baby toe bent under. A thumb-size depression near the small of her back. The seamless curve of her buttock. Hair he could drown in. Eyes.

He started to say, It's just for a few days. "I'm going mad," he said.

"*You're* going mad?" Rachel stifled a laugh.

And what would he tell Elizabeth? That he wanted to tear this house down, board by board, until it was nothing but dunes and weeds? Its corridors were shadowed with memories. The faintest smell of cut grass took him back. Even his father had grown up in this house, run up and down its stairs, swam off its beach. Rachel's ancestors may have gone in fire. His went in camphor and faded chintz.

The ghost-pains of Woody's amputation were one thing, but his acutely felt sense of family permeated the walls, the tarnished engravings of silver, the beds slept in by generations. Even now, the presence of long-dead skin still clung to sheets, breath on the mirrors, the litany of stories told and retold.

In the end, he couldn't bring himself to tear this house apart. He hadn't the courage. Staring at the sheets in Rachel's hands, he thought of the thin beds they would shroud.

"Woody!" his mother called from the porch. "Look who's here!"

Woody could hear the crunch of gravel as he made his way to the front of the house. The Buick pulled up, and Jonah opened the rear door. Out came a slim foot in a black high heel.

"Lovely girl!" his mother called down. "You've brought the weather!"

Woody watched her from the porch. It was part of Elizabeth's trousseau, this talent for weather and looking lovely. Why shouldn't she have brought these flawless skies, this wind-ruffled water?

"Oh, go on," said his mother. "Go down and meet her."

The moored boats clanged in the gusty breeze that whipped the scarf around Elizabeth's throat. He knew that throat. Tan in summer, pale in winter, traversed by a faint, blue vein. How many months since she had stood at his hospital bed, held his hand? When the nurses changed his dressing, Elizabeth had turned away.

Now she was holding her arms out, her blond hair frothy, the gesture at once pleading and possessive. If he went to her, embraced her, he would have to tell her it was wonderful to see her. Even if she *had* broken off the engagement, she had traveled so far. How could he not?

That evening, Elizabeth found him on the bay-side porch. Dinner was over. Inside, Mandy cleared the table while June bugs, frantic for the light, banged against the screens.

"It's so calm," said Elizabeth. "I feel I could swim right across."

"It's five miles," said Woody.

"Still," she said, "I could do it."

Woody had risen when she came outside. Now he sank back into the glider. It groaned as he moved. It was covered with some kind of canvas, redolent of mildew. The paint on the arms was peeling.

As if she read his mind, Elizabeth said, "This old place."

Was it exasperation or affection he heard in her voice? Woody drew a long, deep breath. "Why did you come, Elizabeth?"

"I should have come sooner." She was sitting in an old wicker chair next to him. Now she drew her knees into her chest, scanned the lake as if it held a thousand reasons. "I thought you were dead, Woody." She rested her cheek on her knee so she could look at him. "Everyone else seemed to be. So when you weren't, it was the most astounding luck."

Some laughter rose on the breeze from a party two houses down. Woody wondered if they had been invited. Either way, he wouldn't have gone.

"You couldn't even look at me."

"And *you* wouldn't talk to *me*," Elizabeth finished.

"I'm sorry."

She put two fingers against his lips. "No," she said, shaking her head. Suddenly she smiled. "Tell me how well I look."

Slowly, he removed her hand from his mouth, held it in his. "You always do."

"Tell me."

She *was* lovely. It was what had drawn him to her. Tonight, her hair was twisted up. Silver disks at her ears, silver cuffs at her wrists. Linen slacks. She seemed to be on fire with her white blond hair, her eyes, which matched his own, that skin. A fine, rare bird who talked a mile a minute and made him laugh. Now she had come to claim this summer house, its mismatched wicker, its faded photographs, him. If she had her way, her picture would hang here, too, her smile both broad and beautiful.

"Lovely," said Woody. "Lovely and exotic."

"*Anything* looks exotic in northern Michigan!" she said with a pout, but he could see she was pleased.

The sky had darkened almost to black.

"Look," said Elizabeth, "the first star!"

Woody followed her pointed finger. "It's not a star," he said. "It's Venus."

"It *has* to be a star," Elizabeth insisted. She touched his arm. "I've already wished!"

The hills to the east were barely visible in the morning sun when Rachel, heavy with fatigue, started up the walk. Not even September, and already the maple trees were tinged with red. Soon the houses would be boarded up, the furniture sheeted, the boats led to dry dock across a green autumn lake.

The kitchen smelled of cinnamon and frying eggs. Mandy, stacking toast in a silver rack, was breathless.

"Hand-stitched," she said. "Solid with beads. The entire dress!"

"What else?" said Ella Mae.

Mandy closed her eyes. Her words were delicious as syrup. "And a cashmere cape. Same color."

Ella Mae glanced at Rachel, who was hanging up her sweater. "That Parker girl is rough on cashmere. I seen what she done to that sweater she threw out."

"I don't think she'll be throwing out this cape," said Mandy. "The dress neither."

Ella Mae hooted and turned to Rachel. "What would the nuns think, a dress like that handed down end of summer?"

Rachel put on her apron, tied it behind her back. Lifting the kettle from the stove, she poured hot water into a china pot. The steam rose up and burned her cheeks.

"Rachel," Ella Mae said when the buzzer sounded, "you take Miss Elizabeth her tea."

She seemed to be studying Rachel for a reaction, but Rachel had set her face like stone. I am rock, she thought as she carried the tray up to Miss Elizabeth's room.

She knocked. Knocked again, then cracked the door. The bath was running, so she set the tray on the table by the window. She had looked from this window many times—changed the linen, collected the towels. Today, she found the view too narrow. She touched the clothes strewn over the back of a chair. Butter-soft leather, good for moccasins. On the dressing table—lipsticks and silver earrings, a string of pearls, a tortoiseshell case for cigarettes. She fingered the pearls.

The faucets in the bathroom squeaked off.

"I've brought your tea," said Rachel. She stared at the door for a minute. Finally, a splash, a thud, the sound of water draining. "Your tea?"

The door opened. Miss Elizabeth, in a towel, peeked around, her wet hair knotted on top of her head. "Could you toss me my cigs? They're on the bureau."

Rachel picked up the tortoiseshell case, handed it to Miss Elizabeth, and started to make the bed. Through the half-open doorway, she could see the steamy, white-tiled bathroom, a cigarette balanced on the edge of the sink. From beneath her lids, Rachel studied the back of Miss Elizabeth's neck, her foot perched on the toilet seat, the crimson paint that bloodied each toe. The smell of polish was sharp. The color overwhelmed her. Suddenly nauseated, Rachel turned from the room, dashed down the hall to an empty bathroom. Kneeling, her stomach convulsed, but gave up little. A bit of breakfast. Some tea. The lingering taste of sand and lake.

In the living room, Rachel emptied ashtrays into a silver dish, fluffed the pillows, eavesdropped. In the dining room, Mrs. March was speaking to Miss Elizabeth, saying any child of hers would rise above his disabilities. It was no use for Woody to dwell on these things. The ones who came back in '19, the ones who didn't forget—they fell into despair. Remember how Uncle Maynard twitched and had nothing to say?

Rachel sniffed a vase of black-eyed Susans and found the water had turned.

"If he won't see his friends, we'll bring them to him," Mrs. March said. "He'll come around. You'll see."

Rachel wondered how Miss Elizabeth could stand Mrs. March with her constant instructions, her blessings, and her plans. If *she* was Miss Elizabeth, Rachel would tell Mrs. March to mind her own business.

In a sulky voice, Miss Elizabeth said, "And if he doesn't want me anymore?"

"Has he said anything?"

"He hasn't begged me to marry him, if that's what you mean."

Rachel leaned against the wall.

"Let me tell you something about Woody, Elizabeth," said Mrs. March. "He can be convinced. What he needs is a wife and children. And once you have the children, the thing is set for good."

"And if he can't?"

A hand on Rachel's shoulder made her jump. She turned to see Woody's eyes, inches from hers. His mouth.

"Rachel," he said.

His face was drawn and gray. She wanted to take him into her, puncture his skin, draw her nails across him till he bled.

Rachel was shaking a rug out on the porch when Miss Elizabeth found her.

"Oh, there you are! Would you be a darling," said Miss Elizabeth, holding out a blouse to Rachel, "and touch this up? I meant to give it to Mandy this morning. The suitcases ruin everything."

Rachel took the blouse.

Back in the kitchen, Rachel held it to her cheek. The blouse was the color of sea foam. There were vegetables to clean, a soup to stir. A short cold snap had given way to a late-summer heat. Rachel tossed Miss Elizabeth's blouse onto the table. The heat had made her restless and more. Enervating. That's what the nuns had said.

"This heat is something! I wish I had me some ice cream," Mandy said. "And you look green as old cheese."

"I'm fine."

But Ella Mae laid her hand on Rachel's forehead and looked into her eyes. "Mmm, mmm."

Tears collected as Rachel chopped onion for the soup. She had wiped her nose with the back of her hand and gone back to chopping when the knife slipped.

"My soul!" said Ella Mae, grabbing the nearest cloth and pressing it into Rachel's hand.

"I'm all right," Rachel said, but the cloth quickly soaked through with red. "It doesn't hurt."

"It will."

Rachel unfolded the bloody cloth, realized it was Miss Elizabeth's blouse. She liked the rippled patterns of red the creases made. For one whole week, she had checked her underwear for the same sort of stain.

My hand bleeds, she thought. My knees. Nothing else.

CHAPTER SEVEN

A cross a field of damask, Woody watched his childhood friends laughing in the candlelight. Jay Hewett had aged, filled out since the war—one of those men who came back invigorated rather than spent. Max Bailey, Serena's fiancé, had gone from a pimply adolescent to pompous and jowly in a few short summers. Some girl Woody couldn't remember was there with Lambert Redding who smoked all through dinner, saying nothing. Lambert's sister, Diedre, looked dour next to Elizabeth, who was stunning in her strapless dress. Standing beside his hospital bed the year before, Elizabeth had looked like a picture. But Woody had lost his taste for pictures.

Max Bailey was trying to form words with a mouth full of salad. He jabbed his fork at Jay Hewett. "Luff them up before the mark so they'll have to tack."

"And if they ask for room?"

"Make them beg for it. Mast to beam."

"So competitive! Won't Max do well at business school?" Elizabeth said, her eyes fixed on Woody.

Woody almost laughed. Elizabeth's smile seemed to say, We used to laugh so much!

Max's voice buzzed in Woody's skull. Woody dipped his finger into his champagne glass, ran it slowly and evenly around the rim. A low hum, ominous at first, crescendoing into a high-pitched whine.

Diedre clasped her hands over her ears and said, "Ooo!" but Elizabeth was delighted.

"Again!"

Rachel was in the kitchen. She had served Woody and his friends on gold-edged plates, taking care not to clatter the silver, returning with Mandy, back and forth, back and forth.

Once more, Woody concocted the eerie, crystal harmony while everyone listened.

"Funny stuff," said Max, turning back to Jay Hewett.

Woody didn't stop. He ran his finger around and around. The laughter this time was dampened, the politeness forced.

Although she was smiling, Elizabeth's voice cracked. "Woody?"

Working a piece of ice between his fingers to soothe his flesh, Woody half-expected an after-dinner game of musical chairs, little Jay-Jay Hewett crying because his chair had toppled over, Max standing upon his, crowing that he had won. Who were these people? Had they ever been friends?

He raised his glass, drank it empty. "Well, then. Brandy on the porch."

"Oh, please," said Elizabeth. "The smell!"

For the past week, the beach had been littered with alewives. Once every decade or so, scads of the dead fish would wash up, perishing all at once for no particular reason. The yardmen would have to rake the beaches, bury the offending corpses. This summer, their stench was particularly strong in the harbor.

"The bay-side porch, then," said Woody.

"I'll ring for the girl," said Elizabeth, feeling with her foot for the buzzer.

"No," said Woody, "let me. I'm the only one who can ever find the damned thing." He sank beneath the table. Finding the lump beneath the rug, he pressed it, sending a soundless signal to invisible ears. "There," he said, heaving himself back into his chair, "I've called the girl."

Below on the beach, waves broke, pulled back. It was a warm evening, and they were going to play bridge. There had been martinis before dinner and later, wine. Serena was already tottering. The other girl's lipstick was smudged. One face, then another, moved in and out of focus. Elizabeth helped Woody to the porch. Someone—possibly Jonah—had brought out candles. A moth fluttered near the flame. Woody flicked it away. The cards were dealt. Two tables of four.

"Woody," said Elizabeth, "your bid."

Woody bid two clubs, folded his hand. From the porch he could see Rachel clearing the table. Out here, the sound of the lake, the flickering of shadowy faces. Inside, the woman who smelled of lake water. My mistress is serving me, Woody thought. Covering his eyes, he erased the image of her working. He spread his fingers, and she became his wife clearing the table. Fingers closed again, he made Elizabeth disappear, his mother's will, the sense he had of a plane bearing down. Spreading them wide, he saw only Rachel. His fingers closed and opened.

Rachel piled plate upon plate. She wasn't supposed to stack the china, but she had gone up and down the stairs at least ten times. Her legs hurt. She found it hard to breathe.

Woody was drinking too much. Once she had leaned over him and asked if she could help, but he turned away from her, spoke to someone else. They talked of people she didn't know, subjects she didn't understand. She remembered sitting among the elders as a child, their murmured Odawa difficult to her ears. She had moved behind Woody's friends, removed their plates, replaced them with others. Someone said thank you. Miss Elizabeth even smiled. Rachel had lingered, smelling Miss Elizabeth's perfume.

Woody and his friends had gone out to the porch. Helping Jonah with the coffee, Rachel set the cups on a tray, followed the old butler outside. She offered sugar. Woody asked for brandy. Rachel felt his stare.

Suddenly, he turned to Miss Elizabeth. "What?"

"Your face."

He threw down a card. "My face? My face is made for poker."

"Really?" said Miss Elizabeth. "That was a terrible bid. And you're tipping your hand."

Something in Miss Elizabeth's expression made Rachel almost sorry for her. How did Miss Elizabeth do her hair that way? So many pins to make it smooth. Rachel wanted to pluck one out.

"So, Jonah," said one of the men, speaking to the butler, "how's the fishing this summer? When're you going to live up to your name, old man, and catch a whopper?"

One of the women laughed and said, "Whenever Max drinks, he starts sounding English."

"Quiet, wench!" said the man. "Better an aristocrat than the landless bastard of some potato farmer." The woman laughed louder.

"Aren't we all?" said Woody.

"Aren't we all *what,* old boy?"

"Displaced. Bastardized." Woody swallowed some brandy. "Whatever it was you said."

"See here," said the man, with an amused look at the rest of the group, "sounds like you flew a bit too close to the Russian front." In a loud whisper, he added, "Got a soft spot for the peasants, have we?"

The conversation stopped. "Bastard," Woody said under his breath.

A moth flew into the flame, ignited.

One of the women looked from Woody to Miss Elizabeth, then kicked the man under the table. "Honestly, Max. Play the game."

"But I am."

Woody threw down his cards and said, "You'll have to excuse me." His chair tipped over as he rose. A drink overturned.

Elizabeth stood up. "Woody, I'm soaked!"

Passing by Rachel, Woody muttered, "I need a shot."

Rachel wanted to follow him, but Jonah stopped her. "Rachel," he said, "get Miss Elizabeth a napkin."

Woody lay across his bed. Through the open window, he could hear Elizabeth saying good night. Would her voice always be this forced and cheerful?

"Just one little kiss, Elizabeth. C'mon."

Serena's sharp voice. "Max!"

Any minute, Rachel would come to give him a shot. Just for her, he had gone for weeks without it. She had become his drug. But now he felt as though he was arcing through air, falling into the sea. Icarus ignited. How could Rachel begrudge him?

The turquoise beam of the lighthouse swept across his ceiling with indifferent regularity. Woody could hear the clink of bottles as Jonah restocked the bar. His mother would be home soon. She shouldn't see him so drunk. Why hadn't Rachel come?

Resigned, Woody pulled himself up and limped to the bathroom, took a syringe and a vial, returned to his bed. The need was more urgent than ever. He tapped the glass of the bottle. Did his leg hurt? He was certain it did.

In his upper arm, a prick and a burn.

"Woody?"

He looked up to see Elizabeth staring at the needle, his pulled-up sleeve. Her lips were parted. Her hair had come loose. He waited for her protest, the dull assertion that he mustn't.

She came to him, sank to her knees. He could feel the divine shift as his body left him.

"Shall I call the girl?"

He started to laugh. She smiled but couldn't find the joke. He was laughing about nothing. His breathing evened, slowed. Elizabeth's face turned toward his the way a flower turned toward the sun. It was a lovely face, he tried to tell her. She was pulling him down, but he kept floating away, tossed in the waves of morphine.

"Woody," she said, "do you love me?"

She was grasping him. He tried to say, I can't, but the words ebbed before he spoke them. She kissed him, bent her ear to his lips. Almost distractedly, he pushed up her dress, ran his hand up her leg. She wanted him to say her name, to hear it the way she imagined on their wedding night, clearly and lovingly, not the way he said it now—mumbled, slurred, sounding like the name of another girl.

"Tell me."

Her dress unbuttoned, he pushed apart her thighs. Her skin became his as their teeth knocked together.

The dim beam of the lighthouse traced the walls. A limp tress of hair dangled from Elizabeth's forehead as she pulled him into her. There were footsteps in the hallway.

"Tell me," Elizabeth groaned in a voice that wasn't hers. One of her sandals had fallen to the floor. On her skin, the stale, sweet reek of Shalimar.

The beach was quiet as a holy place. A path of moon tracked across the bay. Rachel stood, her arms crossed, looking out. The water was too big here. Somewhere there was a smaller lake, warmer, its bottom soft with clay and rotted leaves instead of rocks that cut and bruised.

Everywhere—the stink of dying fish. Rachel flinched as her knees hit the beach. The water rushed across her thighs, her belly. She wanted to wash away what she had seen through the door. She thought she had heard Miss Elizabeth crying. But why would Miss Elizabeth cry? Who would cry, knowing they had everything? If she were Miss Elizabeth, Rachel would not cry—not as she was crying now, tears like stones, hard and bitter.

CHAPTER EIGHT

Woody stood in the door of his mother's room. He had rehearsed all morning. He wanted to tell his mother that everything had changed, that Elizabeth was right to call off the engagement. She shouldn't have come. His mother needed to see it through Woody's eyes the way he had seen bodies floating past, the girl on the dock under a silver moon.

But now he was going off on a tangent, telling his mother instead about the kamikaze and how it felt to have a plane bearing down. *They blew right into us. Can you imagine that kind of resolve? Not even Lip. . . .*

His mother wasn't listening. The phone had rung, she had lifted the receiver and said, *Yes? Yes?* Light spilled onto piles of books beside her bed. Jesus looked down from the wall. When Woody was a child, he used to love to pick up the receiver and listen to the prim operator voice ask, *What number, please?*

"Mother?" he said.

The phone had fallen from her hand. His mother's eyes glistened, and her skin seemed bloodless. Woody could hear the distant sound of a plane, possibly a B-29 from the airstrip in Manistee. His mother's hand as she reached for him was cool and brittle, her words as garbled as his memory of Elizabeth the night before.

"Your father's heart," she said.

Woody suddenly felt self-indulgent, as if what he had to say meant nothing. Now the plane seemed to be aimed at his heart. It was terrifying to know he was a condemned man, and yet so oddly comforting. He pulled away from his mother, turned to call for Jonah. His mother rose, took her Jesus from the wall, held it to her chest. Stroking his crown of thorns, she rocked him like her child.

Wheels shrieking, the train pulled out of Moss Village, picking up speed and slowing again at Pont du Lac. Woody could still see the edge of white sand as it curved around the bay, the trees, hills, the church spire, but the houses on Beck's Point were now merely specks. Summer receded. The train sped up. Soon the trees blocked the bay.

My God, he thought. And then, as if to evoke a divinity who would intercede, turn the train back, make him become something he was not, he said it again. But Woody had never really believed in God. Even his mother's tenacious Catholicism had failed to move him.

Elizabeth laid her hand on his as they rumbled past a quarry. Rachel would have arrived by now to find the Buick gone, the trunks brought up from storage. Would she find the letter he had left on his bedside table? His hand had shaken, and he could hardly write the words. *Love. Sorrow. I can't.* He had started it three times. *Rachel,* he had written, telling her he was a coward. That he had cared for her in spite of himself. He had written these words, torn them up, started again. *I cannot shirk my responsibility. I am to be a banker, sooner than I thought. I am half the man my brother was. I am in no way fit to be a husband.*

The train turned inland, rattled on.

Jonah was dragging in the wicker porch furniture as Rachel came up the steps. In the kitchen, Mandy was scrubbing the oven. No cooking smells, only the sickly tartness of bleach and Borax.

"You heard?" said Mandy.

Rachel shook her head.

Pious-eyed, Mandy wrung out her sponge. "Mr. March," she said with relish, "had himself a heart attack."

"Rachel!" Ella Mae snapped as she came into the kitchen. "You strip the beds. Sheets and linens can be ironed later. We gotta be on the train back to St. Louis tomorrow."

Mandy leaned over and whispered, "He'll be dead by tonight!"

Taking the stairs two at a time, Rachel ran up to Woody's room. She pulled open his desk drawers, his bureau, scanned the top of his tables. Nothing. She tore back his bedspread, patterned with anchors. Surely there was something! Perhaps that piece of driftwood or the sand between the floorboards was meant for her. Would he go and leave her nothing? She smelled the bristles of his shaving brush, opened books, shook out pages. The radiator hissed like a snake. Soon, the pipes would be drained, the house bled out and emptied.

In the bathroom, she found some hair in the sink, a dropped towel, a crushed pack of Camels. A rock like a clenched fist drew her attention. She placed it in her pocket.

"There you are," said Ella Mae, holding a box of rat poison. "And when you're done here, the fireplace needs emptying."

Mandy's broom scratched in the hallway. Rachel asked Ella Mae if she thought the Marches would come back.

"All the way from St. Louis? Uh-uh, girl," said Ella Mae, shaking her head, her eyes drifting toward the bedside table. "This summer's done."

CHAPTER NINE

Rachel rested her cheek on the confessional grille. "Father forgive me for I have sinned."

"How long since your last confession?"

"Three weeks." She dug her nails into the soft brown wood.

"Too long. What is the nature of your sin?"

Rachel considered the question. Outside the confessional, one of the girls was scrubbing tiles. The mop swished back and forth, the sharp bite of ammonia mixing with Spic and Span and incense.

"I have had a vision, Father."

The priest waited, but Rachel said no more. Cloistered in darkness, she knew what he wanted—what they all wanted: for her to speak of lust and sin. Purge yourself, he would tell her, and she would say, I tried. She had gone with a man and she liked it. She would do it again, even though he was spoken for and now she was with child. That was what he wanted—Father Tom with his sad, spotty flesh—so he could make her tell him what it was like, what they did, where and how they touched. Rachel, close to the screen, smelled something foul and salty the priest had had for lunch. In mutual darkness, they would come together, divided, so that their lips almost touched, and Rachel would say, "Here, Father. He touched me here." And he would make her say rosaries all through the night and crawl across the yard on her knees until they bled like the wounds of Jesus.

"A vision? About what?"

"The son."

"The Son?"

"My *employer's* son," said Rachel. "Woody March."

A pause. Rachel imagined the priest stroking his lips, examining the tips of his fingers. The confessional was too warm, the velvet of the curtain too cloying. She breathed in the sweet smell of communion wine, counted the seconds, a hundred years since the Odawa handed their land over to the Jesuits.

"What vision could you possibly have had about Woody March?"

She touched herself, her hand clenching to the sound of the Father's breathing, her fingers finding the place that Woody March had found. Pressing into herself, she rubbed.

He touched me here.

Father Tom whispered her name, but Rachel, cleansed, confessed, heard only the residue of hymns.

"What did you say to Father Tom?"

Rachel stood in front of the nun's desk, her hands folded behind her. Sister Marie stared back at her, Rachel looking more deranged than she had as a child, filthy with lice when they found her, lips cracked and bruised, her grandmother dead for days.

"Nothing, Sister."

The rug was beige and comfortless. On the walls, framed photographs of priests—clean-shaven, Jesuit, and pale. There was a purple blotch on Sister Marie's face—like the red mottling of the rock she had found in Woody's room. Now the blotch pulsed furiously.

"You're in trouble, aren't you?"

When Rachel didn't answer, Sister Marie crossed herself, cupped her head in her hands. When she looked up, Rachel saw the face of the Madonna, bereft, marred, so sad she almost wanted to comfort the nun, to say it was all right, the blood would come. Burnt cedar could make you bleed rivers. The pollen of goldenseal brought on cramps. Rachel would chew on mint leaves, the dried bones of seagulls. Any day now, the blood would come.

Sister Marie sighed, asked hopefully, "A workman?"

Rachel shook her head.

"One of the help, then?"

Eyes met eyes. Sister Marie was the first to look away. She drummed her fingers on the desk, lined up the pencils, studied Rachel's raveled braids, her knees gone black and blue.

Shaking her head, Sister Marie pressed her thumbs into her lids. The girl had been her responsibility since she was fourteen. Her mouth drawn into a line, Sister Marie said, "This is what you're going to do."

It was not the first time that she had laid out instructions for penitence. There were novenas to be said, candles to be lit, saints to be prayed to. Rachel would stay at the convent, take her classes. Toward spring, when the evidence of her shame grew too apparent, Rachel would go to a place where girls like her could go.

"A station, if you will, of the cross."

Rachel ran her tongue across a chipped tooth. She wondered if the nun was worried more about her or what the Marches would say. Would Rachel be able to talk to Woody? Could she write? She had no address, but she could still steal out and fly down the road, past the piers and the gate, to the now-empty house, locked surely, yet nothing was impenetrable. There were drawers full of letters, slips of fine paper.

As if she had read Rachel's mind, Sister Marie said, "You shall speak to no one of this."

Rachel touched her belly, gleaned the thin, sharp tug of something growing. For a moment she imagined the baby, one-legged like its father, but the image blurred, rearranged itself, and a scarred face turned its eyes upon her.

"We're all sinners, Rachel," said Sister Marie almost compassionately. "We reek of it."

Autumn was slow to come. Rachel watched the trees in the yard lose their green, become suddenly, violently red. She spread her arms wide against the fence.

Grass paled to the color of straw, dead things collected in gutters, were raked into piles, and everywhere the smell of burning leaves. Rachel imagined forests, the woods of her childhood, a bonfire of birch and ash. The sun slanted lower in the yard, the shadows flickered, faded, died. A child called for her, then Sister Marie, but Rachel's braids had taken root.

That night, Rachel's devotions to the Virgin went unsaid. The diamonds of fence wire etched faintly into her palms, she untied her braids, set free her hair, praying instead to the great god *Gitchi-manitou,* the hunter *Nanabozhoo,* and silently cursed the Marches. Sleepless, she sorted through her collection of gifts from Woody, feeling each shell, each stone, each piece of glass.

The days shortened until, by dinner, it was dark. Darkness was a mask. One night, Rachel pulled her hand-me-down coat around her shoulders and escaped under a powder of stars. Leaves muffled her steps as, shadowed, she glided under trees and through gates of Beck's Point unseen. Arriving at the Marches' house, her hair loose, she rushed like a bride up the leaf-covered stairs.

Everything was locked up tight. Guiding herself with the railing, Rachel scrambled back down the steps to find a rock by the empty pond. Rock in hand, she returned to the front door, the panes divided by strips of lead, the glass old and thin. The sound of glass breaking was sharp and wrenching. A raccoon, they would think. A raccoon broke the glass.

The house was changed. Everywhere, the gleam was dulled, the furniture sheeted, the rooms dried and desiccated. There were no flowers in vases, no warm smells in the kitchen. The dank odor of emptied pipes and toilets, their basins rusted and evil. Mothballs. Rat poison.

She went to Woody's room. There would be an address—if not here, then in Mrs. March's room. The beds, unmade, looked smaller than she remembered. The light was gray and septic, the floor stained where something had spilled. Upon the shelves, the children's books lined up like soldiers.

Rachel opened the drawer of a rolltop desk to find pencils and postcards, stamps and a letter opener. She fingered a stack of envelopes addressed to Mr. Woodrow March and postmarked in St. Louis. Snatching the letters, she sat on the bed. A cold wind rattled the windows. Rachel's hand shook as she unfolded the paper. The handwriting was brisk and confident. Such pretty handwriting! Descriptions of weather and friends, declarations of love, whispers of concern, assurances of loyalty tumbled in Rachel's ears like tongues. Her fingers traced across words like "Darling, I was being silly," across Miss Elizabeth's signature. The paper was crisp, fine as birch bark. Rachel wanted to tear the letters, crumple them into a ball, light them on fire. Such beautiful things, these letters. Rachel wished she had written them herself.

Snow came early and hard. Flakes twisted and eddied in the corners of the yard, clung to dead things, drifted into shrouds. Rachel had found the Marches' address in a book in Woody's room, scrawled in a childish hand.

The name of the street—Buckingham—sounded like a prince should live there. Ladue, not St. Louis, was the town. Rachel wrote one letter, then another telling Woody of his gift to her, that he had gone and left her something after all. *Darling,* she wrote, trying out the word. *Darling, I tried to stop it, but the pollen of goldenseal, the burnt cedar hasn't worked.*

She bribed one of the girls to post her letters across the street, then waited for his reply. Days. Weeks. Perhaps the address was wrong. By December, Rachel had ceased looking up at lunch when the nun arrived with the mail. She bent over her plate, furtively guarded her food, dropped her fork when someone spoke to her, ate instead with her fingers.

The lake—what she could see of it—froze by inches, flinty as mica, thickening finally into the hardness of stone. It took on the color of winter, faintly blue where the ice broke and piled up again. The horizon merged with the sky. Rachel could not see the canyons of ice or the glowing huts where the fishermen spent their nights. She imagined a deep place where she could swim, but that place, too, was ice.

At night, her sleep worried by dreams, Rachel lay chambered as a nautilus, knees to chest, arm thrust over her head like a child's. She dreamt of baskets—the weavings of bark and sweet grass, the patterns made of quills. Flowers. Clouds. The spread wings of an eagle. When she awoke, she knew she had created something, that her bones, flesh, and tissue were the vessel. A thin echo to her own heartbeat, and her belly, verdant, swelled.

February, and the snowbanks eclipsed the road, stacked halfway up trees, muffled the chickadee's song, giving start to the rumor that spring would never come. The swing in the play yard was buried above the glider, the statue of the Virgin nearly gone, yet nothing was as desolate as what she could not see—the boarded houses of summer, their insides coated with leaves and a filtering of snow, fine as gossamer.

The last of Rachel's sleep evaporated with the clicking of a nun's shoes down the hall. She sat up, face rumpled, hair warm and cat-licked, her white gown loose about her widening waist. Lately, she had marveled at the dark line tracing up her belly, at how her wild locks had grown heavier and wilder still.

Sister Marie's hair was pulled back tightly into her habit. "They're here."

There was little to pack. Nothing fit anymore. Quickly, Rachel shoved her box of shells and rocks into a bag. On the concrete stoop, she scuffed at a brown patch of ice with her heel, pulled at her coat with its ratty fox trim, said "Ma'am" when Sister introduced her to two women whose names she did not catch.

Father Tom put his hand on her shoulder, stroked her braid. "We're awfully fond of our little Rachel."

Rachel's eyes were downcast when Sister Marie touched her other shoulder, put her lips to Rachel's ear. Rachel expected a last little word of advice, some admonition. But the nun's words, hastily whispered, froze hard as the lake.

Forget him. He's married.

Rachel stepped down the first step, nearly slipped. One of the women grasped her arm. Rachel did not look back at Sister Marie or the priest. They drove away, and for the first time, Rachel saw the whole town was white, and that the harbor, too, was a field of snow—frozen water she could walk across to that place where, in winter, no one lived.

CHAPTER TEN

S now as far as she could see. Fields of it covering last summer's thistle and corn, fields she might have run across if she were a child, falling into the snow, making angels. Icicles, sharp as teeth, hanging from the eaves. From the windows of the little house, Rachel looked out on snow interrupted only by a pale line of trees. It came in flurries and blizzards, covering the roads, the walk. Every day, one of the women put on her coat and left with a shovel.

The two women were pleasant enough. Rachel wondered if she could trust them. They didn't talk much, for which Rachel was grateful. Didn't constantly ask how she was feeling and if she needed more meat and if the baby was kicking and what would she name it when it came. It was a no-name baby they would deliver, a no-name baby whose cord they would cut, whose bloody forehead they would clean, whose bottom they would spank till it cried while Rachel lay emptied and spent.

Their names were Ada and Bliss.

Arrangements had been made. Rachel could tell from their talk, though she asked no questions, told them nothing, spoke no words. Words were stones in her mouth. She peeled the potatoes as they told her, sitting with them at their table, looking away when they smiled in an earnest, pitying way that made her stomach turn, trying to win her over with talk of farming and foaling, little jokes about the nuns, comments about how she was lucky because someone had taken an interest. *An interest!* That Rachel had been sent here instead of one of the wards with a bunch of girls like herself—big-bellied and unwanted, scores of them who had trusted some boy.

Forget him. He's married.

What had she been thinking when she lay on the beach with a man who showered her with stones and shells and sand?

Now she was cloistered on this farm in the middle of nowhere with two women who slept with each other in the same bed. It wasn't much, Bliss said to Rachel, but it had been in her family for eighty years.

"Homesteaders," she explained as she rose to light the oven. She limped a little, maybe from an old injury, maybe from arthritis. Ada was always fussing after her, making her take her medicine, rubbing salve into her ankles at night.

Rachel, who had decided to stop speaking, said nothing. Homesteaders, indeed. And whose land had they stolen in the first place? Ever since she was a child, Rachel had heard the stories about how the government had tricked the Indians. Homesteading was just one word for it.

"First-generation Polacks," Ada added knowingly.

"No worse than shanty Irish!" Bliss said, eyes flashing but fond. Turning back to Rachel, she went on. "You should see it in the summer. You'll be delivered by then, but goodness, these acres are pretty. Corn and alfalfa. Sheep in the barley fields."

She was large as a tree, this Bliss. Polish hands, Polish neck, and a smile which, if Rachel were to trust it, warmed up the room.

Ada, on the other hand, was wiry and Irish. "Killarney stock," Ada said, adding with a wink that she was a lapsed Catholic, but don't tell the nuns. This almost made Rachel smile, but she locked her lips against it.

"Still," said Ada, nodding at Rachel's belly, "there's money in midwifery, and a good thing, too." She told Rachel they'd almost lost the farm in the 1930s, but had made ends meet selling bathtub gin to the pharmacist who sold it as cough medicine.

"Till Ada," said Bliss, wiping her hands on her apron, "developed a chronic cough of her own and drank up all the profits."

"Irish," Ada whispered to Rachel, winking again, and Rachel, in spite of herself, smiled.

The room the two women had given her was built into the eaves. Downstairs, the sound of a kettle being filled, a heavy skillet set upon the stove.

Morning came earlier now. In the half-light, Rachel rose slowly, smelling bacon. She almost groaned with hunger. Now that the baby was big in her belly, now that she saw the trails of its feet, felt its elbows in her ribs, she wanted to feed it, nourish it with love, food, air. It had possessed her, this baby she had tried, with roots and goldenseal, to keep from growing. Their entrails knit together, she ran her hand across her stomach and whispered the only words she spoke.

As she came downstairs, Rachel could hear them talking. She stopped at the door to listen.

"You think she'll put up a fight?"

"She never talks. Besides," Ada said, "she has no family of her own."

A station of the cross, Sister Marie had said, but Rachel, trying to fit the pieces together, wondered who was paying for it and why. A pot banged. Inside her belly, the baby flopped like a fish.

"They say a family in Grayling will take it."

A silence. Then Ada spoke. "Don't suppose she'll be working in *that* house again."

Rachel closed the door and tiptoed away.

At lunch, she fingered her bread. A cuckoo clock chimed, sending out a boy and girl who whirled around each other before disappearing behind two separate doors. The women seemed preoccupied with a cow that wasn't eating, wondered if it was the hay.

"No other animals getting sick off hay," said Ada. She pushed back her short, white hair. "That cow's too picky."

Finally, Rachel could stand it no longer. "I do *too* have family."

Bliss, her fork in midair, looked stunned.

"She talks!" said Ada. "A miracle!"

"Rachel," said Bliss, "what did you say?"

This time Rachel spoke up. "I have an aunt and an uncle. They live on a lake."

"And what lake is that?" said Ada.

"A man named McCready owns it, but he leaves us alone." She stared at her food. "*Ke-she-kee-kee* it used to be, but most of us call it 'Horseshoe.'"

"Ah," said Ada. The two women glanced at each other.

"If you don't believe me," Rachel said, "I'll show you."

A green lake in summer, she told them. Gray in autumn. Now surely white.

"And this family?" said Ada, her eyes narrowing, adding up. "You think they'd want you?"

Rachel bit her lip. Of course Sister Marie would never have mentioned it to Ada and Bliss. She herself barely remembered her Aunt Minnie and Uncle Jedda, not fit to raise her, according to the nuns. Not fit to raise *any* girl, that drunk of an uncle, that aunt with her pagan ways.

"Absolutely," said Rachel.

That afternoon, Rachel pulled on the coat she could no longer button and climbed into the truck with the women. The salt-pocked highway was black with ice as they drove more than two hours in the direction of Moss

Village, turned off the State Road onto Pinconning when Rachel told them, and headed west. The banks were as high as the windows of the truck. Studying the sky, dark with snow-plump clouds, Rachel prayed for a sign.

Finally, Bliss broke the silence. "Do you have any idea where we're going?"

Rachel looked for a landmark. "It's a lake shaped like a *U*."

Again, the two women glanced at each other. Ada sighed, as if she were dealing with a finicky cow. "If it's the pain you're scared of, Rachel, we'll give you something."

Rachel didn't answer. She'd hardly thought about the pain, though she'd seen babies born before. Twice, her own mother had crawled around on the floor, her haunches shiny, her backbone quivering as she pushed those babies out, the first one all white and pasty, born too soon. Two years later, the second child, Rachel's little half-brother, his big head looking up from between her mother's legs. Aunt Minnie had caught him as he slithered out, cleaned him up while Rachel's mother lay panting. Next day, the mother had tied the baby to her front and gone off to find the father, leaving Rachel with her grandmother, who said it was all for the best.

"Perhaps," said Bliss, noting Rachel's silence, "it's not the pain."

"Little gi'l," said Ada, her voice assuming the broguish authority of her ancestors, "do you know what happens to Indian orphans?"

Rachel pulled her coat tighter. She was wedged between the women. "It's not an orphan." She would bring up the child as an Indian, make sure it learned a language she herself could barely speak.

Ada rolled her eyes and stared past the windshield, whistling. "Keep in mind," she added during a pause in the tune, "the convent's for the lucky ones."

When Rachel didn't answer, Ada drummed her fingers on the steering wheel and continued to scan the landscape.

"How long," Bliss asked, "since you've been to this Horseshoe place?"

The road rose, fell. Trees became years moving past. Ada turned on the radio, but there was only static. Then from beneath the crackling reception came the faint beat of a polka. Up ahead, Rachel saw a splayed cedar tree, ripped by lightning.

A no-name road. "Turn here."

An old barn. A stand of oaks. Rachel recalled them vaguely, misread them once so they had to circle back. They found an unplowed road where the tracks should lead into Horseshoe, but there were no tracks now, none that a truck could drive on. Some marks made by snowshoes, the hooves of deer.

Ada turned off the truck, pulled on the brake. "Looks like we're walking."

"Sweet Mary," said Bliss.

"You don't have to come," Rachel muttered. But she knew the women wouldn't let her out of their sight. Someone had paid for her care, paid dearly from the sound of it. Fine, thought Rachel, let them trudge along.

The snow was almost to their knees. Their breath escaped in clouds as they pushed through the woods where Rachel had played a million summers before, where the fallen, moss-covered trees made beams she could walk on, testing her balance, where the sandy soil yielded up mushrooms, ferns, and Dutchman's-breeches between the roots each spring.

All was white now. A slick coat of ice had formed a crust. Rachel lurched through it, her legs reddening from the cold. The two women struggled behind her. Ada cursed from time to time, saying it was a goose chase, that there was nothing here. But *everything* is here, Rachel thought, recalling her prayers. Her grandmother would show her once again how to make baskets by the lake, and Minnie would be frying bread. Old Jedda would be mending his snowshoes with deer gut, singing in that high-pitched wail.

But the beach was empty. The cabins and wigwams—what were left of them—stood like frail elders. Perhaps the men were off in shanties on Sturgeon Bay, their eyes glued to the ice. Perhaps the children were indoors or had made the trek to the schoolhouse in Manitobee three miles away.

Three shacks—lonely boxes of corrugated metal and tar paper—crouched at the edge of the beach. The one that was Minnie's listed to the side. From its pipe came a thin plume of smoke.

"Auntie!" Rachel called.

The women shivered. Ada slapped her hands together, blew on them. "Pretty damn welcoming."

"Auntie?"

The door creaked open a crack, revealing a figure wrapped in a blanket. All they could see was her face and not much of that, but Rachel knew it was her aunt, that horsehaired woman who had scared her as a child with her murky language, her dirt-eating, and her fits.

The old woman's coal black eyes narrowed. *"Nee-ne-chaw-nis?"* The word came out choked and rusty.

Awkwardly, Rachel thrust her body toward her aunt. "It's me."

Minnie took Rachel's face in her hands. On her breath Rachel smelled the jerky she had probably been eating for months.

"So tall, Crazy Hair!" Minnie said. "So pretty!" Minnie's face was lined, her fat cheeks spotted. She ran her hands down Rachel's face, chest, belly. *"Taw!"* she said. "What now?"

"If you don't mind," said Ada, "we're kind of frozen."

Minnie peered at Ada. Her lips curled slightly, but she held the door open.

Inside had little warmth, but they were sheltered from the wind. Leather, straw, and grass hung from the ceiling. Boxes of teeth and bone, beads, bits of feather, bells.

"Sit," said Minnie, but there was only the floor. She pulled a deer hide off the wall, told them to wrap it around themselves, since she was out of wood and they'd probably freeze. "Anyone got a smoke? It's not for me, you understand. It's for Winnay." She jerked her head backward to an empty corner of the room.

"Auntie," Rachel said in a low voice, "you *know* Grandmother's been dead for years."

"I know that. You think I don't know that?" She leaned toward Bliss and Ada. "This girl's grandmother was my sister Winnay. Older than me. Still"— she pulled one of Rachel's braids—"we're related."

"Ma'am," said Bliss, "Rachel wants to come back."

"And who are you?" said Minnie.

"We're not nuns, if that's what you think," said Ada.

"Hardly," said Bliss, explaining they were midwives. "Sometimes, the nuns send us one."

"If she's special," Ada added. "Like Rachel here."

"Special?" Minnie sniffed. "Oh, she's something all right. You should have seen her when her grandmother died. Barely got her out before the worms got in. And stubborn! I can tell you stories. This girl . . . well, you can call her special if you want."

"Either way," said Ada.

"Auntie," said Rachel impatiently, "where *is* everyone?"

"Look around you," said Minnie.

But there was no one to come home to. Scattered quills. Half-made baskets.

"Where's Jedda?" said Rachel.

"I kicked him out." Minnie reached into a pouch, pulled out a worm-chewed tobacco leaf. Sooner or later, she said, someone would kick out the rest of them. Luck had gotten them this far, and if Rachel had half a brain, she'd take this chance and stay away.

"They're okay," Minnie said, nodding at Bliss and Ada. "You go with them." She shrugged as if to say, What else could she do? They could see for themselves how it was.

"But my baby!"

Minnie's hand flew out and struck Rachel on the cheek, but the look in her eye was more threatening than her fist.

"Don't be stupid," Minnie said. "Go be a nun yourself, and let someone else raise the kid."

Rachel wanted to tell her she was wrong. They *could* make a life here. Why not? But Minnie had a point. There was nothing here but skeletons. Even the spirits had fled.

Snow fell slowly during the long ride home. Ada hummed and snuck a look at Rachel. They'd had quiet ones before and some who talked her deaf. Some had thrown themselves onto the bed and wailed into the night. Others had wandered off or been picked up by a dewy-cheeked boyfriend, fresh out of uniform and having second thoughts. One ate detergent—not to do herself in—just liked the taste. Loose cannons, that's what they were.

"Some family," Ada said.

Rachel was studying the windshield like it was a map of the world. In the headlights, the snowflakes danced hypnotically. Rachel sighed.

"Spit it out," said Ada.

"That family in Grayling?"

"Who told you about that?" said Bliss.

"Are they Catholic?"

"Goodness, yes!" said Ada, downshifting and turning into their driveway. "It was one of the terms."

"Are they Indian?"

"All these questions." Bliss sighed. "Honey, it isn't often one of our girls wants to keep her child."

Rachel's eyes started to fill. She didn't want to cry, but Bliss's voice was so sweet. The farmhouse ahead of her looked almost welcoming.

"I want her named Winnay," said Rachel, "if it's a girl."

"And if it's a boy?" said Bliss, pausing as she opened the door.

Ada abruptly pulled on the brake. "Now don't you two be naming. Things go all haywire once you start to name."

It was dawn when Rachel felt the tug, hazy as the light of winter sun. For days, she had hovered beyond her body, finding no room in her flesh for two. Her spirit seemed to float in a safe place of dreams and dead grandmothers. With stitching fingers she traced across her belly to find the hard spot which lay lower than before but, according to Ada, still not right. She willed it to turn, was answered instead by the pull of an opening womb.

By morning, the ringing in her ears resembled chanting, the pitch of drumbeats. With coaxing words, Ada and Bliss lifted up her nightgown to see.

"There's not much time," said Ada.

Rocking into a crescendo of pain, one that flipped her over and onto her knees, Rachel tried to do as her mother had, crouched like a dog, but she could not move.

Ada stuck her face into Rachel's. "I'm going to have to reach inside."

As Ada's hand pushed up between her legs, Rachel screamed and cried out to her grandmother, to Minnie, to her own mother even, summoned them until she heard their whispers. Marry your pain, they told her. Call it your lover. She thought of Woody as her water broke, releasing a flood of lake, sea, and tears. She tried to remember his smell, touch, taste, taking the pain into her the way she had taken him, bathed in moonlight at the edge of the lake.

Ada put the stethoscope in her ears and strained to hear a heartbeat. "I'm going to give you something for the pain."

I am rock, Rachel thought.

"Damn you," Ada whispered. She looked at Bliss, who nodded and wet the cloth. She leaned in close to Rachel. "You've got to push."

Bliss's hand clamped over her mouth, but Rachel twisted her head. She heaved herself onto her elbows as they lifted her legs. Shivering violently, she was dimly aware of Ada screaming, "Push! Push!" And Rachel, gritting her teeth, pushed against the pain, knowing she would tear apart.

"Again!"

The baby wouldn't come. Rent with pain, she tried to say, I can't, but the pushing consumed her until she was rocking with it. The room darkened and swam. A screaming, grinding ache, and Rachel's back arched as Ada lifted something dark and wet from inside her, the cord wrapped like a snake around the furry head. Rachel reached for it, expecting to hear a cry.

Nothing.

Rachel, unable to move, felt something wet run down the inside of her leg.

"Sweet Jesus," said Ada, staring down at the still thing in her arms, blue as the evening lake.

Rachel was watching from her bedroom window when Sister Marie arrived. Across the field, grackles scavenged for seeds. She could hear the screen door slam, Ada's tread on the porch.

A thaw had caused the gutters to weep freely. For days, Rachel had listened to their dripping, her own body dripping, too, breasts and tears, the sweats that came at night. No one had told her. Not about the blood that kept coming. Not about the emptiness that wouldn't stop.

She could hear the women talking on the porch, the nun's insistence that she'd been calling for days. Why had no one answered?

"The baby was stillborn, Sister."

A trickle of milk worked its way down Rachel's breast. She leaned her head against the window.

"And the girl?"

"Said she was eighteen."

Sister Marie muttered something.

"Either way," Ada continued, "she's gone. A truck came and got her."

Silence except for the drip of gutters.

The nun finally spoke. "Perhaps it's a blessing."

"Funny kind of blessing," said Ada. Rachel could imagine her tough little face, made for poker or staring down girls while she told them what to do. The kind of face that added up, made plans, shifty as the wind—not a kind face like Bliss's, but smart and shrewd. The way she'd looked when she turned to Rachel after they'd breathed life back into her son and said, *This is what you're going to do.*

Rachel held her baby to her chest, sniffed his warm, dark head. She hadn't decided on a name. He had been born like the lake. Hungry now, he grew insistent as the waves.

"Sshhh," she said, pulling away from the window. Rachel opened her blouse. Milk ran freely down her still-ripe belly. You can stay here for now, the two women told her. We can use a hand.

Her hair hung loosely where her braids had been. She had cut them herself, coiled them into the box with Woody's gifts. He had grasped that hair, inhaled and kissed it. Who was she to need braids now?

She leaned forward. The baby's mouth opened like a bird's, clamped eagerly around her nipple. Rachel shuddered with the pinch of it, almost laughed at his little fist pressing into her chest. Sister Marie was getting into the car, turning to speak to another nun behind the steering wheel. Had they believed Ada? Would they continue to send girls here? For a moment Rachel wanted to run down and tell them Woody March had a son. But Woody was gone, married, and the station wagon had already pulled out of the driveway and disappeared.

Part Two

CHAPTER ELEVEN

1956

Years. Years drifting by like snow, like leaves, like dandelion down. Autumns hardening into winters, winters bleeding into springs. In the fields, meadow rue gave way to hawkweed, hawkweed to thistle and Queen Anne's lace, until the grasses browned, dried out, were covered with snow.

"You can stay here for now," Bliss had told Rachel after the baby was born.

"But keep the kid out of sight," added Ada.

Rachel raised the ax, brought it down. The two women never had asked her to leave. Then came the first harvest. And the next. Rachel learned to reach her hand inside a woman, to feel the size of the opening, the hard patch of head. She had held girls by their elbows as they pushed, their eyes rolling back like those of animals made crazy by thunder. She could say "shhh shhh" when she needed to, "damn you" when a girl started to fade.

In the Indian summer evenings, she sat on the porch with Ada and Bliss, listening to the story of the girl who'd almost bled out, the story of the baby with the unformed twin. One girl, they told her, had eaten detergent. *What's with that?* they asked her. *Detergent and stones.* But Rachel couldn't tell them where the craving had come from. For as long as she could remember, most of her band had chewed on stones. It was more than hunger; it was sustenance. A desperation to consume the land.

"Mineral deficiency," Ada had said, putting an end to the discussion.

Together, the three women had watched Rachel's baby become a toddler, then a small boy who was curious about everything, who pretended he was a plane chasing chickens in the yard. Rachel's hands had grown tough from farm work—nine years with Ada and Bliss, nine springs including this one—tilling fields, planting seeds, splitting logs, and helping girls to push.

Though the winter of 1956 had been bleak and relentless, it had started out mild enough. By Christmas, there had been little snow except for a dusting on browned-out grass. In January, three storms chased one another down from Canada, dumping ten feet and freezing the lake north of the straits. Pipes broke. Cats froze. A five-car pileup south of Onoway injured a busload of Sunday schoolers, killing one. After that, the Virgin was sighted on the back of a snowplow headed north on the Grangeville Road.

Spring had arrived with a vengeance, flooding half the fields. Ada always said she could predict the birthing season based on how the weather changed. Since March, the lake had risen, devouring beaches, submerging docks. Sunny mornings turned to hail in the afternoon. The boyfriend of one of the girls who came to deliver had been stranded off Sturgeon when the ice broke up, setting his shanty adrift. He crawled on his belly from ice floe to ice floe until he reached the shore. *Now,* said the girl, *if only he'd marry me.*

But the girls who came here rarely got married. Most of them gave up their babies. Some held them close and wouldn't let go. The girls who went home empty-handed seemed hollow, chastened, relieved. Rachel wondered how they could stand it—to feel something grow inside, feel it quiver and surge, suffer through that pain, only to let another family come and call it theirs.

And then there were those who came back, sickening Rachel with their stubborn, dumb hope. Retreads, Ada called them. The kind of girl who wouldn't learn.

Not me, thought Rachel, making an oath that no man would touch her again. Raising the ax for a second stroke, she split the wood. This year, the births would be difficult.

Now it was April, and the fields were sodden with marsh. Four more cords to chop from the oak they'd cleared last summer. Across the pasture, the trees were greening, and a breeze carried the hint of wild leeks. From the shed Rachel could see her boy tossing grain to the chickens, saying "Chickie! Chickie!" the way he had since he was small. Even as a baby, his eyes studied everything, blue and intent—a puppy who ran from her arms as soon as he could, running up to the biggest rooster and saying "Cluck! Cluck!"

What's the Indian word for beaver? Ada would say. *What's Indian for* humming-bird? But Rachel had forgotten these words. Her mind searched for names whose sounds she could not recall. Running Brook. Shifting Dune. But none of these seemed right, and finally she called him Ben-oni, as Rachel in the Bible had— "Son of My Sorrow"—although the biblical Rachel had died. *Well, I died, too,* Rachel had thought when she gave birth. She had cut off her braids to prove it.

Ada, covered in grease, leaned her head out from under the hood of the tractor and called to Ben. "Hey, Monkey-Bones, get me a wrench."

For nine years, it was all he had known. A mother and two aunties. He was copper-skinned like Rachel. Dark-haired. Blade-faced. But his eyes were his father's.

Rachel watched as he flung the rest of the feed at the chickens and raced off to help his auntie. Anything mechanical drew him. Anything that needed taking apart and putting back together. What was the Odawa word, Rachel wondered, for Good with Hands?

"Crap," said Ada, kicking the side of the tractor.

Rachel set down the ax and watched as a faded green truck drove past the driveway, slowed, stopped, reversed. It made her uneasy when people came to the farmhouse. Someday, she thought, those nuns are going to come back.

"Go inside," she said to Ben as the truck turned in.

The truck curved up the driveway. Rachel leaned on the wood block, wiped her brow. She was wearing a man's shirt tied at the waist above her jeans. She had kept her hair short, brushed it only when she had to.

The door swung open, and a man got out. Rachel could see he was Indian. Army pants. Crew cut. Tall. A face that was vaguely familiar.

"Can we help you?" said Bliss.

The man leaned on the door of the truck and nodded toward Rachel. "Sign on the road says you got some firewood to sell."

Rachel rested her hand on her forehead and squinted. She studied the line of his brow, the way the hair cut straight across it. Ten years since she'd seen him, but she remembered how she'd felt ashamed when he'd come to sell wood and seen her in the Marches' kitchen.

"Honda?"

His hair was short and bristly. She thought she saw a flicker of recognition in his eyes, but he didn't let on.

"You know this man?" said Ada.

"Honda Jackson. He's from Horseshoe Lake," Rachel said, crossing her arms, trying to match Honda's cocksureness. "At least, when I was a kid."

"Oh, *that* lake," said Ada. "Anyone still living there?"

"They are. And people call me Honda Jack." Honda Jack gave Ada a look that meant business. "The wood?"

Ada stared him back. "Ten dollars a cord."

"Ten dollars? *I'd* have to sell it cheaper than that."

Ada glanced at the man's truck. "Ten dollars is ten dollars. We aren't running a charity."

"Maybe not." Ignoring Rachel, Honda Jack surveyed the house, the fields. "But from the look of things, you could use a hand."

Ada scratched her head, making her hair stand up on end. "Honda *Jack*, is it?" She chewed her lip as she did when she was thinking, that same lip chewing she'd done when she'd bent over Rachel years before and said, *This is what you're going to do*. "Crazy name," Ada said. "You know how to fix a carburetor?"

That night Honda Jack, his pants now as greasy as Ada's, joined them for dinner. As he helped himself to string beans and onions, to steamy bread, and thick slices of pork, he told them about growing up on Horseshoe Lake, about how they used to make a living fishing and cutting down McCready's trees till the lumber company closed, about how he'd left to find work, ending up in Korea, where he'd half froze to death.

"What was it like in Korea, Mr. Jack?" asked Bliss.

"You grow up here, ma'am?"

"All my life."

"Well, then," he said, chewing his meat, "you probably think you know what it's like to be cold."

"What's your point?" said Ada.

"What I'm trying to say is that Michigan's tropical compared to North Korea," he said. "Friggin' Siberia, that's what." He told them how he'd hauled half a dozen bodies out of bunkers, not to mention the miscellaneous pieces that had been blown to bits. "It'll be a long time before I look the same way at dead meat."

Ben had been staring at Honda all through dinner. He was like this whenever a man came around. The butcher. The doctor. The farmer from down the road. "Yeah," he said, "but you just ate your pork chop."

Honda Jack threw back his head and laughed. Rachel could see a gold tooth the army had probably paid for. She drew her tongue over her own chipped teeth. "Tell me about my Aunt Minnie."

"I can tell you this," Honda said, not laughing now. "She wonders why you've never come back."

Bliss and Ada rose to clear the table.

"Go help your aunties," Rachel told Ben. What were her choices? Men went to war. Women had babies. At least she had a life of her own, a roof that didn't leak. Furniture, even if it wasn't hers. She turned back to Honda. "Do you remember the rest of my family?"

He nodded. "I remember your grandmother. Winnay always kept after me. But I was pretty young when your mother left the lake."

"So was I."

Honda leaned back in his chair. "So why don't you come home? We've got a garden now. A couple of campers. Almost a village again."

"Home?" Rachel said, her voice ripe with disbelief. Even so, she could smell the musk of quills, the earthy scent of clay. Honda's teeth, like hers, would be chipped from chewing rocks, his toenails black from standing on the ice in thin-skinned moccasins, waiting for the flash of silver that would feed them for a week—the crackle of cook fires, the fish caught and shared. "You don't even *own* it."

Honda threw his arm in the air. "Any more than you own *this*."

Rachel saw the tattoo on the back of his hand. A coiled piece of rope. Perhaps a snake. The doors of the cuckoo clock snapped open, the boy and girl came out, whirled around each other, danced away. "I'm surprised the McCreadys haven't cleared the whole place for lumber."

"You think McCready cares? He's got, what, two thousand acres? Why should he bother us?"

Rachel rose to clear the rest of the table. "I think you'll find those kind of people keep track of what they own."

Honda slept on the couch that week and helped around the farm. Ada and Bliss paid him in firewood, which, Rachel suspected, he would sell for three times as much as they would have charged him. Not that it mattered. Forty acres needed planting, and with Honda helping out, the work went twice as fast.

"Mama," asked Ben, "can we go out to Honda's lake sometime?"

"What do you know about that lake?"

But Ben wouldn't take no for an answer. He followed Honda everywhere. Honda would tell him about water so smooth and clear, it was like swimming through velvet. There were spirits in the lake. The whole damn place was magic. "You're not really Indian," Honda had said, "till you live in a place like that."

Ben would lie belly-down on the porch for hours with the crayons Bliss had given him. He drew pictures of the sky and water, his memories of a beach where they had taken him each summer. Now the crayons were worn to stubs, their wrappings all but peeled away. Still he played with them the way he played with the blocks Ada had whittled out of maple, the drum Rachel had fashioned from a goat's hide. Scraps for toys, but Rachel understood his love for them because she, too, had hoarded scraps—bits of beach glass, sand, and driftwood.

"That's beautiful," she said, looking at the waxy smudge of blue. "It looks like water."

Each day, Ben tagged after Honda on the tractor, riding with him side by side. Rachel watched from the porch as the man leaned over Ben and whispered secrets, wild tales, lies. Possibilities Rachel had kept from the boy. Ancestries, histories—legends of the Anishinabee.

"Tsss," said Rachel to Honda one afternoon. "Why are you filling his head?"

"And why have you left it empty?"

He looked at her so hard she looked away. She knew he wondered about the boy's father. Let him think it was some buck who'd run out on her, some gas-pumping no-good who'd hit the skids as soon as he got a bottle.

She wondered if Honda had a girl. A family. But Rachel didn't ask, pretended not to care. Besides, it wasn't her business. Hers was to help with the cooking, to clean, to split the firewood and hunt wild leeks in the woods. Soon it would be May, and June would tumble into summer. There would be fields to tend. By then, the tractor would be broken again. Honda would be gone, and with him, a truckload of firewood.

"Don't you want Ben to meet his people?"

His people. Over the years, Rachel had gone to Moss Village only once. She hadn't the nerve to go to the Marches', but someday she would stride right up the front steps, her dark-haired boy in tow, ask to see Mrs. March, present her with her grandson. You prayed for children, she'd say. I heard you.

"You were there when my grandmother died," Rachel said to Honda. "You saw it."

"I saw a shack burn down. Nothing else. I saw a girl crying for her grand-mother."

Honda's dark eyes were shot red from sun, his skin leather. A deep scar split his eyebrow. There were pockmarks on his cheeks. A face that would look better when his hair grew out, when it fell to his shoulders as it was meant to, dressed with feathers and bands of beads when it was pulled back into braids.

Up till now, it had seemed too risky to take Ben out to Horseshoe. Someone would tell the nuns. Besides, what had living there ever gotten her?

"You're lying," she said.

"No. I heard what you'd seen. Wished I'd seen it. But I don't have those kind of eyes—those *wabeno* eyes—and you were the only one."

"*Wabeno* eyes?" Rachel said with a little laugh. She shook her head. Sorcerer's eyes, indeed.

She sat on the porch with the two women and Honda. In front of them, Ben ran in circles on the lawn, becoming a bird, the wind, a rushing river—she couldn't tell. He made chirping sounds, then howled and groaned, dove into the grass, somersaulted.

"Weird kid," said Honda. "What's he doing?"

"He's got an imagination is all." Rachel herself had pretended to be a bird or a fish when she was a child, swimming upriver, soaring above trees. When her uncle was drinking, she could always pretend to go under water.

"He's like any boy," said Bliss.

Ada nodded. "He licks rocks." Her eyes slid to Rachel. "Most mothers would smack their kids if they did that."

Rachel shrugged. She had taught her son the subtle tastes of rock and dirt. *There are secrets in the soil,* she told him. *It will always bring you home.*

"I'm a plane!" shouted Ben. "I'm a kamikaze!" He jumped up and began to fly in circles, arms spread, engines roaring. He rushed right at them, pretending to crash into the porch, to burst into flames. Ada and Bliss hooted at him, but Rachel didn't laugh. She sat silent, wondering what had made him think of crashing planes when all they ever saw out here was the occasional prop plane headed to Mackinaw or Beaver.

"Aaaaaargh!" screamed Ben.

Rachel flinched. He should be playing with other children, not always showing off for her or dancing with the wind. He was nine now, and if he'd been living with other Indians, he'd know the steps and the songs. As it was, he made up his own, or sang "Tipperary" with Bliss.

As if he could read her thoughts, Honda said casually, "That old nun who used to come out to the lake? The one with the thing on her face?"

"Sister Marie?" said Ada. "The look *she* gave me last time I saw her . . ."

"Well, she's not giving anyone looks now," Honda said. "Passed away like that." He snapped his fingers. "Right in the middle of confession."

Rachel shuddered, remembering the nun's hand pulling her away from her grandmother. What had Sister Marie confessed to? She had told Rachel of Woody's marriage, then sent her away to give birth. Rachel's gaze returned to Honda's.

"Kid's going to be a dancer," said Honda, staring her down. "I can tell you now." He had rolled a piece of tobacco between his fingers the way Rachel's grandmother had done. His profile, too, looked like her grandmother's— haughty and amused.

Maybe they *should* go back to Horseshoe Lake, even if for a day. See the new trailers, the latrines, the garden Honda was bragging about. The sun set, the sky grew orange. "When I was a girl," Rachel said, "my grandmother said never to trust a Jackson."

Honda laughed. "A lot of people feel that way." He whistled for Ben, signaled him over. When the boy arrived, Honda reached into his pocket, bent in close to show him a dull metal coin. "This here's Japanese," said Honda. "You can tell by the hole in the middle."

Ben held out his hand, drew the coin up to his eye, peered through the hole, then handed it back to Honda.

"This one's Korean," said Honda, holding up another coin. "Worthless shit. You can't patch a hole with that coin."

"Can I have it?"

Honda looked over at Rachel. "I've got more of this stuff out at the lake. Why don't you come and see for yourself?"

Horseshoe Lake. Nothing but shacks. Not enough food.

"Maybe we will," Rachel said.

C H A P T E R   T W E L V E

The next day they set off in the truck heading west on the highway, past acres of farmland, sea-vast and emerald, an occasional island of deciduous woods.

"I was up to here in latrine shit," said Honda. "Most of my buddies were dead, and this Korean guy comes over to where I'm hiding. I'm thinking I'm a goner. Next thing I know, he opens his pants to pee." He glanced sideways at Rachel. "That's about the most blessed rain that ever came."

Rachel closed her eyes. She thought if she kept them shut, she could become a girl again, driving with old Jedda down the road to the lake. They would have been to the general store in Conway to buy string and fishhooks and whiskey. Jedda would already have opened a bottle with his teeth, driving the truck with one hand, pointing out some tent caterpillars attacking a tree, a secret spot for sweet grass.

"Smell that?"

It was Honda speaking. Rachel breathed in deeply the lingering scent of balsa.

"I've been collecting that," he said as he turned off onto the no-name road.

"I got a real production line going. Pine sachets, moccasins, little hatchets, and whatnots. You know. Stuff the tourists buy."

Ben perked up. "You got boat models?"

"The tourists come all the way out here?" Rachel said, opening her eyes. She recognized the woods now—birch and ash, flashes of torrey pine. They were winding among the duney hills, the ones they called the Sleeping Sisters because of their generous curves.

"Hell, no," said Honda. "We go to them." They hit a bump. Ben shrieked with delight while Rachel grabbed the window frame. "Here's my plan," Honda went on, telling her how he was setting up a little store over in Moss Village where all the rich people came in the summer. They'd sell Indian trinkets. "Other stuff, too. I'll import from Japan."

"Real native stuff," said Rachel.

"You think they can tell the difference?"

Trees rolled past them. The smell of pine. Damp soil. Lake. Honda stopped the truck and cranked on the brake. Rachel could already smell the smoke—the constant smoke of fires she remembered from childhood, whether or not there was something to cook. Smoke calmed the spirits, and even the suggestion of a meal was better than nothing at all.

"*Bozhoo,*" said Rachel under her breath, eyeing the trailers perched on cinder blocks.

When she was a child, it had been a village of shacks and bark-clad wigwams along with a couple of tepees. The air had been full of campfire smoke and the distant sound of sawing. Now it smelled tinny with rust and gasoline. There were cabins—three times as many as before. From one of the porches, some women poked fun at two men leaning over the hood of a car. Several kids played tag among the laundry flapping in the breeze. One fell down, then stood up crying till they all came over, laughed, and ran away. Where did all these children come from?

Ben jumped out of the truck. Honda whistled, and they all looked up.

"Hey," said Honda, "this here's Rachel Winnapee."

Embarrassed, Rachel gave a little wave. The women stared back as if she was a foreigner. She wanted to declare that she had lived here as a child, and surely that entitled her to something, but twelve years had wiped her tracks from the beach. Rachel tried to smooth her hair, but it sprang back up. Tucking in her shirt, she started down the path. Her sneakers sunk into the clay. On the end of the beach was Minnie's cabin. Next to it, the empty place where her grandmother's had been.

Taking Ben's hand in hers, Rachel strode to Minnie's, pounded on the door.

"What now?" came from inside.

"It's me," shouted Rachel. "Your niece."

"What niece?"

"Your only niece, Auntie. Open the door."

The door swung open, and Minnie stood there in a man's plaid shirt and a skirt printed with daffodils, a straw hat pulled low across her forehead. Pinned to her chest, a rhinestone crab. "So now you come crawling back?"

"I'm not coming back. Besides," said Rachel, her eyes raking over Minnie's getup, *"you* told me not to."

Minnie dragged on a tobacco leaf rolled into a cigar and looked down at Ben. "This yours?"

"Can we come in?"

The door slowly opened with a familiar creak. The room smelled of something undigested, but Minnie seemed large as ever, her arms and legs the trunks of trees, a horsetail of gray tumbling from beneath the hat. She took another, sharper look at Ben. *"Au-nish aus-way-be-sit au-way?"*

Rachel could feel Ben studying the woman's crazy clothes, the dingy cloth pulled across the windows. "He doesn't understand."

"Taw," said Minnie. "What have you been teaching him?"

Rachel looked around, expecting to see her uncle's boots, his knife and fishing rod. "Still haven't taken Jedda back?"

"I did. Then I kicked him out again." Minnie jerked her head toward the window. "He lives across the lake."

Ben picked up a sharp claw from a box. "Put that down," Rachel said.

"That's wolverine," Minnie said to the boy. "For headdresses." Ben stared at the boxes of feathers and beads, fang and nail, fur, hair, shell and hide.

Jabbing her cigar in the direction of the boxes, Minnie said, "I can make you a costume out of those."

Ben touched a dress covered in hundreds of metal cones which clattered like hail on a metal roof.

"Hear that?" said Minnie. "*Ken-say-totem naw?* That's your ancestors laughing."

"Oh, for Pete's sake," said Rachel.

Minnie moved in close, crouched down to see Ben's face. Her dark eyes met his blue ones, traced them for clues. She took his shoulders in her hands, rubbed the length of his arms, turned him around, palmed his back, felt his legs. Ben tried to wriggle away, but Minnie pressed her thick, blunt nose to his face and sniffed.

For the first time, she smiled. "Stone licker," she said.

They stayed into the evening. Rachel sat with Honda as they watched Ben throw pebbles into the water. On the opposite shore, a lantern burned. Was it Jedda, waiting for Minnie to take him back? They'd never married because, as Minnie said, *Why bother?*

Honda looked at her. "It's good, don't you think?"

Drained of color, the lake mirrored the heavens. As a child, Rachel had lain next to her grandmother, watching the sky until she knew it by heart—the darting stars she thought were spirits, the shapes she named *Mi-she-kae* and *Wa-boose*. Pleiades and Orion. The night rainbow, aurora borealis, which surely was a *manitou*. "You see too much in the night sky," her grandmother had told her, but Rachel always felt she didn't see enough.

On the beach, the Indians had started a campfire. Honda's face reddened in the light. Watching the snake on his hand flicking to some imaginary beat, Rachel wondered if he had other tattoos. On the small of his back, perhaps. A girl's name on his upper arm.

"So," said Honda. "I got a proposition."

The low, sweet hoot of an owl. Rachel listened for its mate.

"Your grandmother was the best quill artist around. People were collecting her stuff all the way back in the twenties."

There. The answering cry of another.

" 'Course they sold for nothing. We could get more at the shop."

Rachel roused herself. "How much more?"

"Twenty, thirty dollars a box. You could stay here, work with Minnie."

She shook her head. "Those boxes weren't worth the porcupines who died for them."

"The way I see it," said Honda, waving his hand across the lake, "if the store's successful, we could afford to buy this land eventually. Bring in electricity. A better road."

Rachel flicked away a moth. The bonfire glowed. She tried to imagine it, to see what he was seeing, but all she could see was a collection of castoffs on another man's land.

CHAPTER THIRTEEN

In the summer, when the fields buzzed with crickets and grasshoppers and clover-hunting bees, Ben hid behind the barn or under the lilac bushes, even though there was no one but his aunties or mother to find him. Sometimes a girl came to the house—a different one each time—but they were always cranky or sleepy, not good for anything.

He would play war, a stick for a gun, bounding and ducking, falling to his belly and covering his head. He had seen planes overhead and became one of them, dropping bombs, exploding into flames. When he was lonely, he would lie on the ground, taste it. It was a gritty, happy taste that spoke of vanished forests.

The tractor in the barn was the giant hulk of a beast. A stegosaurus, maybe. One of the words he had learned in school. He would go to that school every autumn, three miles down the road where they made leaves out of paper and tissue snowflakes. But now it was June, and there was no school. The sun came up each morning over the hill with the elms, and the mist on the field would lift so that by breakfast, the air was thick as cream.

It was cooler at night when the maple outside brushed against the screen, and the sky was full of stars. Whenever one shot across the horizon, Bliss or Ada would say, "Quick! Wish!" and his mother would say, "For what?"

But Ben was full of wishes. He wished he had a bicycle so he could ride down the road. Or that there was a cool stretch of lake close by to swim in. There were mostly women in his life. The girls who came here didn't have husbands, but Bliss had told him that even Mary had Joseph. Ben had seen horses mounting each other in the spring, the bulls with the cows. He knew where babies came from, but his mother was always so vague when he asked, he thought maybe she was the Virgin after all. Still, he would have liked to have had a father. And when he had seen the boats crossing the straits to Mackinaw, he longed for one of them, too.

Bliss told him that Mackinaw used to be an Indian meeting ground. "I bet you have ancestors buried on that island."

Ben thought about asking his mother if his father was buried on Mackinaw Island. She had been bent over the kitchen table for weeks, pieces of bark and quills spread out before her. Maybe Honda would come back soon, and they would ride on that tractor. Everything was growing now. Corn. Alfalfa. Wheat. There was a new lamb in the barnyard, and Ben had asked if they could keep it, but Ada said no, that they had to sell all their lambs. There was a plaque on the wall in the parlor that said JESUS LOVES HIS LITTLE LAMBS, but Ben wondered, if that were true, why did they have to be butchered?

Ben fingered the porcupine quills, sharp as the stalks of feathers. There had been feathers in Minnie's shack. She had sewn some of them together, wrapped it around his head to show him what it would be like. If he had one of those headdresses, he would dance around the yard like an Indian and scalp the cowboys when they attacked.

A drop of his mother's blood was smudged on the table. He came in close, sniffed her skin. She was the warm thing he always drew near to, knowing the taste of her the way he knew the taste of milk or sugar or stones. There were berries in the yard, but his mother told him not to eat them. *They'll make you sick,* she said. When they went to the beach, Ada would scrape the sand from his mouth, tell him to spit it out, but he liked the taste and would hide some in his pocket for later.

Who, he would ask his mother, was his father?

A soldier and a sailor, she told him. A brave man. One who was killed in the war.

Ben imagined his father's hands. Were they tough from pulling lines? Did he steer his ship into battle?

When his mother finished the boxes, Honda would come to see them. Ben traced the pattern his mother had made on a round piece of bark. It felt uneven, crooked as his own drawings, but he liked the way it zigzagged like patterns in the sand after the waves pull back. Ada said his mother was becoming independent, but his mother said it was a useless thing to weave quills.

The linoleum on the kitchen table was royal blue with white swirls, same as the floor. Ben liked to pretend it was Lake Michigan seen through the eyes of a gull. Sometimes he flew over that lake, studying the whitecaps, the undulating waves. Looking down, he could see a ship tossed on the peaks, disappearing into troughs. The waves crested and cracked across the bow, his father steering it, his fist clenched upon the wheel. His father was a sailor and a warrior. The ship capsized and sunk.

"Someone's here," said his mother.

Ben stood up quickly. Even before he saw the truck, he was running toward the door, across the porch, down the lawn. Honda got slowly out of the truck, knelt down so that he was eye to eye with Ben.

"Hey, kid," he said as Ben ran up to him, stopped short of embracing him.

"Honda," said Ben, "will you take me swimming?"

Honda ruffled Ben's hair, which was growing long around his ears. "Where's your mother?"

Ben pointed to the house, then followed Honda, two feet behind, back to the kitchen where his mother was bent over quills. The two boxes she had made were pushed to the side. With a cloth, she blotted her hand.

"So," she said.

Honda pulled back a kitchen chair, strode it backward, his legs and body so big the chair looked like a pony straddled by a giant. "What've you got?"

Ben watched Honda examine the two boxes, holding each as if it were an Easter egg. Still grasping the towel, Rachel said, "I barely remember how to do that pattern. It needs finer quills."

"I can get you the quills," said Honda.

"Can you get me some dye?" she said. "Ones that will last?"

"Your stitching could use some work."

"You think I have nothing better to do?"

Ben looked out the window. The lamb in the barnyard was being suckled by its mother.

"No hurry," said Honda. "I've got plenty of inventory already. Moccasins and the like. Headdresses. But when you're ready, Minnie says she's got room for you and the kid."

Ben shot a look at his mother. Her mouth quivered but didn't smile.

Honda tugged on Ben's arm. "Get a load of this." Out of his pocket he pulled a small wooden box, flat and narrow. "Watch," he said to Ben, sliding open the box to reveal a quarter. He waved his hand over the box and smacked it. "Now you try."

Ben opened the box to find the quarter gone. "How'd you do that?"

Honda laughed. "Magic. What'd you think?"

"There's no such thing," said Ben's mother.

"No?" said Honda. He waved his fingers over the box again, told Ben to open it. The quarter had returned. Honda, his eyes still laughing, told Ben to take it. From his other pocket he produced a clamshell like the ones on the beach at Horseshoe Lake. "Here. Put this in some water and see what happens."

Ben filled a jelly jar from the faucet, dropped the shell in. It made a little "plop," then sunk to the bottom where it lay like a giant mollusk. Through the glass, he could see the linoleum of the table. He could imagine fish swimming past the wreckage of submarines buried in the sand. The clam suddenly opened. Tiny paper flowers—pink, yellow, green—rose up and began to wave.

"Honda thinks you'd make a good dancer," his mother said.

"Wow," said Ben, dazzled at the garden.

"Maybe," said Honda. "I only said maybe. But if you are—and we'll see about that—you can compete in the powwow in August."

From his pocket, Ben took the Japanese coin Honda had given him and dropped it into the glass. Making its way to the bottom like a sinking ship, the coin landed in the clam, flattening the flowers. The garden shuddered, engulfed the coin.

"What do you think?" said Honda.

Ben could see that his mother thought it was a waste of time. He turned away from the glass and stared out the window to the fields. Later, he would take the coin and bury it along with the army knife he found last summer. He buried all his treasures at the edge of the yard where the taller grasses grew. His mother kept hers in a box. In a month or so, the corn would be harvested, and they would have corn on the cob for dinner.

"Will I get to wear a headdress?"

"Maybe."

In a couple of months, the bushes beyond the maple woods would be thick with berries. He would go with aunties to pick those berries to make a sweet and sticky jam. Hunt where the sumac grows, Bliss had told him. Be careful of your hands. The thorns on the stalks of the bushes were sharp, and his hands always bled like his mother's.

By the middle of June, it was so hot that Rachel and Ben lay side by side on the kitchen floor just to stay cool. Rachel pressed her face to the flecked linoleum. Summers made her half-delirious, haunting her with longings. On certain nights, she could smell Lake Michigan, hear the waves, feel the pebbles of the shore press into her. In the morning, the palms of her hands were bruised.

"There are other beaches," she said to Ben when he pestered her to go back to Horseshoe.

But Ben wanted to swim in the still, clay-bottomed lake, to see that woman—that old woman with her wild collection of feathers and bones.

"She's a crazy woman," said Rachel. "Forget her."

Ada came into the kitchen with a pail, stepped over Rachel, then Ben. "Do I have to mop around you? Or do you just want to squirm around and do the job yourself?"

Ben laughed. Rachel sighed and lifted herself up to sit cross-legged. "Ben wants to go back. And Honda wants us both to go stay a while with Minnie."

Ada filled the pail. After a long silence, she said, "And what's so bad about that?"

"You should see it," said Rachel. "It's even worse. And now Honda's got everyone making 'authentic Indian' junk for sale like it's going to be their salvation."

"In this heat, the only thing that's going to salvage us is a swim." Ada turned off the spigot. "So what'd you tell him?"

Rachel traced her finger across the linoleum's lacey patterns. Ben was watching her, waiting for her answer. Give the kid a taste, Honda had said. Let him know what it's like to be Indian.

Rachel didn't meet Ada's eye. "Maybe," said Rachel. "I told him maybe."

Two days later when Honda came again, Rachel had packed their things in an old suitcase of Ada's. It's just for the summer, she told the aunties. Still, Bliss spent most of the morning in the kitchen pitting cherries, and Ada's eyes were strangely red.

"Nine years," said Ada, pulling back her short white hair.

"It's not like we're dead," said Rachel.

"Now, don't you worry," Bliss said. "We got two mothers-to-be coming in August, so it's just as well we'll have your room."

"You ready?" said Honda, hoisting the suitcase into the truck.

Ben had gone to the edge of the yard and dug up his treasures, stuffing them into a sack. The clotted soil that clung to his hands smelled faintly of manure as he ran back and climbed into the truck with his mother.

A door slammed, and Bliss hurried from the house, thrust a bag through the window. "You'll need these for the drive."

Ben opened the bag, reached in, drew out a cherry. Biting into it, he tasted the dirt on his hand. Honda had jerked the truck into gear. His mother was staring straight ahead, but Ben twisted around to see his aunties grow small on the porch. He raised his hand to wave, but they had vanished.

His mouth was juicy with cherries. It was only for the summer, his mother told him. They would be staying with Minnie in her cramped little house, and Ben would see how good they had it on the farm. He knew he would miss it. He thought of the aunties, the lambs, the fields—but the lake drew him now, the sound of drums. They were going to live with strangers in a forest where his mother had lived as a child. As the truck sped past farms and meadows, crickets shrieked while the corn, knee-high, rustled in the breeze.

Down the road, Rachel could see the bent tree marking the place where they turned toward the lake. Ben had been quiet for most of the trip, but Honda was humming. Every time he jerked the gears, Rachel grabbed the window frame. The woods were steamy, and chickadees were calling *all-ye, all-ye oxen free* to one another from among the branches. Remembering the days when she'd gone with her grandmother to peel birch bark in this very woods, Rachel searched for the telltale rings around trunks, the parchment-fine skin harvested for boxes that would be lashed together with strips of leather, trimmed with sweet grass, covered with quills. They'd been cutting down trees, Honda told her, pointing out a bare spot in the forest. They needed the firewood, and he was planning to sell a few cords.

Rachel peered over the top of Ben's head. "You think you own this place?"

Honda laughed and said maybe he did, but the truth was McCready *wanted* the trees cleared. A favor for a favor.

"I thought McCready never bothered you."

They pulled up on a grassy spot close to Minnie's. Honda climbed out of the truck, looked sternly at Ben and jerked his head toward the lake. "Git." Then he grinned, and Ben smiled, too, and jumped out of the truck.

Watching her son run down to the lake, Rachel wondered if she was being unfair to McCready. It was McCready, after all, who had let them stay here, even after the lumber mill shut down. So what if he wanted some of his land cleared? Sniffing the air, Rachel shook her head and looked at Honda. "After all these years?"

"It's not like he's asking us to *leave*," Honda said. "Besides, it's a chance to make some money."

Maybe, maybe not, thought Rachel as she pulled her suitcase from the back of the truck and started toward Minnie's cabin. It would be close, crabby quarters, and if Rachel had half a brain, she would turn back now. A crazy, old woman—her shack packed with bones taken from birds and beaches, sequins from old clothes, exotic and worthless.

Minnie was waiting on the porch. As Rachel drew near, she forced herself to look at the older woman's face, the face of someone who had stayed, was dug in and rooted, lichen on a tree. Minnie's hands would be punctured from quill work. As Rachel drew close, Minnie raised one marked palm to greet her and mumbled something incoherent. Rachel, her memory of the language as chipped as her teeth, willed herself not to turn away.

"*Ah-neen,*" said Minnie.

Rachel braced herself for the onslaught of language, some sly insult. But there were no more words. *Ah-neen* hung in the air, startling in its simplicity, the Odawa word for *welcome.*

Mornings came early with the smell of cooking, the harsh turnover of car engines. By sunrise, someone would be telling their child to hurry up, there were chores. Cars pulled out, heading to jobs at service stations, lumberyards, jobs washing dishes at breakfast joints or sweeping someone's walk.

His mother spent mornings sorting quills with Minnie, talking over patterns. Each afternoon, Honda called Ben to the clamshell-covered beach. For the longest time, Ben couldn't see any difference between what he was doing and what Honda showed him, over and over. The drumbeat had sounded sad at first—like the wind in autumn when the last leaves fell. But now it was becoming faster, stronger, almost wild.

"You've got to *stomp* the earth," Honda said. "Get low. Think of something that makes you real mad."

Ben dipped his face so close to the beach he could almost lick the clay. From the stoop of Minnie's shack, his mother paced back and forth as he learned to move like eagle, snake, deer. It made him laugh to hear the bells on his wrist and ankles as he moved across the beach, whooping like an Indian, clapping his hand over his mouth, crying, "Woo woo woo!"

"Where'd you hear that?" said Honda.

"The radio."

"Forget the radio. The radio's shit. You see any radios here?"

Ben shook his head. No radios. No lights. Not even a stove like the one Ada and Bliss had in their kitchen. Honda banged on the drum and wailed. *Be a reptile, low in the grass! An owl in the top of a tree!*

Gently, Ben struck the beach with his toe.

"Harder!"

Again he struck it, this time more like a kick.

"Think of an eagle, Ben. *Soar.*"

He thought of all the times he'd pretended to be a plane high above the cornfields, and soon he was moving, striking, twisting. The wind blew down from the trees and carried him up. Like a bird he rose, a cry rising in his throat. Tomorrow, Honda was taking him and his mother to see the new store in town. There were boats in the harbor, Honda promised.

Ben opened his mouth, spread his wings and flew higher, higher. Below, the rivers veined, worked their way to oceans. The continents grew smaller. Ben's feet worked the beach hard until they grew white from clay. Whatever Honda told him, he would do. Honda could be his father. For all Ben knew, Honda *was* his father. His knees hurt, his back felt strained, but Ben was dancing now, lungs straining for joy in air too thin for sustenance.

CHAPTER FOURTEEN

Less than a mile from Moss Village, Rachel saw the first glimpse of lake as it cut into the landscape, announcing the shift from farm to town. Soon they were driving down Main Street, past the five-and-dime and the butcher, the drugstore and the bank. Had that fudge shop always been there? Ahead, the spire of the Catholic church rose above everything. Rachel tensed, reeling from memories of the confessional, the rank, prying breath of the priest. With Sister Marie gone, would the nuns still know her? Or would she be just another girl, grown up?

"So," said Honda, "is it like you remember?"

In all these years, Rachel had only come back once. Ada had warned her to stay away, that it would be best if everyone thought that Rachel Winnapee's baby had died, and she had disappeared. Even so, Rachel had made her way one winter onto the frozen peninsula, the houses and the guard's shack boarded and desolate. She had sat upon the porch of her lover's house as she had done one autumn many years before, staring out at the hard, gray lake, recalling the warm sand of beaches now buried under ice. She had never gone back after that.

"I was only a girl," she said.

Ben cupped his hands to his eyes like binoculars and was staring at the boats in the harbor. A cluster of sails shifted in unison like seagulls in the wind.

"My dad was a sailor," Ben said, his eyes sliding toward Honda.

Honda's eyebrows shot up at Rachel. "Really?"

"Do you know how to sail, Honda?" Ben asked.

Honda laughed, said he might take a canoe out now and then. Rachel could see the disappointment flash across the boy's face as he looked away.

Rachel tugged at her hair. It wasn't a lie, the part about his father being a sailor. She had given Ben scraps of stories the way Woody had given her seashells and torn pages. Whenever Ben pressed for more, she would tell him it didn't matter. *Not even a picture?* he asked her. But she told him there weren't any, that scraps would have to do.

As they pulled up to the curb, Honda slammed on the brakes and came around to Rachel's side, holding the door for her impressively, like he owned the sidewalk. She knew what she'd see—some back-alley shack held together by duct tape, some dump of a place. No one will come to this store, Rachel thought as he led her down an alley between two buildings. How would they find it? But when they emerged into a sunny spot, she gasped.

It was little more than a stand, really. Bark-clad, tin-roofed—like a jewel box of a wigwam behind the long-established brick buildings that fronted Main Street.

"And look at this," Honda said, demonstrating how one whole side could be opened up like a garage, its hinged doors spreading like arms inviting everyone in.

Inside was filled with stacks of baskets, leather clothing trimmed with beads and fur, moccasins, birch drums, pipes, and headdresses. "Gosh," said Rachel, running her hand across a claw-studded breastplate.

"I knew you'd be impressed."

"You *knew*," she said, eyeing the hand-painted sign reading TRADING POST and trying not to smile, "no such thing." She drew her finger across the counter, wrote her initials in the dust. "Give me a cloth."

I could be in the woods, Rachel thought, in the middle of nowhere. Not blocks from the convent. Not half a mile from Beck's Point.

Ben was already cross-legged on the floor, playing with a birch bark canoe, making it dip and weave through imaginary waves. For a moment, Rachel felt safe and peaceful in this tiny, bark-covered shack, hidden behind other buildings. No one would find her. No one would say her name.

All afternoon, they unpacked boxes, stocked the inventory on dusted shelves. Honda was planning to serve fry bread and beer for the store's grand opening. Minnie would come and tell stories to educate the customers about the lore of the Odawa.

"Here," said Honda. "Get a load of this." From a box he pulled a child's headdress, gaudy with feathers, marked MADE IN TAIWAN. The beadwork looked slapdash, but Honda insisted they'd sell a ton.

"You want it?" he said to Ben.

Ben took the headdress. To some imaginary drummer, he began to move. Already he could turn himself into a bird.

"What are you smiling about?" Honda asked Rachel as he hit a button on the cash register, making it ring.

Rachel picked up a dream catcher—a wire circle covered in leather, trimmed with beads and feathers, its woven strips of gut resembling a cobweb. It was supposed to cast out nightmares and preserve happy thoughts. The whole store was a jumble of real and not-real. What, for instance, was that pipe used for? Those tiny, carved bears? But Honda insisted they were tribal, if only vaguely so, and not necessarily Odawa.

"How come you could borrow money for all this," she said, "and not for that land you want so bad?"

"Land?" Honda laughed. "Washington won't do squat about our land. They'll lend money for business. But for land?" He shook his head. "The government," he said, "in its wisdom."

Above her, seagulls screeched, battling for pieces of bread thrown by a child. Rachel had made it to the piers today, the farthest afield she had gone after coming into town each day for a week. The first day, she walked only a block before turning back. The sight of the harbor, the hint of the church steeple made her queasy with dread.

Now she was willing herself to stand at the end of a dock and stare down Beck's Point. A few days before, watching Honda with the boy, Rachel had thought of Woody—the palms of his hands, smooth as wax, faintly singed. She had thought of his thigh, the abrupt termination of flesh. She had thought of his mouth. The taste of his lips on hers.

He had never written her. Not once. She had thought of asking for money, was sickened by the thought. She'd rather split logs, sow the crops, weave quills, if it came to that. She was a quill weaver, after all. Even now, her palms throbbed from the awl.

The masts of sailboats clanged, the church bells chimed three. At the end of Beck's Point, clear as day, stood the Marches' house. Fiercely white and unchanging, it seemed oddly isolated and full of ghosts, as if the family who lived there would pass skin through skin, bone through bone, blood through blood, untouched.

I dare you, I dare you, Rachel thought. Suddenly lighthearted, she turned and beat a different path back to the store. Honda would be hunched over a price list, looking up occasionally to tell Ben to stay lower when he danced, to hold his shoulders like so. Feeling almost jaunty, she passed the five-and-dime, the hardware store, inhaled a sugary blast from the fudge shop. In the awning-covered windows, she could see a reflection, wondered whose it was. Surely not the girl whose path was beaten solely between the convent and Beck's Point. Here was a woman, braidless, face and arms brown from too much sun. Tough hands still, but the girl who had cleared the dishes was gone.

The truck-bed was filled with a pile of chopped wood. Ben leaned his head against the window. Toward the east, a faint horizon glowed. Honda leaned over, fiddled with the radio, but there was mostly static. All the way into Moss Village, Honda had been talking about the dancing, about the pow-wow, about how when *he* was a boy, the art was almost lost. Now, he said, things are different.

"Different how?" said Ben. His mother had told him not to take Honda so seriously.

"Oh, you know. . . . Better," Honda said over a crackly voice announcing a baseball game. "Minnie teaching you some words?"

Ben nodded, but it was like catching water to remember a whole word. River-fast and crazy. They tumbled together like waves, snapped like ice breaking up in March.

Across the lake, the sunrise streaked a path of red. "Red sky at morning," said Honda.

In a few hours, the Fourth of July parade would start. Honda had promised to take Ben and his mother to watch the parade and, later, the fireworks. Now they were pulling through the Beck's Point gate, waving at the guard, driving past houses three times as big as Bliss and Ada's.

"This used to be Indian land," said Honda. "We were robbed."

Ben adjusted his headdress. No lights shone except from some of the basement windows. Honda stopped the truck, cranked on the brake, leaving the motor idling, then signaled for Ben to follow him to the back entrance of a house so big and rambling it made the boy wonder if ghosts lived there.

The stone stairs leading down to the cellar kitchen held an odor of mildew and old food, but inside it smelled warm and buttery. Tipping his hat to the two dark women sitting at the old scarred wood table, Honda said, "Ladies?"

"Can't see needing a fire in a heat like this," said one, her skin darker than Minnie's.

"You know what they say," said Honda, "about Michigan weather."

"Moody weather," said the colored cook. She turned to Ben, eyed his head-dress. "Well, now, honey, that's a nice hat. You must be a help to your daddy here."

Ben didn't move.

"Come here now," she said, nodding toward a row of twisted dough. She was big and black and shiny. "Try one of these."

The other woman—the younger one—laughed. "He scareda' you."

"Child," said the fat one, "you'll like this."

She picked up one of the sugary pieces and set it on a plate. Ben liked the sound of her voice, the way the words fell slow and warm. His mouth filled with spit.

The cook bent low. "You're a real handsome boy. Don't know where I've seen such eyes."

"Takes after his mother," Honda said.

"Does he now?" said the cook, studying his face. Ben studied hers back, read something ancient and mysterious. Rows of crops. A field of blackbirds taking flight.

"There now," she said. "I'm Ella Mae."

Taking a bite, he said, "Ben."

"You going to watch those fireworks tonight, Ben?"

Ben nodded. His mother had promised. A buzzer made him jump, and suddenly the two women were up, pouring coffee, stacking plates. While Honda headed back to the truck, Ben slid into a chair and eyed the younger cook. As she ladled oatmeal into a bowl, the door swung open and a boy, still in his pajamas, walked in. The boy's hair was white and fine, twisted into snarls. Draping himself into a chair, he dropped his head into his arms. Slowly, he turned and looked at Ben. "What are you eating?" Ben, licking his fingers, shrugged.

Ella Mae handed a tray of food to the younger woman and turned back to the fair-haired boy. "Sweet child, you run up and take a seat. I'll bring yours directly."

"I want what he's having," he said, jerking his head toward Ben.

"You'll *have* what he's having. Just get."

"I want to stay here. Gaga's done and Mommy's still in bed. And Daddy's thrown up."

"For landsakes." Shaking her head, Ella Mae started for the stairs.

Again, the boy's head dropped into his arms. His hands were so white as to be faintly blue. Honda was outside calling for help, but Ben could not take his eyes from those soft, white hands. If he were to touch them, his flesh would pass right through.

The boy twisted his head and regarded Ben through half-shut lids. "My mother bought five new dresses yesterday."

"So?"

"Do you want to see them?"

Ben shook his head.

The boy pointed at his plate. "Can I have some of yours?" Ben pushed the plate toward him. The boy's fingers greedily tore off a piece of cinnamon twist and stuffed it into his mouth. Bits of frosting clung to his chin.

"My name's Rory."

Ben held up his palm, sticky with sugar. "Ben."

"Where'd you get this?" Rory reached out and touched Ben's headdress.

Ben told him about the shop down the alley, about the beads, bones, and teeth. "Maple candy, too," he said, "if you like sweets."

"My mother lets me eat fudge."

Honda shouted again from the stairs.

"Gotta go," said Ben.

Outside, Honda was pulling off leather gloves, wiping his brow. They had five more places to deliver, he said as he tapped Ben on his back. Five more, and if he ate like that at every one, he'd be sick as a gopher before the parade.

"Can you believe it?" Honda said as they drove past the broad lawns and wide porches. "They only live here in summer."

Seeing these houses—big enough for five families each—Ben wondered what their winter houses must be like. Honda told him that their own people used to pack up their wigwams and move them inland before the snows came. But these houses were too big to move. They had to be left behind.

"You know what the Indians used to call America before the white man came?" asked Honda.

Ben shook his head.

Honda turned the truck out of the gate, glanced in the rearview mirror. "Ours!" he said, laughing, showing gold.

The air burned with the smell of hot dogs and the tart metal of sparklers. As the sound of trombones drifted down the street, Ben pushed in front of the lawn chairs on the curb to get a better view.

"Hey, kid," someone shouted, "get away from the line."

"He's okay." Honda reached down and lifted Ben to his shoulders. Rachel caught her breath. Maybe it was his tattoos or his size, but no one wanted to argue with Honda.

Ben's gaze was fixed on the convertible at the front of the parade—a boat of chrome and red. From its cushioned depths, a fat man and his wife were throwing candy. Quick as a flash, Honda reached up and snatched a Brown Cow out of the air. "There you go. Compliments of the mayor."

The sucker in his mouth, Ben raised his hand in a salute as a car full of uniformed vets motored past, followed by kids on bicycles, their spokes twirling crepe paper red, white, and blue. Sequined majorettes in Uncle Sam hats propelled their batons dizzily upward, and Rachel noticed that, for once, Ben looked exhilarated, as if he had the best view in all the world and nobody could bring him down.

Far below, another boy, one with colorless hair, was holding a tiny American flag and gazing up at Ben. With a sudden, sharp thrust, he poked Ben in the leg.

"Hey, now," said Honda, glaring at the boy.

The boy's flag hung limply from its stick. Rachel had the urge to lean over and wave it. Uninterested in the parade, the boy's mother flicked a cigarette, adjusted her sunglasses. At first Rachel barely noticed her, but then the cold talons of recognition sunk in. Rachel's legs became unsteady, her head light, and she was suddenly aware that her fingertips smelled of quill musk, that her hair was an untamed bush. Staring at the blond hairs shiny with perspiration on the back of the woman's neck, Rachel inhaled her scent, gleaning beneath her smoky perfume the smell of laundry soap and starch. Rachel could hear the hiss of an iron, feel the drag of fabric as she tugged it across the board.

Prickling with shame, Rachel started to whisper, "Miss Elizabeth?" when Ben suddenly shrieked.

"Horses, Mama! Look!"

Honda turned and studied Rachel. "You look like you've seen a ghost."

Not a ghost, Rachel thought. The woman floated away, the boy's hand grasped in hers. Down a sidewalk swollen with locals and summer people, their two pale heads moved in such a way as to touch no one. They disappeared into a crowd of sunburned tourists and sticky children, but before she lost sight of them, Rachel swore she saw that boy turn and look at her, raise his flag and wave it.

The sun took forever to go down. Even then, the dusk seemed to hang on and tease as bottle rockets from across the harbor screamed their false alarms. Each explosion made Ben look up, expecting to see a fine, smoky trail, but it was nearly ten before darkness finally fell.

As they sat on the seawall, wrapped in blankets, Honda pointed out the barge in the middle of the harbor. It was flat, unimpressive and squat, but with the first volley of the cannon, it became a naval ship, an aircraft carrier, an entire fleet. Ben smelled the gunpowder, tasted the ash raining down. From time to time, the water sizzled and popped.

Five big booms, and the sky bled crimson and white. He could hear the people on the docks of Beck's Point. Ben thought about the way the cinnamon twist had tasted, how Ella Mae had called him "sweet boy." Whistles, applause, the blare of horns. The pops came quicker, the thunder deepened. Dense in the summer sky, the stars mingled with the fireworks, flickered and fused until Ben could no longer tell which was which.

CHAPTER FIFTEEN

Woody stood leaning against the porch rail and, with his good leg, toed the post. "Whole thing's rotten."

The dew was still upon the lawn. On the beach, gardeners were picking up bottles and spent sparklers from the night before. Woody stood with his mother and a painter, the house looming three stories above them—four, counting the turret and the half-story of basement where the kitchen and servants' quarters lay.

Woody's leg hurt. The pain would almost disappear, then return with a deep, arthritic vengeance. He didn't want to be here, hadn't wanted to come. Each summer, it became more of an effort. The train ride. The steamer trunks. Elizabeth's concern about invitations and clothes. Please, Woody, she would say. Try.

In the end, he would go. It was a fatal combination, Elizabeth and his mother. Useless to argue against their assertions that their friends would miss him, that the house needed his attention, that it was for Rory's good. He had to agree. His marriage, never strong, was more tenuous than ever. Besides, the steamy St. Louis summer was nothing if not debilitating.

The painter scratched his head, cap in hand, saying that they'd had a heck of a winter and he wasn't surprised.

"It's indoors, too," said Mrs. March, "under the refrigerator and in most of the baths."

Woody sighed. Even with a crew of yardmen, the gutters were rusted and split. Paint blistered, peeled off in sheets. Some of the windowpanes were cracked. "We should tear it down," he said, turning away before his mother could start in on how it had been built by her grandfather. Think of what it *means,* she would say.

"And Rory?" she said to his back.

"He'll go broke trying to keep it up."

Besides, there wouldn't be much of a bank left for Rory to run. The assets were dwindling, loans had gone bad. Woody had never coped well with making decisions. The ones he did make seemed consistently wrong.

Woody stared at the harbor, found it difficult to concentrate, difficult to care. Already the headache was creeping around the base of his skull. By the end of the day, he would be praying to die. "Where is Elizabeth?" he said, flinching at his own peevishness. Had she actually used the word *pathetic* to describe him that morning? Or was it *pitiful? Look at you,* she had said after she found him in the bathroom. *I thought you were done with it.*

But the morphine always won.

"Hell," the painter said, "these old houses, some of them tilt so much, it'd make you sick to walk across the floor."

"Nonsense," said his mother. "This house was built strong and fine. It's been in our family forever."

"Fungus," the painter replied. "That's what."

Woody pecked at the railing with his cane. Rory was upstairs, recovering from the fireworks. A weak child. Pale. They had watched the display from the end of the dock, seated in the pavilion. Woody had tried to enjoy them, but the sound of the blasts made him flinch. The interminable wait, the expectation, the harsh crack reminiscent of bombs. He'd always hated fireworks.

"There she is!" his mother said brightly as his wife appeared on the porch, wearing slacks the color of limes. "Elizabeth! We're trying to make a decision!"

"About?"

"The paint color," said his mother.

"Whether or not to bother," said Woody.

Elizabeth shrugged. Her hair was pulled back beneath a white silk scarf, and her eyes were hidden behind sunglasses. "It's your house, Woody." There was no use arguing with her. When they were first married, he would go to her, and she would sip her martini, drag on a cigarette, and say, *Don't*. She had known he didn't really want her. Elizabeth was always right, just as his mother was always right, and suddenly, he wanted to drink from their rightness, to dribble it on his forehead and be blessed.

"Golf?" he said.

"What?"

"Are you going to play golf?" He imagined her teeing up for a drive, grasping the shaft, the pro placing his hands on her stomach and shoulder and saying, *Here, like so, Mrs. March. Move from your hips.*

"Actually," she said, "I'm waiting for Rory. We're going into town."

"You won't let him eat fudge, will you?" Woody's mother said. "Because it'll make him ill again." She turned to the painter as if it was his fault. "We never used to have such things as fudge shops. It's the tourists. Ever since the war."

Elizabeth pushed her glasses up on her scarf. Her cheeks were flushed, and her eyes seemed bright. "Chartreuse," she said.

"What?"

"Paint it chartreuse. That way, all the neighbors will have something to talk about."

"Honestly," said his mother.

Rory came down the steps in his too-baggy shorts. As Woody watched his wife take his son's hand and head down the sidewalk, he decided to call Dr.

Harbison for another prescription. The breeze dusted up quicksilver at the edge of the bay. I should go swimming, Woody told himself. It's been so long.

"She was kidding, right?" said the painter. "About the paint?"

Woody felt bone tired. He needed to rest. The electrician and the plumber were coming that afternoon to talk about the leaking toilets, the addition of outlets. He wondered what it would be like—to swim and swim till you could swim no more. To slip beneath the surface, to watch the light grow dim.

Picking up his cane, Woody turned to the painter. "White," he said. "It's always been white."

Rachel was unpacking rabbit's feet. For luck, Honda told her. Burn tobacco at the full moon for the corn to grow, hang a dream catcher over your bed for happy thoughts. But nothing beats a rabbit's foot for luck.

Fascinated, Rachel held up the amputated paw dyed in a sickly shade of pink, rubbed her cheek with it, touched it to her forehead, chest, shoulders, willed her fortune to change.

"Excuse me?"

She hadn't heard the bell over the door. Turning, Rachel caught her breath. She had been hoping for days to spot a glimpse of Miss Elizabeth. Now she was here, holding the hand of a boy. For a moment, Rachel couldn't speak. Achy with curiosity, she clutched the rabbit's foot tightly and stared. She must think I'm a fool, Rachel thought.

Miss Elizabeth smiled. If anything she was prettier, though perhaps a little thin. She carried a purse that looked like a basket. On her hand, that big, blue stone. Rachel waited for her to say, "Oh, it's you!" But Miss Elizabeth stared at her blankly, as though they had never met. My hair, thought Rachel. My clothes. Or perhaps Miss Elizabeth had never really seen her in the first place, seeing only the hands that passed her the cigarette case and took away the tea.

The boy yanked Miss Elizabeth's hand. "Mother!"

"My son's been pestering me for a headdress." When Rachel said nothing, Miss Elizabeth went on. "You know, the feather thing? He was told he could find one here."

"This is your boy?" said Rachel. Her voice seemed far away. How idiotic she sounded!

"Not to look at him," said Miss Elizabeth, still smiling. "He could use a little sun."

"His eyes," said Rachel, seeing Woody in the boy the way she saw him in Ben.

"Allergies."

"*Mother!*" said the boy, yanking Miss Elizabeth's arm so hard, Rachel expected her to cry out.

Instead, Miss Elizabeth shrugged and rolled her eyes. She looked around the shop. "This is new, isn't it? I've never seen anything like it. Beats the five-and-dime."

Rachel's hand shook as she took several headdresses out of their cellophane wrappers and opened them, one by one, till they made a parade of feathers across the counter.

"Beautiful," said Miss Elizabeth. "That's really something." She took a Salem out of her purse and lit it.

The boy ran his fingers across each one and shook his head. "His was better."

"Honestly," said his mother. She nudged the boy, then began to move around the store. She fingered a dream catcher, tapped lightly on a drum. She stopped at a case filled with quill boxes. "What are these?"

Rachel was standing so close to Miss Elizabeth she could see the way her lipstick marked her cigarette, see her pick a tiny piece of tobacco from one of her teeth. For a dizzy moment, she wanted to take the cigarette from Miss Elizabeth's fingers and draw from it herself.

"How cunning," said Miss Elizabeth. "Who on earth takes the time to make them?"

"Mother!" said the boy.

But before the boy could start wailing, Ben came through the door with Honda. Miss Elizabeth looked up and smiled. "Oh, hello! You're the wood man." She held out her hand.

She's dazzling him, Rachel thought, just the way she's dazzled me.

"Your wife was showing me these lovely boxes. Honestly! I can barely needlepoint!"

Honda's eyes drifted away from Miss Elizabeth to Rachel, his eyebrows were raised as if to say, My *wife?*

"We're not married," Rachel said.

"Oh," said Miss Elizabeth. "I'm sorry."

Rory tapped Ben on his shoulder and pointed at his headdress. "I was wondering if I could have yours."

"Well, you can't."

Rachel laughed suddenly, a little spastic laugh. Again, Honda looked at her. She covered her mouth.

"Good for you," Miss Elizabeth said to Ben. "No one ever stands up to Rory."

Together, the two boys bent over a case of arrowheads.

By the time they were ready to leave, Miss Elizabeth had decided to purchase a headdress, a tiny log cabin that held incense, and a pair of baby moccasins. "What's that?" she said, pointing to a quill box on the table behind the counter.

Rachel picked up an oval box, a blue heron stitched on the lid. "It's not quite done," she said. Rachel wondered where Miss Elizabeth had found those pale green pants. They were the shade of a freshly mown lawn. "I still have to sew on the sweet grass." Almost against her will, Rachel told Miss Elizabeth she could bring the box to her when it was finished.

"That would be lovely," said Miss Elizabeth. "My husband's boat is called the *Blue Heron*." She narrowed her eyes. "Say, you look sort of familiar."

Rachel's cheeks burned, but Miss Elizabeth had already turned away, her curiosity as fickle as light on water. Rory, in the meantime, had reappeared—a strange, white child now top-heavy with feathers.

"How!" he said, holding up his hand.

Miss Elizabeth laughed. Honda groaned. In the distance, the church bells began their midday crescendo.

There were only six weeks a year when the trees would give up the bark. Rachel's grandmother taught her that. Any other time, it would have to be ripped off, and the tree would no longer be their friend.

Thank you, Tree, for parting with your skin, Rachel thought as she fingered the base of the box. Plucking out one of her own black hairs, she picked up a skein of sweet grass, braided it in. With strips of nylon, she lashed the braid to the edge of the box, the scent recalling days sitting with her grandmother on the banks of streams, sniffing the air, her grandmother saying, *Here!*

And now she was haunted again, seeing the green of Miss Elizabeth's pants in the early summer leaves, in the meadow grass, or floating upon ponds. Once or twice over the past week, Rachel thought she had seen her coming down the walk, turning the corner, but when Rachel hurried to catch up, there was nothing.

The night before, she dreamt she was on a dance floor beneath a galaxy of stars. Rachel had felt the cheek of some nameless man, smelled his aftershave, tasted the martinis, one after another, that she and Miss Elizabeth drank. The music swayed her faster and faster until she noticed her dress had become heavy and loud with the clanging cones of a jingle dress. Everyone else had stopped to watch her. She tried to stop dancing, but couldn't. Shimmering in a mirage of silver cones, she spun like a spirit imprisoned in their light.

The next morning, she could barely work.

The box was finished. Her hands shook as she tied off the knot. Not one of her best boxes, but a good one. Rachel ran her fingertips across the lid, read the evenness of quills. Her stitching had improved. Her grandmother would be proud.

"What's got into you?" Honda asked when she jerked her head up whenever the bell over the door rang. Honda eyed her dress. He'd never seen Rachel in a dress. It was one she'd been given as a hand-me-down and, though it was in good shape, it was dated. The collar, for instance. The way the waist dropped. But Honda said nothing. All morning, he had been preoccupied, tapping his fingers, doing numbers on a pad. Rachel wondered if the store was making money. It seemed to be—they'd had a steady stream of customers, mostly children wanting maple candy, headdresses, and leather wallets. But a surprising number of summer people were coming in, buying baskets and quill boxes mostly, the occasional beaded belt.

Rachel, too, was preoccupied. When she had gone with Honda that morning, she had left Ben at the lake. She didn't want to answer his questions, didn't want to answer the Marches' if she showed up with the boy. She would go to the house alone, see it for herself. Would Mrs. March even remember the girl whose wrist she had held and touched with scent?

God divines all our purposes, Rachel.

And what had been her purposes exactly? To make Woody laugh? Walk? Dance? Hadn't Mrs. March wanted to see some color in his cheeks— *anything*—when he looked so close to death?

The noon whistle sounded. Rachel rose. Honda pushed back a lock of hair grown long enough to hang into his eyes. "See if they need more wood, will you?"

But Rachel barely heard him. She had wrapped the quill box in brown paper, tied it with twine. Her head was buzzing and her breath came in short puffs. The door behind her banged, the bell tinkling, as she started toward Beck's Point.

The house needed paint. In the sun's harsh glare, it was a crone's face. Rachel stood on the harbor side, eyed the cracked panes, the sagging gutters where birds had built their nests. She could see a bit of curtain in what had been Miss Elizabeth's room—the same printed chintz. Did they sleep in that big, flowery bed? Or in Woody's room lined with its children's books and toys?

She would not go down to the kitchen. Instead, she walked up the stairs to the porch. On a wicker table, the pages of a newspaper lifted and fell. A fly buzzed around a half-eaten sandwich on a tray, landed, took off. Rachel knocked on the door.

Everything was quiet. She could hear voices, but they seemed to come from next door. Should she call out? Clutching her parcel, she turned to leave. It had been insane to come. She didn't know if Woody was here, or what she would say to Miss Elizabeth or Mrs. March. Would they even know her name?

I can come back tomorrow, she thought. Or have Honda deliver it with the wood.

The door swung open. "Yes?"

Rachel turned, expecting to see Jonah, but it was Mandy—an older Mandy—standing at the door.

"Hello," said Rachel.

Mandy stood there eyeing her, her mouth open. Rachel started to tell her about the box, but Mandy spoke first. "Lord, girl, what happened to your hair?"

"My hair?"

"Your braids."

"I cut them off."

Mandy's eyes narrowed.

"Anyway," said Rachel before Mandy could ask why she'd come, "I'm here to see Miss Elizabeth."

Mandy's own hair was pulled back in a net. She was getting heavy like her mother. Rachel wondered if she was still so pious. Would she pray for Rachel's soul?

Mandy straightened her back, blew up her cheeks. "Mrs. *March*," she said, as if correcting Rachel, "is not here at the moment." Again, those slitty eyes. "And why you want to see her anyway?"

Beyond Mandy in the hallway, Rachel could make out a girl—was she Indian?—vacuuming the stairs. The scent of onions and beeswax. A spider spinning a cobweb in the window.

"I brought her this." Rachel held out the parcel.

"The ladies have gone out."

And Mr. Woody? But Rachel didn't ask. What was it to her anyway? She had no business here.

"Will you make sure Miss Eliz . . . Mrs. *March* gets this, please."

Mandy took the parcel, shook it. "My mama told me you'd moved away. Went to school or something."

"Or something," Rachel said. After a pause, she added, "Why didn't your father answer the door?"

"Dead," Mandy said. "Two years."

Rachel remembered Jonah's hooded eyes, inscrutable as her Uncle Jedda's. Who would be serving the Marches drinks now? "I didn't know."

"Why should you?"

Why, indeed. Rachel knew she wasn't going to be invited in. Life had gone on without her. She might as well go back to Honda's store. "Say hello to your mama, then."

Mandy opened her mouth to say something, then stopped. She nodded at Rachel, watched as she turned and walked down the steps to the sidewalk. Across the lawn, Victor was pruning the hedges. Rachel raised her hand to wave, but his back was turned. Instead, she crossed around the other side of the house. At least she could walk back on the bay-side beach. Maybe take a swim.

Rachel moved down the rocky edge of the beach. The houses on the ridge of Beck's Point seemed to glare down at her, purse their lips, accuse her of trespassing. She held her shoes in one hand and swatted away a horsefly with the other. Soon, the beach grew wild and desolate. No place for children. No place for lovers. But the memories tided around her ankles, clung to her like sand.

Ahead was the dune. She would lie on that dune, cradled in its warmth, before going back to the store. Pushing up the rise, she came to the crest. A man was seated below her, facing the lake. Hypnotized, she studied him. It was his neck she recognized first. She knew that neck, the smell of it, the fine rope of carotid and bone. His hair betrayed a barber's touch. If she wanted to, she could lean in close, say his name. She fought the urge to cry out.

He seemed to be waiting, watching as if seeing the lake for the first time, his cane nestled in his lap like a child. She clamped her hand over her mouth. A layer of cirrus clouds had whitened the sky. A shadow surrounded the sun. "Hello," she said when she finally found her voice.

He raised his head and squinted at her, smiling politely as if at a stranger. Her memory had betrayed her. He had been thin before, all hollows and bones. But now he seemed depleted. Her eyes traced across his hands, the pulse at the base of his throat. She wanted to lay her head upon his chest, feel the heat of him through his shirt. She wanted to slap his face.

She waited.

Woody couldn't see the woman clearly. She was haloed like an angel by the hazy sky. He cleared his throat, composed his features, ready to say, *May I help you?* when, in an instant, he recognized her.

"My God!" he said, trying to rise, but the sand made him awkward.

"Please," she said stiffly, "don't get up."

He couldn't if he tried. He had a strange sense of falling backward. "I didn't recognize you."

"It's my hair."

Abruptly, she sank to her knees beside him, her eyes taking in his face. He remembered that wariness, that way of looking as though she was about to turn and run. Not a figment. Not a memory. He drank in her breath, the fact of her presence. He closed his eyes, calmed his senses, and the thought of her became the air in his lungs. He exhaled with relief, opened his eyes to find her staring at him.

"They told me you had left," he said.

She sank back into the sand so that she was sitting, her eyes searching his face. He noticed she was barefooted, that her feet were brown against the stark white sand. She seemed to hesitate, selecting her words.

"You have a son," she said.

"Yes," said Woody, wondering how she knew about Rory.

Why had she come here after all this time? He had a million questions, but they popped like bubbles as they hit the surface. All he wanted was to touch her.

"You *knew?*" Her hand shot out and struck him on the cheek. He raised his arms reflexively as she started to strike again. "Rachel!" he said, grabbing her fist.

She was breathing hard now. "You never answered my letters!" Her eyes were wild with tears. "You never said good-bye!"

"*What* letters?"

Down the beach, some children ran, laughing, racing each other to the lake. A breeze kicked up. The shadows seemed to flatten and disappear as the color ebbed from the sky. His fingers tightened upon her wrist. Rachel's hair was short now. It frothed in the wind. He studied the blunt lines of her face. "But I left *you* a letter!"

Between sobs, Rachel said, "You could have at least told me you'd gotten married." She touched her shaking fingers to his eyes. "Your son's eyes are this color."

He let go of her wrist. "You've met Rory?"

"No—your *other* son."

Suddenly, like sand, his world shifted. He searched for answers in her eyes, nose, cheeks, saw an entire history in her stare. Again, he could not speak. The shadow around the sun became a dark, hard ring, the wind shifted to the east. Down the beach, the children scrambled from the lake, wrapping themselves in towels.

"Hurry up!" a nanny called. "Rain's coming!" While all around, the dune grass flattened against the sand.

Woody turned back to Rachel, but she was staring at the lake. The wind whipped her hair, blew it into her eyes. Pushing it away and gaining control of her breath, she nodded.

"Ben," she said. "I named him Ben."

CHAPTER SIXTEEN

R achel got back to the store to find Honda, screwdriver in hand, kneeling behind the cash register. She shut the door, pressed herself against it. Her hair was wild, and her shoes were filled with sand.

"Jesus," said Honda, shoving aside a tangled wad of receipt ribbon, "you can't count on a goddam thing!" He slammed down the register lid. "Register's broken, and now McCready's gone and done it."

Rachel's wrists still pulsed where Woody had gripped them. It had started to rain on the beach. She had helped him to his feet, started up the path. Had Woody been crying? Or was it only the rain? Her dress was soaked clear through.

"He didn't know," she said to no one in particular, still amazed and angry that Woody had never received her letters.

"Like hell he didn't," said Honda. "After all these years. These guys—they're all the same."

Rachel started. "What are you talking about?"

For the first time, Honda seemed to see her. He set down the screwdriver. "Holy mackerel, what happened to you?"

Rachel pushed her damp hair back. How could she tell him her son had a father, living?

"Have you heard a word I've been saying?" said Honda.

She shook her head.

"McCready," he said. "McCready's selling the lake!"

For a moment, Rachel couldn't think who McCready was.

"Twenty *thousand* dollars!" Honda pounded his fist on the counter, and Rachel recognized the old rage of the Odawa at their great-grandfather's grandfathers who had lost their land in a bogus treaty. All these years, the band had acted as if the lake was their own. Who else had fished on the ice in winter, hunted its woods, raised their children in the cluster of almost-buildings by the lake? Even Rachel's grandmother had come to Horseshoe Lake as a girl, leaving Moss Village after the beaches were sold off. Before that, the Odawa had camped up and down the water's edge. Someone in a canoe lingering off the shore at night could see the beaches dotted with campfires, hear the songs, smell the tobacco.

"What are you going to do?" she asked Honda, thinking of all those people with no place to live.

Rubbing his fist, Honda shook his head. Twenty thousand dollars was steep, but McCready had dollar signs in his eyes and wasn't going to settle for less.

"Christ," said Honda, "the Hewetts from Beck's Point are thinking of making it into a fishing and hunting lodge. *Our* lake!"

That damn lake, thought Rachel. It was all Honda could think about. Redemption, he had told her, lay in the land. Land it was, and land it would be to bring justice to the Indians.

Indians. Rachel almost spat the word. Rootless people with no place to go.

"Why not buy the lake yourself," she said, "if you want it so much?"

He looked at her like she was crazy. Perhaps she was. She couldn't stop thinking about Woody, how his long-fingered hands had grasped her.

"Buy it?" he said. "You think moccasins and dream catchers are going to raise that kind of money?"

Rachel rubbed her temples. Her head was aching with words. She would go to the dune tomorrow to talk to Woody. He promised he would be there, just as he had been, years ago, when they met each day at three. They would talk about their lives. They would talk about Ben. Perhaps they would make plans for him to meet his son. She wished she could help Honda, but Horseshoe Lake seemed a far-off place, as distant and insubstantial as memory.

She came the next day as she said she would. Woody noticed she was wearing the same dress. It was a pretty dress, frayed at the hem. He wanted to touch her, but she recoiled from his touch as if she might evaporate like his dreams after a morphine sleep.

They sat in the cup of the dune, out of the wind. Rachel had pulled her knees under her chin and wrapped them in her arms. Woody was stretched out, trying to get comfortable. It wasn't easy. Even after all these years, his leg still hurt like hell.

"Your wife came into the store where I was working," Rachel said, staring out to some middle distance on the lake. "Does she know you're meeting me?"

Woody flinched, but it was a fair question. He remembered standing at the altar with Elizabeth, the satin-covered buttons tracing down her vertebrae like shiny white peas. The sweet smell of lilies had overwhelmed him. Or had it been roses that smelled so sweet that day?

Woody pointed to the rocks. "You see that shoal? How far out do you think that is?"

"I don't know." Rachel shrugged. "A pretty easy swim."

"Exactly. Not much space between here and there. A quarter, maybe half a mile of channel where it's deep enough to sail a boat. That was the test when I was a kid. Whoever made it through that shoal. Port tack on a westerly, and if you got knocked down, you were stuck." He looked at her. "My brother was something of a hero."

Lip had loved sailing, had loved to work the boat through the swells, to play the wind shifts to the best advantage. He must have hated dying on that road in Belgium, landlocked, far from the smell and mist of lake.

But Woody was nothing like Lip. Lip should have returned from war, should have been the one to run the bank. That had been the plan. He knew how to run a bank, had tried with little success to explain to Woody about revenues and dividends, principal and income, explained it as carefully as if he were talking about sex, and made Woody swear that he would never sell his stock.

But Woody hadn't cared. There was always plenty of money. He had only to call his man at the bank. He didn't care much for possessions, but occasionally he needed something. Books, for instance. A gift for Elizabeth. But it wasn't until they were actually engaged just before the war that Chinnery, the vice president, had called him in.

You see, said Chinnery from behind a very large desk, *it's a matter of allocation.*

Woody had sat across from Chinnery, his navy cap in his hands, his uniform neatly pressed. Lip had been off fighting for a year.

Chinnery went on, his spectacles flashing opaquely upon his waxen nose. *Although it's more than sufficient, it must be preserved. The principal, that is. The corpus. For your descendants.*

Corpus. The body. Like a cadaver.

Two weeks later, the telegram came. The Battle of the Bulge, it was called. Thousands had died, but only one had mattered.

Lip.

"Did he make it through?"

Woody roused himself. "Excuse me?"

"Your brother? Did he make it through?"

"Not only that. He caught a header and managed to tack while three other boats ran aground."

"Sounds to me like he was lucky."

"No," said Woody. "He was a hero." He could feel Rachel watching him. "I'm no hero, Rachel." He tried to read her eyes, but they were unyielding. Again, he tried to touch her.

"No," she said. "I've sworn."

He looked away. "I didn't know you were religious."

"You think that's what it is?" Rachel shook her head. It was seeing the girls, she told him, who came one after another to Ada and Bliss for help. She'd taken an oath, cut off her braids.

Woody couldn't blame her, really. When all was said and done, she had raised the boy herself. "Your son," he said, looking back to the bay where three sloops chased one another's spinnakers downwind. "*Our* son. You say he likes boats?"

That night Woody sat with his mother and Elizabeth on the bay-side porch.

"We should trim the trees," said Elizabeth.

His mother sniffed. "I've been saying so for years."

"Cut the trees, pave the roads . . . ," murmured Woody.

The bay had turned a lurid shade of blue that came at the end of sunny days. Now that Jonah was gone, it was Woody who fixed them drinks—Elizabeth's usual Gibson, his mother's sherry. His own martini sat untouched.

"I'm going to take the *Blue Heron* out in a few days," Woody said during a lull in the conversation. "She hasn't been out in years."

His mother almost spilled her sherry. "Woody!"

He could see she was pleased. For a moment, he felt embarrassed, as if he'd suddenly announced he was going to take up polo. Elizabeth was looking at him the way she always did—sideways, secretly checking to see if his hand shook.

He cleared his throat. "Rory could use the exposure."

"Rory," Elizabeth said, "detests the water."

"He could learn."

"He gets seasick."

"You coddle him, Elizabeth."

Surely his mother would agree with him! She was always critical of the way Elizabeth was raising their son.

"Well, Mother?"

His mother leaned back, inhaled deeply. She was pursing her lips, as if the sherry had turned. "Do you smell it?"

Woody threw up his hands in frustration. No wonder his father had rarely spent time at home, preferring instead the office or club.

Even so, there *was* something brackish in the air, almost foul.

His mother had set down her glass. "I believe we're going to have alewives again this summer." Twice in the last decade entire schools had washed up on the shore—the inscrutable multiyear cycle killing off countless tiny fish for no apparent reason.

"God," said Elizabeth, "can we move inside?"

On the dim opposite shore, Woody could make out the faint lights of Chibawassee, where the Jews from Chicago summered. There had been a golf tournament once. Years ago. His father and some other men had hosted the club from Chibawassee. They'd had his father's foursome for dinner, and afterward, his father had shown his new friends his sailing trophies. Woody remembered the smell of cigars, wondered if his father, too, had been smoking.

"Nothing from New York, Charles?" one of the Jews had asked. "Only the Great Lakes?"

"I prefer to sail on Lake Michigan," his father had answered lightly.

"Really?" said the man. "Me? I'd like a trophy from that yacht club in New York."

After they had left, his mother had opened all the windows to air the house of smoke. For years, Woody's parents had laughed about "that yacht club in New *Yawk*," and always his mother would add to that story her memory of the terrible smell.

"You can't get away from it," Woody said to Elizabeth, but she was already rising.

"Oh, Woody," she said, exasperated, "we can always *try*."

Ben waited, his hand in his mother's. She had told him he was going sailing, and for the last few days he had been imagining what the wind would feel like, the cold slap of water. Would the boat tip and buck? Capsize and sink?

Now they were standing on the big pier in town. A sudden gust of wind caused the moored boats to change directions. Those that were docked clanged, groaned, strained at their lines. His mother tried to hold on to her hair, but pieces escaped and whipped around her face.

"Soon," she said, scanning the harbor.

The lines running up the mast of the big boat at the end of the dock went *ting ting ting*. He was eyeing the top of the mast, wondering if he could climb it, when his mother's hand tightened on his.

"Look!"

A motorboat rumbled its way slowly toward them, spewing fumes. The man driving the boat had short, dark hair.

"Ahoy!" said the man as he pulled up to the dock.

Ben's mother laughed, and he looked at her, wondering what was so funny.

Perhaps this man wasn't a sailor. Perhaps they weren't going sailing after all—just for a ride in a motorboat.

The man held out his hand. Ben would have to hold it to step down. The boat rocked gently against the dock, and the man said, "Come aboard."

Ben looked at his mother, who jerked her head toward the boat. "Go on," she said. "You know you want to." As Ben took the man's hand, his mother added, "This is Mr. March."

"Hello," said Ben. He tried to get his hand back, but Mr. March held him long and tight, looking at Ben as if he was some kind of birthday present.

"He looks like you," said Mr. March, releasing Ben and turning to help his mother.

"Hardly. Look again."

Pushing off from the dock, Mr. March turned the boat back toward the harbor and headed to Beck's Point. The wind carried off the smell of diesel fuel, and soon they were zooming across the water tailed by a frothy V of wake.

Ben pointed to a sleek blue boat tethered on a mooring. "That your boat?"

"That's the *Blue Heron*," said Mr. March. "Hank from the boat shop is coming along to help out." He turned to Ben's mother. "And I've decided to bring Rory."

His mother was sitting in the back of the boat. Ben had never seen her back look quite so straight. Her hair seemed to have a life of its own, dancing this way and that. He wondered if she was scared to be on the water, or if the look on her face was for something else. The dress she was wearing seemed wrong somehow. Shouldn't she be wearing pants? Lately, she had been wearing lipstick, too. Even Honda had noticed.

Mr. March went on, looking over at Ben. "First time on a boat, then?"

Ben didn't answer. He had been waiting forever to be out on this lake, gliding across the water. Even if he'd never actually *been* on a boat—a thousand times in his imagination must surely count for something.

They pulled up next to the moored blue hull. The sails batted angrily against the mast. A man with a sunburned nose leaned over, held out his hand.

"This is Hank, Ben," said Mr. March. Ben let the man haul him aboard. Next came his mother, and finally Mr. March, who had tied the motorboat to the buoy.

"Got 'er?" said Hank, bracing Mr. March. Ben saw Mr. March wince as he got on board, noticed the stiff way he moved and how he had to help his leg over the rail by holding it.

"Rory," Mr. March said to the fair-haired boy in the cockpit, "come over here."

Rory was sitting in the cockpit, his arms wrapped around his knees. Wearing an orange jacket that made him look strangely bloated, he stared off into space as though he was willing himself to be onshore.

"Rory?" said Mr. March. "This is Miss . . ."

"Call me Rachel. Please."

This time the boy didn't even look at her, just nodded, as if the rest of his body was paralyzed. But none of this mattered to Ben. All that mattered was that he was on a boat in the middle of the harbor, and that the wind felt fine, and that any minute now, they would be casting off.

Rachel was still barely able to speak. She felt as if it were all a dream—this boat, the lake, Woody. Woody had held out his hand, and Ben had taken it, and now they were on the lake. She looked at the father, the son, saw each in the other, and had to look away. She wished she had worn a scarf. The wind tossed her hair, and suddenly she felt tired, as if she hadn't slept in years. They rounded the end of the peninsula, and she realized she had never seen Beck's Point from this angle, that the houses looked smaller from this distance. She could almost smell the potatoes boiling, the naphtha soap, the lilac perfume on an old woman's bureau.

Hank yelled that there were some gusts ahead. Rachel grabbed a winch and held on. The boat heeled, and Ben laughed. Rory looked ill. For a moment, Rachel pitied him. She could see Ben had all the blood—the electric blue of Woody's eyes, the honey-rich skin of the Odawa. The other boy looked sapped, the tree that wouldn't make it.

Woody was explaining to both boys—to Ben really—how the sails worked, how you trim them like so, and when the wind goes this way, this is what you do, and if you don't, this happens.

"You shouldn't touch that," Rory said to Ben, who had started to pull on a line.

The boat tipped and took on water. Rachel screamed. Rory grabbed his seat, but Ben laughed, and Woody laughed, too, because Ben looked so happy, laughing.

"I had a brother like you," Woody said to Ben, again resurrecting the long-dead hero.

But before Rachel could say to Woody, *Stop. You're confusing him,* Ben called out to Rory, "Do you come out lots?"

Rory nodded and forced a ghastly smile. "Sure," he said. "All the time. See that house?" He pointed to the big white one toward the end of Beck's Point. "That's *our* house."

"So?"

"It has twelve bedrooms!"

Ben was silent, but Rachel felt sorry for the boy. He looked so sick, and Woody hardly noticed him. Even Hank stepped over him as if he were nothing more than a winch. "My!" Rachel said. "That's a lot of beds to make."

The boy's watery blue eyes fixed on hers, and his cheeks flushed slightly. "Yes," he said slowly. "But we don't make them ourselves."

The boat bucked, sent up spray.

"Either of you boys want to steer?" said Woody.

"Nope," said Rory. But Ben practically jumped into Woody's lap, and for a moment, Rachel's eyes stung. She wanted to believe it was the wind, the sun, anything but this wave of gratitude and loss that rushed through her like a tide. Ben was taking the wheel now, and Woody's arms were around him, showing him how to pick a course, saying, *Look at the sails, Ben. Look at the water.*

Ben looked up at Woody. "Who taught you how to sail?"

Woody's eyes fixed on the horizon. After a moment, he said, "My father."

The boat plunged through the waves. They were in the middle of the bay now, the houses onshore barely visible. Green hills, the occasional gash of dune.

"Ready about!" yelled Woody.

Rachel could see he was in pain, that he had to brace himself not to lose his balance. At one point, she almost grabbed him but, thinking of Rory, pulled away.

Hank jumped into the cockpit, undid the line from one cleat, leapt to the other side, and began to crank madly. Still holding Ben, Woody pulled the wheel all the way over. The sails swept across the deck. Ben screamed with delight.

"Ease her off, Hank," said Woody. The sails relaxed, the wind softened. It was quieter now as they headed back to shore. Catching the roll of a wave, the boat surged forward.

Rachel looked at Rory, who was practically green. "Woody, have you got something to drink on board?"

"What we got, Hank?"

"Pops. You boys want a pop?"

Nodding at Rory, Rachel said, "I think it would be a good idea."

Woody was almost happy. He pushed back his hair from his lake-misted face. On port tack, he could brace himself with his good leg and sit on the windward side, although from leeward it was easier to watch the sails. His father had taught him that. Look at the luff, he would say. Use the wind. See how the draft bellies out? That's what you want.

Ben was watching the sails, studying them, his gaze tripping up and down from line to shackle, trying to understand how it all worked. He can *see* it, Woody thought. He can see how the wind drives the boat.

Rachel was sitting erect, almost prim. He wanted to touch her, but he knew she would pull away.

Your son, she would say. Your wife.

Woody longed to tell her he hadn't touched his wife in ages, but it seemed vulgar to say it, even to the girl who, all those years ago, had made him think there was hope.

But there had never been hope. Not really. One couldn't elope with the Indian maid.

"You okay, Rore?" he said. Rory nodded, but his eyes were fixed straight ahead.

Woody remembered his own father's impatience with any display of weakness, fought the same urge in himself. How many times had he been compared to Lip? *Look at your brother,* his father would say. *You should be bolder, Woody.* But boldness never suited him. It was easier to acquiesce, do what his mother told him.

"So," Woody said to Ben, "your mom tells me you're practicing for a contest?"

Yes, Ben said, his chest puffing slightly. He was going to be a Fancy Dancer.

"Is it Indian or something?" asked Rory, who seemed less green now, gulping down a Coke.

Woody had been brisk with Rory that morning, barking out orders. *This is the way you coil a line, Rory. Not a* rope. *A line! This is the painter. Yes, it goes here. The* bow, *not the front!*—and only mentioning in passing they were going to take along the boy Rory had met in the Indian store. Rory had looked at him as if he'd lost his mind. Now he was regarding Ben with nascent condescension, already patronizing. Woody could see it in his son the way he had seen it in others of his class—the feigned interest, the elaborate politeness.

"Look," Woody said, "you see over there? Where those waves are breaking? That's the shoals we see in the distance from the house."

Indeed, the Marches' house rose in the trees beyond. Woody could almost make out the figures of his mother and Elizabeth standing on the porch.

"When you come around the point on a tight reach heading up in a westerly," he said, "you can sometimes get a little lift in there. The wind comes off the bluffs and shifts direction."

"What's that mean?" asked Ben.

"You ever run a footrace and take the inside corner? The more you can cut in, the less distance you have to go. It's the same on a boat."

"So it's cheating?"

"No," said Woody. "It's only cheating if you fall off a little and drive the boat below you into the ground." For a while they watched the waves crest, then break upon the offshore strip.

"You ever do it?" asked Ben.

Woody shook his head. "I was on a boat when my brother did it. The wind has to be perfect. Any other way, you get too pinched. You can take the keel off a boat that way."

Ben crossed his arms, stared at the distance. "Doesn't look that hard."

Woody laughed. "Oh, it doesn't, does it? Well, we'll come out another time, give you a chance."

"And if he hits the ground?" Rory said.

"Hank here'll come get us. Right, Hank?"

"Towed more boats than I can count off those damn rocks," said Hank.

Rachel looked preoccupied. She was staring at the Marches' cottage, her lips tight. Woody followed her stare, saw clearly the two women at the rail. The

Blue Heron was cutting close to shore now. They would need to jibe to clear the point.

Woody said in a low, even voice, "They knew we were going out today."

"Did they know you were bringing us?"

He didn't answer. "Pull in the sails, Hank. We're tacking. Heads down, everyone."

The boom groaned across the deck, then snapped loose with a loud crack. For a second, the boat pitched, heeled to starboard.

"Tighten up."

Woody moved to the other side of the cockpit with effort, heading close on starboard toward the middle of the harbor. His mother had been trying for years to get him back on the boat. If he wanted to give a kid from town a ride, what of it? He could say it was charity—something she would understand.

Ben had moved up to the bow now. Again, Woody was reminded of Lip. The boy's hair was scruffy at the neck, but the way it danced in the wind was captivating.

They could come out again. Woody was sure of it. It was something a father should do. Teach his son how the wind worked, the language of waves on the water. Woody knew this bay as well as anyone. He would teach the boy to sail.

CHAPTER SEVENTEEN

W oody leaned against his mother's bureau. He was looking out her windows toward the bay, sparkling in the late-morning sun. This summer the water was shallow over the shoals. A flock of gulls had lit upon the rocks, though from this distance, it appeared they were standing on water. For two weeks, he had been taking Rachel and Ben out on the *Blue Heron,* crossing up the stretch of lake nearly to the horizon and back. He had never meant to stay at Beck's Point for more than a week or two. Now the visit was extending into a month.

"Those people you've been taking sailing?" said his mother. She was sitting at her desk. "I'm curious."

Why did his mother insist on such heavy curtains? They were like everything else in this house—dated, falling into disrepair.

"Woody?"

Only yesterday, Elizabeth had commented on the faded upholstery, but his mother had insisted that the fabric was perfectly fine. They'd had it sent up from Chicago.

Woody roused himself. "Excuse me?"

"I watched you through the binoculars the other day. Are they friends of Hank's?"

Woody crossed his arms and surveyed his mother's room. He had stopped taking Rory out after the first few times, the boy begging off because of seasickness.

"What do *you* think?" he asked his mother. God, how he loathed that crucifix over her bed.

His mother set down her pen. He could see she was making a list. "I don't know what to think."

The emaciated body of Christ dangled from the cross. Blood trickled down the Messiah's wrists, feet, and brow. "Do you remember," Woody asked, "that first summer after the war?"

His mother's eyes traced his stare to the wall and back again. "It was a difficult time," she said. "Awful, in fact."

"Yes." He nodded. "I had to learn to walk all over again."

His mother paused. "But you *did* walk. You walked and you danced. And then you married Elizabeth."

"I married Elizabeth. Exactly."

"What does this have to do with sailing?"

"Nothing whatsoever."

Every day when they went out, Ben would point to the shoals and ask him, *When?*

Soon, Woody told him.

His mother went on. "You don't sail with Elizabeth."

Woody turned to face her. "It's none of your business, Mother."

His mother picked up a sheaf of stationery, straightened it on the desktop. "It's her, isn't it?"

That bloody Jesus. He wanted to rip it from the wall.

And now his mother was sounding sanctimonious, her face as serene as the Virgin of the Pietà. "That girl. The one who worked here."

"She has a name, you know. Rachel. And the boy's name is Ben. But then, you thought he was dead, so why would he have a name?"

He couldn't tell from her face whether she was fighting back disgust or satisfaction. She closed her eyes, as if she was adding up her rosary, wondering which saint to appeal to. Finally she looked at him and said, "So."

"So?"

"What else do you want me to say?" She gave a little laugh. "It's ridiculous, really."

"That I have a son?"

"He's not a son, Woody. He's *not*. Rory's your son."

"And Ben?"

"A little Indian boy. Who knows where he came from? Honestly."

Woody's head snapped up. "He's my *son*, Mother. As much as Rory is my son. My son and my heir. As I am *your* heir. You can't change the terms."

For a second, her smile flickered. When she spoke, her voice was hard. "No?"

"Father to son."

"I'll deny him."

"I won't."

"Oh," she said in that tone she'd used with him since he was a child. "I think you will."

"What's this guy to you?" Honda asked later that afternoon as Rachel got ready to go sailing again.

Pulling her hair back into a bandana, bobby pins sticking from her mouth, she shot him a look. "I've told you. I worked for their family when I was a girl. You remember."

"That's what you've told me," Honda called after her as she walked out the door.

Later, as they waited for Woody to pick them up on the dock, Ben asked, "What's Honda so mad about?"

"You tell me."

"Is it Horseshoe Lake?"

Rachel held her hand over her eyes and squinted toward the harbor. "What do you know about the lake?"

Ben's eyes drifted sideways, the way they did when he knew more than he should. "I know that everyone's going to have to find someplace else to live."

But before Rachel could say it wasn't so bad, that they'd figure something out, Woody and Hank were pulling up to the dock. Rory, as usual, wasn't with them. Rachel waved.

They sailed far into the bay that afternoon. The wind had dusted up from the west, and it wasn't until they were halfway to Chibawassee that Woody decided to tack. Even on port, he told them, they could clear Good Hart, follow the wind past Sturgeon, and maybe cut east to Mackinaw. "Which would take all day."

"Let's keep going!" said Ben.

"Wind's perfect," said Woody, raising his eyebrows at Rachel.

It's true, she thought. It's a perfect day. The deep blue of the sky meeting the deeper blue of water. Everything was sun-washed. Everything seemed clean. Somewhere in those hills rising faintly away from the shore, a small band of Indians was preparing for a gathering. They would be clearing a field on the far side of the lake just beyond the woods. First the trucks would come, then the tepees. There would be a rope around the ring, and in the middle of that, beneath a structure of twigs and branches, the drummers would sit alongside the chanters.

Tomorrow night, Ben would be dancing. Now he was staring off the edge of the boat as if he knew exactly what was up ahead. Suddenly, Rachel felt tired, as if it was too much to hold together. Two lives, one of them secret. Every time she was with Woody, she fought back the desire to touch and hold him, to trace his veins with her tongue.

Again, Ben's expression struck her. She'd seen that look of rapture when he'd taken something apart, figured it out. Now Woody was teaching him to make the boat dance. No small dinghy, either, but a big, gleaming, full-sailed yacht.

"We'll go out again," Woody told the boy.

"I've never seen a kid learn this much this fast," said Hank. "Even your brother, Woody."

Woody looked almost proud.

The following afternoon, Woody waited at the dune. The day was heavy with heat and humidity, windless and waiting. Any minute now, Rachel would come over the crest. He had asked her to come, and she had promised. Reluctantly. "The powwow," she had said, telling him she had to get back to the lake to prepare.

A dull ache crawled up his spine to his neck. What if she refused him? He hadn't thought of that. Even that morning when he went to the attorney's—a thin, sallow man whose experience with probate and estates was limited to the transfer of farmland.

Your wife? the attorney had asked. *Is she aware?*

And Woody had stared down his impertinence until the man turned back to the letter Woody had dictated and said, *Sign here.*

There, Mother, thought Woody. You never thought I had it in me.

It was exhilarating, like the first time he swam to the shoals—a hero in spite of himself. For a moment, he felt heady with resolve. He had never had the

audacity of Lip. Now he was truly compromising everything. This is what con-
viction is, he thought. The singularity of purpose the kamikaze pilots must
have felt.

Say your rosaries over this one, Mother.

"Woody?" It was Rachel's voice. That deep, throaty sound he loved. As she
sat beside him and dug her feet into the sand, he reached out, took the ends of
her hair. She didn't move. Her hair, damp with sweat, was wind-crazed and
coarse—not the angel's silk of Elizabeth's. Rory had hair like his mother's—
fine, almost colorless.

"So," he said. "Should I come to this powwow?"

Rachel laughed. "In your blazer and tie?" Her smile was sweeter than a
drug. "You ever been to a powwow?"

"Every year in St. Louis. It's the most sought-after invitation of the season."
She looked at him seriously. "You're joking."

He matched her seriousness. "I never joke. You know I'm morose."

Rachel looked away, trying not to smile. "You even know where Horseshoe
Lake is?"

"I can find it."

"It's a ways from here. It's past the hills."

She had described it to him, years ago. The glow of the huts in winter. The
green of the water. He closed his eyes, imagined the lake again. Better than the
reality, no doubt. Still, he wondered. "Is it as green as you said?"

"Excuse me?"

"The water. You said it was green."

"Only one way for you to find out. But you'll never come."

He shifted his weight, rubbed the place where his leg stopped. "I've gone to
an attorney." He spoke carefully, as if to a child. He wanted her to understand
that this was important, that he was determined, but she looked past him, the

smile of a minute before vanishing. "You see, I want Ben to have what is his. . . ." Woody's voice trailed off.

He had come back from the attorney's office euphoric. Hadn't the trust been his to direct? *I have a son*, he'd told the man. *Another son whom I want to have remembered*. And he signed the letter saying it was so.

Impassive, Rachel stared at the lake. A bead of sweat trickled down her cheek. He cleared his throat. The terms of the trust, he told her, were clear. There was less money now, but it was still substantial. And now that he had *two* sons, Ben would benefit as well.

"Why are you telling me this? Do you think this is what I want?"

Woody's cheeks burned, and he looked away. It had never occurred to him. "Don't be stupid . . ."

"It's you who's stupid."

He turned back to her and grabbed her shoulder. "You're right." His voice broke off. He tried to touch her face.

Shaking him off, Rachel rose. "You think too little of me."

After a pause, he said, "I think of you all the time."

With a loud caw, a crow flew up from a tree. On the bay, Woody could see the wooden-hulled gleam of a boat, its motor buzzing persistently. After a while, the boat changed course, turned back toward the harbor. Woody could feel Rachel next to him, wanted to touch her, to pull her down to him and say, Forget my mother. Forget Elizabeth. It was a mistake, don't you see? I hadn't the courage then, but today I recognized my son.

Rachel leaned down and picked a stalk of dune grass, held it between her lips. "He thinks his father is dead."

Woody lay back on the dune, wondered if perhaps he wasn't. For the first time in a week, his leg was throbbing. He thought of the morphine the doctor had sent, lying in the drawer, untouched. Each day, knowing he was going to see Rachel, he'd been able to resist it. *I dare you, I dare you,* it said. The waves whispered, *Still, still.* And still Woody wanted to touch her.

"He's a good sailor, Rachel."

The look she gave him was beyond pity. He thought perhaps she was crying, but her eyes were dry and hard. "Yes, but you should see him *dance.*"

That evening, Woody leaned on the rail of the patio of the Beck's Point Club and drew on his cigarette. Inside, Elizabeth was dancing with another man. Max Bailey, most likely. Dinner was finished. Waiters in tuxedos were clearing the plates, the band had struck up, and now the silhouettes of diners moved across the windows to the low buzz of conversation and the occasional laugh.

Woody stared at the shawl in his hand. His mother had told him to fetch it from the patio, even though the evening was warm, and now he couldn't bring himself to go back inside. The music was too loud, the beat too manic.

Mere alcohol doesn't thrill me at all . . .

Why had he and Elizabeth married? Surely she had other prospects, though at the time the world seemed smaller, life shorter; and there was the yearning for the familiar in a universe that was spinning apart. Woody had found comfort in despair, in its inevitability, in its delicious, dull ache. To know the worst, to feel the heat beneath your palms, the jab in the thigh, and know that, for the moment, you are exempt.

But I get a . . . KICK . . . out of you!

Now it was faintly disquieting to realize that there might be other possibilities after all. He had seen his own face in Ben's in a way he hadn't in Rory's, and the boy's wide-eyed wonder had made him reconsider. Perhaps one's transgressions *could* yield meaning. Perhaps life was more than a sentence to this thin band of existence, its ceaseless repetition.

"Woody?" His mother was standing beside him. He could smell her perfume even before she spoke.

"Mother."

"You said you would come in." For a moment, they were both transfixed by the view of the harbor, streaky with the light of buoys and the town. Somewhere, there was another party, but the noise from the club drowned everything out until it seemed this was the only place to be.

"You know what I think?" he said.

"I never seem to."

"I think"—he jerked his head back to the brightly lit windows of the club—"that my wife is having a perfectly wonderful time with someone else's husband."

His mother was silent. Finally, she took his arm and said, "Let's walk." He picked up his cane, and they moved away from the club, toward the gates of Beck's Point. Passing beneath the lights of streetlamps, watching their shadows grow long and shrink to nothing, he listened to his mother describe how when she was a girl, she would walk along this very sidewalk, some young man at her side, someone she didn't marry, but who at the time had made her laugh.

"There were no wars then. Life was good."

"There are always wars, Mother."

Her grip tightened. "Not here."

There was no use arguing with her. To his mother, as long as there was Beck's Point, whatever was happening anywhere else was irrelevant.

A couple passed them on the sidewalk, murmured good evening. After they'd passed, his mother said, "I never know who anyone is anymore."

"I know."

"Do you feel it?"

"For years now." They stopped at the dock. The music from the club had faded. A car door slammed. In the distance, Woody could pick out the faint thread of drums, the pale strain of chants. He knew it wasn't possible. The powwow was miles from here. Thirty minutes by car at least. "Do you hear it?"

His mother cocked her ear. "What?"

"That sound? It's the drumming from the powwow."

He had told Rachel he would go. They had laughed about his tie and his blazer.

"No," said his mother. "I don't hear it."

"Listen."

Behind them, the upbeat quarter time of the club band. From the hills, miles away—the pulse of drums, the pitch of a cry.

"Are you hearing things?" his mother asked. "Because you sometimes—"

He held up his hand. "It stopped."

Grasping his arm tighter, his mother peered at him. "Woody," she said, "I'm worried about you and Elizabeth. If you're thinking of leaving her . . ."

He didn't answer.

"It won't set, Woody. You've made your vows."

For a second, he swayed on his cane. Vows? To hell with *vows*, he wanted to say. His mother's. His wife's. Rachel's. He started to say, To hell with you all, but the look on his mother's face stopped him. There was nothing frail about Lydia March. She had the stony endurance of a saint. In the lamplight, her features looked almost menacing.

"All these years," she said, staring him down, "I've had to listen to the talk. I've defended you before, but I won't stand by while you throw your life away on some Indian girl. I'll say you're unfit, Woody. Chinnery will testify. Maybe even Elizabeth. You can't run the bank. You can't run your life. You'll lose your rights."

"My *rights?*"

Suddenly, Woody felt like a child again, as if he had been caught looking at dirty pictures in a book. He gripped his cane and fought down the urge to strike her. It would be so liberating—comforting, even—to watch his mother crumble. But he knew that she had won, as she always won, with whatever arsenal she had on her side. Drive the leeward boat aground. Leave it on the rocks. Who would believe an addict?

"Don't pray for me, Mother," Woody said, grasping his cane, turning to walk away. "Ever again."

That evening, there were Chippewa, Sioux, Odawa, and Cree dancing together under the stars. It was a thin substitute, this powwow, for what had once been a huge gathering of tribes. Long ago, they had come by canoe or on foot. Now they came in rusted Pontiacs, named after a great chief, long dead.

Since sunset, they had drummed and wailed, ever since the first dancers entered to stomp down the weeds and make way for the others—first the Grass Dancers and then the processional in which they all had walked, not only the little band from Horseshoe Lake, but also the bands that came from Chibawassee and farther north, all the way from the Upper Peninsula and even parts of Wisconsin.

There hadn't been a powwow in years. Not in these parts, anyway. Not since Rachel was a girl, and Jedda had organized one during a brief, sober spell when he thought it was time to resurrect the old ways and pay tribute to their ancestors.

"Of course, only about twenty people showed up," Minnie had recalled. "And most of them didn't know the first thing about dancing."

Now a hundred or more were gathered. The men with their beads and feathers and bones were dressed even more gorgeously than the women. In his cabin, Honda was helping Ben prepare for the dance. The boy had been practicing for months and knew the steps by heart—when to stomp, when to jerk, when to move backward or twist. The evening was warm, and Honda was painting Ben's face with black and white grease until it looked almost fierce. Ben eyed the buckskin pants he had to wear, said something about the heat.

"Indians don't sweat. Only white boys sweat," Honda said, and punched Ben in the shoulder. "You a white boy, kid?"

Rachel bristled. *My son. My heir.* All the way back to the lake, she had thought about Woody's words.

Soon Ben was layered with necklaces, breastplates, bracelets. His hair wasn't long enough to braid, so Honda spit into his hands and wet it into a ducktail before tying on his headdress, cinching a beaded band to his forehead. A porcupine hide, trimmed in silver, trailed down his back.

"Now," said Honda, "hold still." He took a jar of white paint from a tackle box, began to rub it on Ben's face.

"Can I look?" Ben asked.

"Go ahead."

Ben looked solemnly at himself in the mirror. His eyes were lined with black like the bandit mask of a raccoon, but the rest of his face was white. Behind him, Honda was grinning like a crazy, proud father. Rachel knew most kids didn't win the first time, even if they were good. The first time was to show respect and win the respect of others. Rachel knew the most he could hope for was to make it through, to stop on the beat and keep from tripping.

She could hear the announcer describing the upcoming Fancy Dance. Ben was ready to go. Rachel jerked her head toward the door where Ada and Bliss were waiting. "Go show your aunties. They've come all this way."

For a moment, Ben wobbled, as if his legs felt weak, but he pulled away from Honda and started for the door.

Woody sat on the edge of his bed listening to the tattered bits of music that drifted through the window. Any minute now, Elizabeth would be home.

How long had it taken her to notice he was gone? Down the hall, Rory was sleeping. His mother had retired to her room.

You'll lose your rights.

His head hurt. He was still dimly aware of far-off drumming. He had opened the package from the doctor, held the bottle in his hand. The liquid was clear and colorless. He had taken a syringe from his bureau. Now he wavered. It had been more than a month since he last shot up, but the ache in his leg, the conversation with his mother, the futility of it all made the choice seem inevitable.

He flicked the bottle with his nail, broke off the top, drew out the liquid with the syringe, pressed it into the crook of his arm, and squeezed. He lay back against the pillow. Now he was sure of the drumming. Or was that the throbbing in his veins? He closed his eyes, thought of the dancers at the club. Malcolm McGee and the Miller sisters. No, that was years ago. All of them gone.

I never know who anyone is anymore.

Maybe he would go to the dune, wait for Rachel. He rose to his feet. Somewhere in the house, a noise. Elizabeth? He decided to leave before she found him collapsed upon the pillow.

I thought you were through with it.

He made his way down the hall, down the stairs where he almost slipped, grabbed the banister. Then across the dining room to the porch. Outside, the crickets were shrieking; he'd never heard them so loud.

He thought someone called to him. *Woooo-dy!*

Lip! He was sure of it! Lip was out on the water, yelling, *Come on in, you priss!*

Almost laughing, Woody staggered down the steps to the path. He had forgotten his cane and stumbled once, sprawled out on the dirt, tasting the soil, the tiny grains of sand. Rising to his feet, Woody started more determinedly toward the beach. He was sure Rachel would be there. She would come after the party, and they would dance at the water's edge. All those years ago—she had helped him to swim.

You can't run the bank. You can't run your life.

He was at the beach now. The waves beat black against the shore. Somewhere there was drumming. Somewhere, a singer crooned a love song so sad, it made him wince.

Wooooo-dy!

Lip was out there, on the rocks. Not a long swim, really. Less than half a mile. He could make it if he took off his clothes.

I went to an attorney, Lip. I have a son.

He kicked off his pants, tore the sleeve of his shirt. He could smell the water now—briny like tears. He plunged in. Soon he was swimming, and as he swam, his thoughts were on Rachel and the boy. All he had to do was get to the shoal! His arms slowed, his prosthesis anchored him. And the moon! Where else had he seen such a beautiful moon?

In the distance, he could hear the shrill whine of a motor coming closer. Its squeal was deafening. He was frightened, briefly, then panic gave way to relief. If he turned back now, he would only sink before reaching the shore. There was no point really. Everything had been burned away, leaving only the resolve to swim and swim until he could swim no more.

It was growing late. The campfires were lit, the stars were out. Finally, it was cooling down. Ada and Bliss had planted themselves on folding chairs and were commenting on the costumes. Next to them, Rachel pulled a shawl around her shoulders and once again searched the crowd. She knew he wasn't coming, had known it the moment he had said he would. The absurdity of it caught her like a slap.

Still, she searched the sea of faces, the thought of Woody's offer expanding like a balloon. There was a naive earnestness about it that touched her.

She could make out white faces among the Indians. Onlookers, mostly. Some mixed. Rachel had met a girl that afternoon who'd looked more Irish than Ojibwe, had almost laughed when that girl spoke in perfect Chippewa. Well, she thought, what do I know?

But she knew this: he wasn't coming. Ben would dance and never know that his father had expressed a desire to come and hadn't. She would reject Woody's pronouncement. Let Ben go on thinking his father was dead. Not some man on a boat who had sat him on his lap and given him pointers about sailing.

"He's up next," Honda said, coming up behind her, his arm around Ben. "Rachel?"

"Hmmm?" She pulled back into herself and turned to catch Honda staring at her.

"Looks like you're expecting someone."

Rachel shook her head, ran her fingers through her hair. "No."

"Well," he said, "that's what it looks like."

Honda crossed his arms. Again, Rachel was aware of the tattoos on the back of his hands, wondered what it would be like to gouge something into your flesh. She reached out and touched his fist.

"No," she said again. "No one." She smiled at Ben, shook her head. "Well, look at you."

"Scared the bejeezus out of me," said Ada, tapping Ben on his shoulder.

Honda knelt down. "You ready?" Ben nodded yes, his own arms folded like Honda's, his expression fierce. Rachel covered her mouth, turned away, startled to see so much of Woody in him—as much March as Winnapee. Her breath caught in her throat. She almost cried out.

Ben moved toward the ring with the other children and was soon caught in the wave of dancers. He found a spot, stood perfectly still, arms at his side, head down. A singer wailed, high and thin, followed by some drums. Ben lifted his knee, brought his heel down on the second beat, almost missing it, then hurried to catch up.

"C'mon," whispered Honda.

For a moment, Ben lingered over a beat, missed it as if distracted, then began to dance again, fast and hard. Sweat ran down his cheeks, streaking black and white together.

"What's he doing?" Honda said.

Ben seemed to catch himself. He was one of the smallest boys, but he moved quickly and with purpose. Rachel could see that he danced the way his father had learned to walk—every step determined, every step a refusal to give up.

"Will you look at that?" said Bliss.

The other boys—one in particular who wore the markings of another band—had more experience. They'd competed before, probably many times. Ben wouldn't win. Not at this powwow. But later . . .

"You've taught him good," Ada said to Honda.

Honda shrugged, but Rachel could tell he was smiling. Even though the boy would lose, he'd danced with feeling and grace.

Again, Rachel scanned the crowd, wishing Woody could see this. See! she would say. *This* is what he comes from!

But the faces around the campfires were those of strangers. The music pitched higher, seemed to hang in the night air. The stars glittered with a new vibrancy. Silhouetted against them, the sweet undulation of trees. Sparks flew from the fires as the chanting, ringing, drumming came together, and then all at once, abruptly stopped.

CHAPTER EIGHTEEN

Not since she was a girl had Rachel slept on the beach, listened to the frogs, watched the stars, smelled the still night-water. Slowly the campfires died, though she could hear low voices, a laugh from a tepee, the even breaths of sleep. She lay next to Ben, his exhausted boy-body twitching as if he were still dancing in his dreams. Hush, she told him. It's over now.

The futility of it all. These ragtag bands, the poor, rank wretchedness. Most of these people barely had money for cigarettes, much less clothes or cars or shelter. And this sense of communion? Nothing more than shared despair in a keening, gaudy mess. Once, a shack had burned here. Now, there were silhouettes of tepees, the round, smooth forms of trailers. It was odd to think that this was ever home—odder still to think it would never be again.

How people love to huddle together! Even on Beck's Point with its grand houses, all within sight of one another like a ring of children gathered for a bedtime story. She wondered where Woody was sleeping tonight, and if he slept alone. If he had come to see Ben dance, she would no longer be able to deny him.

But he hadn't come.

She must have slept because suddenly dawn was breaking, and she could make out the outline of reeds, of trees, the spindly boards of a dock. Soon the fires would start, their smoke both sweet and terrifying.

Ben rustled next to her. "Mama," he said, "are we going sailing?"

"Not today."

"Are we going to the store?"

Rachel didn't answer him. She wanted to lie here by this lake a few moments more, pretend she was a child again, her grandmother calling, *Rachel! Rachel! It's time to come in!* Perhaps her grandmother would make fry bread. Perhaps she would braid Rachel's hair.

Your hands are too soft, she used to tell Rachel. You need tough hands, like so.

"What'd you think?" Honda asked as he folded up the last of the blankets.

All morning, they had helped the participants and their families pack up. Many people took Rachel's hand, thanked her in English, in Odawa, in Cree. Their voices trailed off—slips of words, familiar, forgotten, strange. Then they were gone as quickly as they had come, leaving the flattened circle of grass, the dark wounds of fires, the smell of tobacco, dust. Minnie put her hands on her hips and nodded. It had been a good powwow. One that would bring them luck.

Now Rachel felt *her* luck was turning. It was Monday. Tomorrow they would sail with Woody as they had every Tuesday for a month. She would wait for him at the pier, and when he helped her into the boat, she would say, *Well, you missed it.* And then she would describe Ben's skill and grace, glancing at Woody from beneath her eyelids to see that flicker of pride she'd begun to suspect in him.

Soon the families of Beck's Point, Chibawassee, and Pont du Lac would pack their suitcases and head for St. Louis, Chicago, Detroit, back to their schools, their clubs, their universities with ivy-covered walls. Rachel knew now what she would say to Woody. She was already practicing her words. *This is what I want,* she would say. *This is what you have to do. Share your riches with him. Teach him to sail, to play golf, to run banks. Anything but to dance in the dust helplessly wailing for what was lost.*

Tuesday arrived. Rachel and Ben went to the dock to wait for Woody, but the day grew late, and the motorboat didn't come. Some children were tossing bread to the seagulls. The birds swooped down, fought one another for the morsels.

"Let's go," Rachel said abruptly.

First the powwow, and now this. But Ben didn't want to leave the dock. He was sure Mr. March would come.

"Come *on!*" said Rachel, yanking his arm.

When they got back, Honda was talking to a man at the counter. He turned, and Rachel recognized Hank, the boat hand from the *Blue Heron*. As soon as they saw Rachel, their conversation stopped.

Honda cleared his throat, held up an envelope for Rachel. "This came in the mail for you."

Rachel took it, saw the attorney's name in fancy print, stuck it in her pocket. She looked from Hank to Honda and back again. "Is there something else?"

Honda pulled his hair back. He looked as if he was choking on stones. Suddenly he hit a button on the register, pulled a bill from the drawer, and said to Ben, "Here's some money. Why don't you go buy yourself a box of fudge?"

Rachel raised her eyebrows. Honda had never given Ben *real* money. But Ben, not waiting to see if Honda would change his mind, snatched the bill and ran out the door.

"What's this about?" asked Rachel.

Hank plucked at his eyebrows like he did when he was figuring the wind. Rachel noticed how pink and peeled his nose was, how bloodshot his eyes.

"There was an accident. At least"—he paused—"it looks like one."

He waited, as if she would know the rest, but she didn't.

"Where's Woody?"

Honda stood up. "There was a boat with some kids in it. They didn't see him."

Hank was looking at her like he wanted to be forgiven. Finally, he threw up his arms. "Why was he swimming at night like that? And him with only one leg?"

But already Rachel's knees had grown weak, her hands covering her ears, the moans breaking from her like waves until her voice choked. Why was Honda touching her? Why was he kneeling before her and taking her face in his hands and pulling her tightly until she couldn't move, couldn't rock, couldn't breathe.

"It was an accident, Rachel," Honda was saying. "It was an accident. He never knew what hit him."

The bells rang early that morning. Rachel hadn't been to the Catholic church in years. Now she stood across the street and watched the mourners filing out, their clothing dark in spite of the heat. They looked like crows. Death birds.

She hadn't gone inside, wouldn't sit among those people and pretend to be one of them. The man they were mourning and the man she knew were not the same. They knew a son, a husband, a peer. She knew a lover. A man with a broken body whose pain she had eased one summer when his mind was still at war.

She waited until they all came out. She watched two women, veiled, get into the Marches' Buick. For a moment, people seemed to linger in clusters, then they, too, drove off or walked in the direction of Beck's Point. Rachel looked around for the hearse. No pallbearers had left the church. Was there nothing left to bury?

Crossing the street, Rachel ran her fingers along the chain-link fence as she walked down the sidewalk past the yard where she used to play. It caught at her hand, begged her to come in. In the garden, the statue of the Virgin bowed her head alongside a sign that spelled out how the Jesuits had built the church to save the orphaned Indians.

"Excuse me?"

Rachel turned. Two tourists dressed in Bermuda shorts, smiling eagerly.

"Do you speak English?"

Rachel nodded dully.

"We were wondering . . . ," they said. They had read the sign that said how the Jesuits had built the convent to help the Indians. Then they saw her by the statue and had seen the resemblance. It would make such a lovely picture. "You *are* Indian, aren't you?"

Rachel began to laugh. Her eyes brimmed over. She must look like some crazed penitent, wordless with contrition. "I'm sorry," she said. "I've just come to pray."

Leaving them agape, she hurried toward the church, paused at the doors, then stepped into the bluish gloom.

"Father?" she whispered.

No one answered. Echoes from childhood—the hushed whisperings of girls, the clicking of rosaries. Rachel genuflected, moved into a pew, crossed herself, and knelt. She bowed her head to pray but could not. She had not prayed for years.

On the altar, vases of lilies and black-eyed Susans perfumed the air still ripe with eulogy. "Father?" she whispered again.

The confessional stood to the side—a chamber of little lies and petty misdeeds, the occasional sputtered truth. She rose from her knees, crossed to its curtained front. Inside the musty space she breathed deeply. What would she tell the priest now? Shrouded in chastity, she had buried her past the way her son used to bury his treasures. She had denied him his father, denied him his feelings, denied his very birth. Sipping from her own words the blood of redemption, she spoke.

No response. No pale echo. Rachel smoothed her hair, her dress, fingered the letter in her pocket. She knew what she had to do. Pushing through the doors and into the afternoon, the sunlight banged her face with a sure, sharp slap.

The Marches' porch was overflowing. The humidity had kept everyone outside. They sat on the porch rail, the glider, the wicker chairs. Men who normally wouldn't remove their jackets were in their shirtsleeves, once crisp, now wilted. Waiters, hired from the club, moved around with trays of iced tea, though a few men and several ladies were asking for a stiff one to ease the tension and make the time go faster. As Rachel passed through the dining room, no one seemed to notice the Indian woman in the faded dress. Perhaps they thought she was one of the help. Or perhaps she was invisible, not even worth hushing their asides about Woody's "little problem" and how Elizabeth might be better off.

The kitchen was even more humid than outside. Ella Mae, dressed in purple and still wearing her church hat, was sitting at the table. Rachel could see she'd been crying. Mandy, on the other hand, seemed dry-eyed and efficient. Redeemed, even, as if she knew all along this was coming.

"Mama," Mandy said, "look who's here."

No recognition crossed Ella Mae's face. She stared at the wall, didn't seem to hear.

"Mama!" said Mandy, louder, impatient.

This time, Ella Mae looked up at Rachel, opened her mouth, shut it. "I heard you was back."

Rachel looked at Mandy, who shrugged.

Ella Mae went on. "I heard it was you he took sailing."

Rachel braced herself for the tirade she was sure was coming. The litany of blame, the mountain of accusations. But Ella Mae shook her head. "I had hoped it might cheer him up. Give him some purpose, you know, seeing you again like that."

"Some purpose," Mandy said under her breath.

"Do you remember," Ella Mae said, gesturing at a chair for Rachel to sit, "how hard we worked to get him to walk?"

Rachel sat down next to Ella Mae.

"How he used to cry out?" Ella Mae continued. "I was sure he would quit. He'd always been partial to quitting. But then when he didn't, I knew there was a reason." With a low laugh, Ella Mae said, "And it wasn't his mama."

For the first time in days, Rachel smiled.

Ella Mae's hands flew up to her head as if she suddenly realized she was still wearing her hat. "No wonder I'm so hot." She took off the hat and used it to fan herself. Her eyes fixed on Rachel. "She told me you didn't come back 'cause you went on to school. That true?"

Rachel shook her head.

In a grumpy voice, Mandy said, "Well, what, then?"

"Mandy," said her mother, "get this child a lemonade."

"Tssss," said Mandy, "she worked here two whole summers. You'd think she'd know where the glasses are."

"I need to see Mrs. March," said Rachel.

"Drink some lemonade," said Ella Mae. "There's no rush. Let her say good-bye to her guests first."

"And what makes you think she wants to see you?" said Mandy.

Rachel turned her eyes coolly on Mandy. "She doesn't."

"But she will." Ella Mae nodded.

When Ella Mae gave her the go-ahead, Rachel started upstairs. She wanted only to tell the truth and hear it told back. In the dining room, a vase of limp gladioli drooped upon a table of uneaten food. A cold leg of lamb, bowls of new potatoes, mint jelly, aspic, and curried beans. Rachel recognized some friends of Woody still lingering in front of the wall of photographs, transfixed by the past. There was Woody on a sailboat. Rachel ached to see him at the helm, his blue eyes a pale gray in the photo. There were a number of stiff family portraits, everyone gathered in garden chairs, on seawalls, the dock, or porch steps. A lovely shot of Miss Elizabeth holding a trophy. But it was the one of Woody as a boy that most pinched Rachel's heart. That curve of his jaw just like Ben's. That widow's peak above the startled eyes.

Ella Mae had told her Woody died immediately, that the kids who were driving the boat thought they had hit a branch. He was too mutilated to be placed in an open coffin, so in deference to the Presbyterian Marches, they had cremated him, baked him to dust.

"Know what the first thing to wash up the next day was?" Ella Mae had said. "That damn leg."

Rachel touched a photo of Woody as if to bless it and started up the second set of stairs. At the top to the left was the guest room, the one Miss Elizabeth had used. The door was closed. Rachel wondered if she had spent the afternoon drinking. She passed Miss Elizabeth's room with the slightest pause to listen, heard nothing, moved on. She felt she should be carrying sheets. Any minute now, Ella Mae would be calling her to hurry up. If she stood very still, Woody would come around the corner, pull her toward him, try to find an empty room.

Down the broad hallway, its Oriental carpets faded and frayed, she came to Mrs. March's room.

Rachel stood in the doorway and cleared her throat. Mrs. March was sitting, as usual, at her desk, stationery spread before her as if she was already answering notes of condolence, thanking everyone for the flowers. Such beautiful flowers! They were strewn about the house.

Rachel gazed around the room. Everything looked the same, older perhaps, but otherwise unchanged. Jesus still hung from his cross. A pare of gray doeskin gloves lay across the pillows. "I came to say I was sorry."

Mrs. March was sitting so stiffly, Rachel thought perhaps she was frozen with grief. Her bird-beaked nose was silhouetted against the window, backlit by the glare of the early-evening lake. A hushed pulse of waves. The low rumblings of lingering chatter from downstairs.

"We had to have him cremated," said Mrs. March. "Do you know what that means to a Catholic?"

Rachel thought of her grandmother's thin, dry corpse within the burning shack. For years, the nuns had told her that Jesus, ascended into heaven, would return to judge the quick and the dead. How, she had wondered, would Jesus judge dust?

"I was raised by the nuns, Mrs. March," Rachel said. "Did they ever tell you how my grandmother was burned before I could bury her?"

Mrs. March's nostrils flared briefly. On her desk lay her rosary. "Did you know I had a daughter who died in infancy?"

The child taken by the flu. Rachel, remembering the empty room with the crib, nodded.

"I used to pray for a miracle," Mrs. March went on. "I wanted nothing more."

"I've done my share of praying," said Rachel.

But Mrs. March didn't seem to hear her. "I've lost all my children." She turned her back to Rachel, seemed to search the lake for answers. "I'd like you to go now."

Rachel looked around the room, took in its bric-a-brac and photos, its too-lacey bed, the fine, polished furniture, the grand view of the bay. Only days before she had wanted this for Ben. Now she wondered why.

Ten years since that summer. Surely, Mrs. March had known. Hadn't she seen the color in Woody's cheeks rising along with his spirit? She had spoken to Rachel of callings and miracles. Hadn't she seen them walking by the beach? Picked up the faintest scent of mothballs from the blankets they'd lain upon in the attic? The backs of Rachel's legs had been tattooed with the tufts of bed-spreads, her braids hastily redone, her own eyes shiny, shinier than Woody's when he woke from his morphine dreams. Surely Mrs. March had seen it! The sand on Woody's arm, the bruise on a young girl's neck. Maybe the nuns had told her. Maybe Mrs. March had seen the letters after all.

But Mrs. March said nothing, and finally Rachel spoke. "I have a letter," she said, "from Woody and his lawyer."

Mrs. March stared out the window. For a moment, Rachel had the suspicion that she was offended by Rachel's mentioning Woody's name.

"Woody," Rachel went on, "wanted everyone to know the truth."

"What *is* the truth," said Mrs. March, turning back to Rachel, "exactly?"

"That my son is his. That Woody claimed him for his own."

There. The truth was out in this confessional of a bedroom with only Mrs. March to hear.

"You can't expect me to acknowledge that."

"It's in the letter, Mrs. March. He signed it."

"Well, then," said Mrs. March, her hands folded in her lap, as if she was willing them to stillness, "you have your proof. What more do you want?"

A drop of sweat trickled between Rachel's breasts. In the end, what she wanted wasn't that different from what Mrs. March would want. That they would be rid of her. That Ben would never know. That Rachel would relinquish the Marches as gladly as they relinquished her.

"I want money," Rachel said, meeting Mrs. March's gaze. Money had its uses. Her grandmother taught her this. Rachel would take what was owed her. No more. No less. It was justice—not charity—she wanted.

"You'll give me the letter if I pay you for it?" Mrs. March's voice was rich with contempt.

"Yes."

"You'll relinquish your . . . rights?"

"I will take an oath."

"I didn't think you'd have the nerve." Mrs. March opened a drawer, took out her checkbook, picked up a pen. "Do you know who the first person was to see the risen Lord?" Seeing the look on Rachel's face, Mrs. March almost smiled. "A whore."

Rachel pushed aside her anger and thought of Horseshoe Lake, its green water choked with reeds, its beach scattered with clamshells. In the forest, the smoke of burning cedar would be snaking out of the chimneys and campfires. Soon, the old men would burn thistle to summon the autumn fish. Perhaps one of them would teach Ben how to cast a line and take him out on the ice the following winter. There would be songs at night. Sometimes there would be drinking. The trees were rich with bark for baskets and sap to heal, the woods dense with wildlife, acres of it, spread over duney hills shaped like the reclining bodies of sisters. They could own this land, this band of rootless Indians.

Thirty pieces of silver, the Bible told her, bought Judas's treachery as well as the life of a slave. Rachel thought of Honda. She thought of Minnie. She named her price.

Part Three

CHAPTER NINETEEN

1970

Heat and more heat. Trees within trees. Grass that cut. The sky, seared and torched by the burned-out canopy, was no color he recognized. Ben was far, far away from the smell of sweet grass, far from the lapping of waves, the creak and groan of pines, light-years from the gentle warmth of the fainter sun of northern latitudes. So he ate the soil, little pieces of it, his tongue searching for familiarity in minerals and microscopic life. *It will take you home,* his mother had told him. He could taste the rotted reduction of leaves and bark, of Pleistocene insects, of small, furry mammals.

For days they had been moving deeper into the jungle, joining up with a unit cutting north through the valley. The things they'd seen, a private named Spenger told Ben.

"Women and kids, man," said Spenger, his eyes stoned on the memory. Their voices were low as they passed through the jungle. "We didn't want to, but the lieutenant said if we didn't, we'd be dead." The private had arrived the day before—one of the new men too nervous to sleep, trigger-happy with fear.

"So what'd you do?"

Shogging along beside him, Spenger held up his gun and made popping noises. "You'da done the same." For a moment, he fiddled with the end of his carbine, then pointed it at himself. "Blam," he said, his voice as hollow as his eyes.

Ben remembered the first time Honda had taught him to use a bow, how he had frozen when he came face-to-face with a deer. Now Ben's head hurt, his skin tender as a veil against the coming danger. Above the kindled trees, the moon flicked in and out of the haze. At home, it cut a clear path down the lake, followed him through the forest as he tracked night animals, turned the snow a silvery blue. Here, in the jungle, it was a dim yellow ball.

"You can't lose your nerve," Honda had said.

Spenger lit a joint, blew out smoke. "We're none of us heroes, man." And Ben, chewing on a bit of earth and thinking about the way the air smelled lately—like rotting leaves—knew they'd find out for themselves soon enough. He'd always known when a storm was coming, when the wind was about to change. His scalp would begin to prickle. Even on those glaring blue July days when nothing bad seemed possible, he could feel a storm before it hit.

He cocked his rifle and looked around. Beside him, Spenger was strumming his carbine like Carlos Santana when, forty feet down the line, someone tripped a land mine.

"Alpha Bravo!" the lieutenant screamed.

A spray of artillery shredded the bamboo, the running-screaming of an ambush. Ben hit the ground and looked up to see Spenger still spastically twanging his gun guitar. Pulling his helmet low, Ben screamed, "Get down!" But Spenger's body kept twitching until it finally dropped.

The air grew thick with humidity and slaughter. Ben rolled over on his belly, aiming his M-16, watching for friendlies, ready to shoot anything that moved. In spite of gutting fish and butchering rabbits, nothing had prepared him for the stench of bowels and blood. There was a ringing in his ears. His pants were warm and wet. Ahead in the torn bamboo, he made out two eyes, darker than his, staring back. I'm going to die, he thought. He raised his gun, lowered it, and in a ragged voice said, "I want to go home."

There were popping sounds from behind him. He heard a blast and buried his face in the dirt, only this time it tasted like forest loam, the sweet balsa of pine. All around him, grown men—boys only yesterday—crumpled and fell.

When Ben looked up again, there were men down everywhere. Some of them groaned. The right side of Ben's face and neck felt sunburned. The first lieutenant got to his knees, took off his helmet, and puked. From the horn on the CO's corpse, a dim voice crackled. *Can you read me?* But the microphone was broken, and they couldn't answer.

"Shut up," said Spenger, bleeding from his mouth. He threw something at the radio, and Ben, thinking it was a grenade, covered his head, but it was only a fistful of dirt.

"Fucker," said Spenger as it bounced off the metal with a loud *ting*. Then he looked at Ben, who was slowly, carefully standing up. "Christ, man. Your face!"

But before Ben could ask him what he meant, the first lieutenant, who seemed to have forgotten he held rank, turned to him. "What should we do?"

Ben touched his cheek. It didn't hurt too bad, but beneath his fingers it was gummy and raw. Shaking, he pinched a wad of dirt, placed it like tobacco beneath his tongue. It tasted like hope—mossy and fertile. He ate some more.

"What the hell're you doing?" said Spenger, whose eyes had turned yellow. Blood was everywhere—splattered across his shirt, all down his face.

"Where you from?" Ben asked.

Spenger's throat gurgled with blood, but his voice came soft. "Mississippi."

"Here," said Ben. "Try this."

The private studied the dirt Ben took from his mouth, looked at Ben like he was crazy, but his lips slowly parted.

"Mississippi," said Ben, placing the morsel into Spenger's torn mouth. "Taste it." Spenger's jaw started to work. Spit dribbled from the corner of his mouth. Just above the cricket song, Ben could make out the staccato thrum of choppers.

"Shit," said Spenger, as if he could smell it now. "It's like home." The mud of the river, the cow dung, the tar on the road softening in the summer heat.

"Swallow," said Ben.

The private's throat spasmed as he gulped the chunk of Mississippi still resting on his tongue. Ben wondered who to pray to as the private's breathing slowed, stilled, stopped. Beyond the edge of the trees, the choppers were landing, kicking up dust. Ben wiped his bloodied fingers across his stinging cheek, shouldered his rifle, and, ducking toward the choppers, started home.

CHAPTER TWENTY

Bending over her table, weeding fine quills from thick, Rachel listened to Country Joe and the Fish on the radio. Soon, the news would come on—a prediction of rain, an update on the war. She had always thought of autumn as the death season. Leaves turned and fell, grass browned. The cooling of water and air. Night hung on too long, and it was well into morning before dawn made gray out of blackness.

The trill of a whippoorwill. Soon, she would smell the smoke from fires in the cabins and shacks around the lake. Rising, she groped her way blindly around baskets of beads and sweet grass, brushed against the jingle dress she had been sewing.

"Shhhh," she said.

Outside, the pungent smells of clay and shallow water. The woods were ribboned with mist as she made her way to the edge of the lake. If she could see a horizon, she would be looking toward it, searching for a sign. But there was no horizon here—only the tips of trees and, in the distance, sloping hills. A loon cut a wake as it swam out of the tall grasses. Already, she could feel the lake grow heavy with the coming cold.

Three weeks since Ben's last call from South Dakota. He was vague about his injury. She had asked him when he was coming home, but the connection was bad, and she didn't catch his answer. He was staying with the family of a trucker he'd met while thumbing a ride. Somewhere in South Dakota, he repeated. That had been in October, and now they were into November, and he hadn't called again. He had been in the States since August. They would have flown him back, but he wanted to take his time. Hitchhike. See the country he'd been fighting for.

The air smelled of damp leaves, fatback cooking in one of the cabins. Rachel could hear Minnie banging pans, the thin cadence of a teapot whistle. Later, mothers would be calling to their children, cars coughing and starting. She would trudge back from the beach, drink some tea, sit down at her table covered with birch bark and quills. She could feel her age lately. Barely forty, but her neck hurt from years of bending over, close work. Tough hands, tough skin.

Every day, Honda asked her if she'd heard anything. It irritated her to tell him she had not.

"He'll be back," Honda said. "We all come back."

It was two years since Ben had left for Vietnam, and in that time he had seen more of the world than he had in his whole life. Sometime after Sioux Falls on the way home, the car he'd been riding in had broken down, and he'd hitched a ride with a girl named Trudy until they'd reached Duluth. Two more rides took him up the southeast shore of Lake Superior.

"Gitchi-goo-me," the man who picked him up had said, beaming a smile as wide as the lake. "You people still call it that?"

After they'd crossed the Mackinaw bridge, Ben had set off on foot from Pellston. He didn't mind the walk. He wasn't carrying much, and the air had none of the deep stickiness of the jungle where he'd marched for miles.

He drove the last few miles of the trip in a Malibu station wagon with a girl who'd offered him a joint. They talked about Nixon and Cambodia, which the girl said was very, *very* wrong. "You'd go to Canada, wouldn't you?"

Ben, watching an ancient apple orchard fly past them, shook his head. "I've already been."

"To Canada?" she said, turning up Janis Joplin and trying not to stare at the side of his face when he turned toward her.

Past the orchard, a field once cleared for a farm about the size of Bliss and Ada's had overgrown with weeds. The farmhouse leaned to one side, as if nudged by a giant hand. "No," said Ben, turning away again. "Vietnam."

She was quiet after that. Joni Mitchell came on, and she tried to sing along, missing the high notes. She let him off where he told her, but before she drove away, the girl leaned out the window and said, "Hey, if you ever need anything . . ."

"Thanks," he said, turning down the road to the lake. Thick with fallen leaves, it meandered through the deciduous gloom. The evening was overcast, threatening rain as Ben, pulling his jacket collar up, made his way home. A sudden blast of sun threw the drifts of leaves back into sharp relief—maple, poplar, birch—but the clouds closed in again, and everything faded to brown. Again, he felt disoriented. He searched for something familiar in the sky, in the circle of buildings, in the water. The beach was like something he once dreamed—a thick residue of silt and bog. At the edge stood the cabins, plain and forthright. People often said that Indians were one with the land, but looking at this hodgepodge of log, chicken wire, and tar paper, Ben wondered.

The creak of a screen door. Turning, he saw her. She froze, mute as if she was seeing a *manitou*. "Mother," he said, abandoning the *mama* he used as a child. She opened her mouth, shouted his name, running toward him until their bodies locked, the smell of her like clay.

They sat across from each other at the kitchen table. He noticed strands of gray in her hair, wondered when those lines had appeared at the edges of her eyes. The cabins were close together, their walls thin. Even as a child, he had heard the night sounds. Snores. Coughs. A drunken argument. Lovemaking.

No privacy here.

"Your face?" said his mother, touching it, drawing back her fingers and pressing them to her lips.

"There was an explosion," he said, wanting to tell her how he'd sat with men who died. With soil, he had guided their spirits home. Sometimes—like now—they would sit beside him, staring him down.

How many years had he been taller than his mother? He remembered when they first came to Horseshoe Lake, how she hadn't wanted to be here. But then the band was able to buy it—a miracle, that was—and his mother and he, with Honda's help, had built their cabin beside the very spot where her grandmother's had stood. *Holy ground*, his mother had told him, and he knew it was true. He could feel his grandmother's spirit. Now his mother's was planted, as firmly rooted as a white pine.

A lantern hung from the ceiling, its light making monstrous shadows from the hanging baskets, the feathers, the animal hides. She showed him the boxes she was making out of bark and quill. She had stopped working in the store years ago, but the boxes she made were in great demand. "Anything Indian," she said.

"Honda must be happy."

"Oh, you know Honda."

Honda was working with the National Council on Indian Affairs, Rachel told him. They had plans. "If we're recognized, we'll have rights."

Taking in the smell of the room, Ben remembered the sweet scent of cooking corn, the yeasty aroma of bread. He'd been about ten when they'd built the cabin. He remembered helping Honda with the roof. A room and a porch, not much more than the shacks he'd seen along the Ho Chi Minh River. Momentary structures, enduring as anthills.

"Rights?" he said.

"You're home now." Again, his mother touched his cheek. Rain was beginning to leak through the ceiling, puddling on the floor. Eyes shut, he could taste the clay passing from mouth to mouth, his mother's to his, generation to generation baked into bone, flesh, and memory.

At dusk, his mother rose to light a fire. "Don't worry," she said. "You'll be dancing again soon. Your hair will grow out."

He wanted to believe her, but already the shadows cast by the bustles and headdresses were turning into demons on the walls.

Winter came, and with it snow, but Ben didn't set foot to dancing, nor hand to drum. Some mornings, he couldn't get out of bed.

"It's okay," said Rachel. "You're home." But his hand, when she touched it, shook and pulled away.

While he slept, she looked at the wound on his face and was reminded of wet sand drying in the sun. His mind was worse. Some nights, he screamed, curled into a ball, held his hands over his head or between his legs. Minnie had cooked up medicines to calm him—root teas, potions made from flowers. Still, he turned toward the fire during the day, wrapped in a blanket, staring into the flames as if he could cauterize his memories.

It was late December when Honda threw open the door. He was dressed in a hunting jacket, carrying a bow and a quiver of feathered arrows. "It's time to get out."

Ben shook his head, looked back into the fire. "Go away."

"You gonna rot here? Let your mother feed you for the rest of your days?"

Ben's hair was growing longer, almost into a ponytail now. Some days, he didn't shave. His beard had been sparse to begin with. Now it was patchy—spiky tufts springing up among the burnt areas.

Honda took a set of snowshoes down from the wall and held them out to Ben. "Get dressed."

Outside, the snow fell heavy. Rachel watched from the doorway as they started across the frozen lake, heading toward the big woods on the opposite shore. When had her son's shoulders grown so broad? He was tall now, taller than Honda. Hunched, they lumbered on the snowshoes like bears dressed in anoraks. Finally, they faded altogether, leaving a webbed chain of footprints across the blanketed ice.

The woods were hushed. Except for the occasional siftings of snow falling from trees, little moved. One of Ben's snowshoes snagged on a stick, snapped it, causing him to swear.

Honda didn't break stride. He pushed on through the trees, forcing Ben to walk faster. It amazed Ben that Honda, who was a large man, could tread so lightly across the snow. All those years when they'd hunted together, Ben had dashed ahead of him, rushing to be the scout, the first to spot a deer, a rabbit, a fox—circle back with the prize.

"Jesus," said Ben, gasping. "Slow down."

But Honda didn't slow. Instead, he started talking, telling Ben how it had been in Korea, how they'd half frozen as they walked for miles across the snow to Huneri to mine the goddam Koreans.

"Only later you find out it's the Chinese all along, and you swear you'll shoot another Chink soon as look at him."

"Not too many of them around here," panted Ben.

Honda shot him a quick look, but kept on walking. "Way I figure, not too many Vietcong, either."

Honda crouched and pointed as a rabbit scurried out from behind a tree. Without a word, Honda drew an arrow from his quiver, threaded his bow, pulled back, and released. A streak of silver, and the arrow plunged into a tree trunk.

"Damn," said Honda. When they reached the tree, he pulled it out, examined the tip, and stuck it back into the satchel strapped across his back. They started off again, Ben wanting to tell him that Vietnam had been different from Korea, that the jungle was a tree whose roots penetrated your skin, probed and strangled. You couldn't breathe. You couldn't piss because everything had been sweated out until you and your buddies reeked of swamp and puke and Spam.

Over there, he'd seen a cat once. At least, he'd thought it was a cat until he got close. And then he saw it was a child.

"There!" said Honda. "See it?"

And Ben saw it, quick and darting, animal in its motions, but before he could say, *Don't shoot, Honda! It's a kid!*, the arrow was already flying until it met its mark.

Ben was running, tripping, shouting, and Honda was on him, and they both went down, coughing up snow, fists flying. Then Honda had him by the collar and was yanking him toward the kill, saying, *Look, Ben! Look! It's only a goddam rabbit!*

And Ben, gasping, saw that it was. "Oh, Christ," he said. "Oh man."

Tears and snow ran together, thawing the snow, freezing the tears. Snow drifted from the trees onto his shoulders. Somewhere in the forest, a branch cracked, birds flew up, then nothing.

"I can't stay here," said Ben.

"It's just a rabbit," Honda said again, his fist plunging into the spattered snow, honoring the kill by smearing Ben's face with the cold, bloody mess.

CHAPTER TWENTY-ONE

T he sound of riveting and hammer blows broke the morning
stillness. Ben shifted his weight from side to side, trying to
stay warm. It had been fifteen years since Mr. March had taken
him sailing on the *Blue Heron*. He had come to the boat shop on a whim, figuring maybe they'd need a hand. The air was thick with the mingled scents of
varnish and brass polish, lubricant and gasoline. Blowing out a cloud of frozen
breath, Ben went up to a guy working on the hoist and asked if a man named
Hank still worked here.

"Nah. Unless you call owning the place 'working.'" He jerked his thumb at
the office.

Ben found the old boat-hand inside, his legs up on a desk covered with
invoices and orders. On an electric burner, some coffee had thickened into goo.
Hank, his eyes still bloodshot, chewed on a pencil and squinted. "I remember
you. You're that kid."

Ben stuck out his hand. "Ben Winnapee, sir."

Hank's palms were still callused, and Ben recalled the vigor with which he
used to trim the sheets. Studying the scar on Ben's cheek, Hank said, "I thought

you'd show up sooner or later. The way you loved to sail." He picked up his coffee cup, made a face, set it down. "You a rigger, Ben?"

Ben eyed the photographs on the wall—boats big-bellied with spinnakers or knocked on their sides by the wind. The same excitement drew him back, and suddenly he was nine years old. "No, sir." He turned back to Hank. For the first time in months, he smiled. "But I can learn."

In the next three months, Ben became a rigger of boats. He learned to check the seams of the sails for frays, resew the batten pockets, to knot the ends of lines and fuse them with his lighter. He followed their paths through the blocks and around the winches, learned how the halyard threaded though the masthead, how the sheets attached to the sails. He sanded hulls and keels. He scrubbed. He got stoned on solvents, metal polish, and lacquer thinner, high on the rush of picking a course, setting the sails accordingly. On sunny days, he worked shirtless, his dark hair slick and ponytailed, the heat on his back. Hank took him out sailing almost every day, testing the boats, making sure they were tight and clean before their owners arrived that summer.

It was in the far reaches of the hangar that Ben first noticed her. He recognized the teal blue paint, now badly faded. He ran his hands along the gunwale, sniffed the hull. He remembered her smell from years ago. Fish. Sea foam. Gulls.

"Hey," he said to the kid who was working with him, pushing the hulls out to the boatyard on their cradles, wet-sanding the keels. "This the Marches' boat?"

"Yeah," said the kid, lighting up a joint as he did every morning around ten. "Can you believe that barge gets put in every year? They never sail it, neither. Just sits there like a lawn ornament."

Ben circled the boat as if it were an injured beast. The rudder pin was rusted, the keel rough from neglect. Most of the lines were snarled, but that could be fixed. Fresh paint on the hull. Sanding the crust off the keel. A *lot* of sanding. Already, he could see how the keel would cut through the water if she was smooth, how the wind would shape the sails.

Ben checked his list. "Says here we're supposed to put her in."

The kid drew hard on the joint, gave Ben a slow, dumb smile. "Hey, man, it's their money."

Later, Ben went to Hank's office. Hank poured a cup of burned, black coffee into a steaming cup and held it out to Ben. "You found a place to stay yet?"

Ben sipped his coffee. For now, Hank was letting him camp out in the sail loft, where he slept under a spinnaker inflated by an electric fan, the silky cloth hovering above him like a rainbow. All night he would listen to the low whir of the fan, the slap of halyards and stays. No artillery. No bombs. Over there, he had slept on the ground, turned muddy with monsoon. Back here, he had slept on the floor by his mother's bed. Sleeping under sails was better. "Not yet."

"There's some messages here for you," said Hank, shoving a few pieces of paper toward him. "Think it's your dad."

"He's not my dad," Ben said, taking another gulp of coffee and putting it down. He knew why Honda was calling. His mother was checking on him, wondering when he would be coming back to the lake. "Hey, Hank," he said, shoving the scribbled papers into his pocket, "you know that boat? The *Blue Heron*?"

"What about her?"

"I was wondering . . . is anyone sailing her?"

Hank swiveled his chair back and forth, studying Ben over the top of his mug. He seemed to be weighing his words. "It's not a happy situation."

Ben nodded. He knew all about people dying suddenly, stupidly. Even so, life went on. His mother told him that.

Hank laughed. "There's this guy over in Chibawassee—Jewish guy—been trying to buy that boat off the old lady for years. You think she'll sell?" He grunted with contempt and admiration. "She's as stubborn as they come."

Ben looked out the window. Across the yard, the kid was lowering the *Blue Heron* in the hoist. Ben wondered just how stoned the kid was, and if he'd chip the paint even more. Good for Mrs. March, Ben thought. "Do you think she'd talk to me?"

Hank pursed his lips and made a whistling sound. "Like I said . . ."

The *Blue Heron* had hit the water. Ben flinched as it grazed the sides of the dry dock. "Shit," he said, "it's worth a try."

That afternoon, after they towed the *Blue Heron* to her mooring in front of the Marches', Ben had the kid drop him off on the dock. Now he stood in front of the old white house that sprawled across the lawn at the end of Beck's Point. To the east, the grass drifted off into dunes. He remembered the first time he'd come with Honda in summer to deliver wood, how scared he'd been of those black women in the kitchen, scared of these old houses with their rambling porches, their towers, their crazy flights of steps.

Fumbling in his pocket for a rubber band, he pushed back his hair and tied it. His fingernails were black, but he'd taken a swim that morning, so most of the grease was gone. As he climbed the stairs to the front porch, he whistled a tune he'd whistled in Vietnam during those black, cricket-shrill nights when they had lain in their tents, trying to sleep, listening, always listening for something that wasn't crickets.

A threadbare towel hung from the rail. Something caught his eye, but it was only a hat made of straw, broad-brimmed, dangling from a chair. It swayed in the breeze, seemed to wave him in.

"May I help you?"

He turned to see a woman standing there. At first he couldn't see her clearly. Perhaps it was the shadows on the porch. The woman's face was half hidden behind dark glasses, the kind Jackie Kennedy used to wear. But that was two presidents ago, and now the glasses seemed old-fashioned.

"I came to see . . ." He started, then stopped. She was watching him intently, gripping a glass. At first, he had taken her to be about his age. Maybe it was the way she wrapped her beach towel around her hips like she knew her figure was good. Her hair was blond. Not the fresh blond of a girl, but an insistent blond—the kind that, once decided, wouldn't give up.

"I came about the boat," he said.

"Thank *God*," she replied in an overly sober voice. "Do you want a drink or something?"

"I'm sorry?"

"Don't be." The playfulness drained from her voice. She looked out at the harbor and nodded at the *Blue Heron*. "I guess summer's official now." She looked back at him. "Do you need to be paid up front these days?"

He crossed his arms. Perhaps he shouldn't have come. "I was just wondering if you had someone to sail her."

She threw back her head and laughed. Her smile was bright and wide, and Ben, infected, wanted to laugh, too. "No," she said, shaking her head. "No one." She plucked the straw hat from the back of the chair and shoved it on her head. It was a child's gesture—a kid mugging for an audience.

"I'm Elizabeth March," she whispered, as if they were sharing a secret. "I'm *not* the one you need to talk to." For a moment, he wondered if she wasn't a little crazy. She reminded him of one of the battle-drunk soldiers who'd suddenly lost their commanders. The hopelessness of it all would be too much, so they'd cry or go silly or puff their chests to stem off the fear. "Follow me," she said.

Elizabeth March led him around to the porch on the opposite side of the house. The house seemed as wasted as the *Blue Heron*. A watering can sat next to a pot of dead geraniums. The eaves needed sweeping.

"Rory?" said the woman to a young man reclining on a sort of sofa set onto tracks so it could be pushed back and forth. "This man has come about the boat."

Dust, like a filmy ash, coated the furniture, and even the spiders hung dully from their webs. With his eyes at half-mast, Rory seemed to be asleep, but he roused himself and sighed, sat up and ran his fingers through hair as fine as cobwebs. Ben recalled the seasick boy in the too-large life jacket, how he hadn't liked to sail. On the table beside Rory sat a Campbell's soup can full of paintbrushes and a tablet streaked with blue. He cleared his throat. "Haven't we paid the bill?" He didn't look at Ben's face, stared instead at his knees. "My grandmother's been ill, but I can call the secretary—"

"No," said Elizabeth March. "He wants to sail it. You know . . . like taking the dog for a walk."

Rory turned to Ben. "Is that it? You want to adopt the *Blue Heron*?"

Ben had no answer. It had been a stupid idea to come here, stupider still to think they'd say yes.

"Have you seen the condition of that boat?" said Rory.

"I rigged her myself."

"Then you know she's a wreck."

Ben held his voice steady to keep it from sounding too eager. "Not so bad. I could clean up the lines, air out the sails better."

"My mother always told me to air out my wedding dress each year," said Elizabeth March.

"Look," Ben said, "if I could just get my hands on her . . ."

Rory laughed in disbelief. "Okay, why not? I'll speak to Gaga and tell her someone has the hots for her old boat. Where can I find you?"

Ben's eyes drifted to the paper on the table. The slashes of blue across it were jagged, almost vicious. "I live at the boat shop."

Following Ben's gaze, Rory said, "Cerulean." With a bitter laugh, he added, "The fabulous blue of my summer memories."

The day was too hot to be crawling along the decks of cradled boats, threading lines through blocks, the grit of a skid-proof surface scratching up his belly. He wanted to be out on the water, catching whatever shred of a breeze might have kicked up midbay, the water slapping the gunwales, the steady lap of waves. Instead, he was breathing the fumes from a can of WD-40, the parts of stubborn jib block strewn before him.

The sun burned the back of his neck, and he pulled off the scarf knotted gypsy-style around his head and retied it around his neck. He could dive into the water off the dock, but the surface was slick and rainbowed with oil. He had been waiting for two weeks for Rory March to contact him, and he was growing edgy.

"Damn," he said as a pin he was trying to jam into a pulley broke in two.

For two weeks, he had patrolled the beaches of Beck's Point at night in a little outboard, checking mooring lights and buoys. He had counted the houses. Sixty of them, from what he could see. He would kill the motor, drift. Even before Vietnam, he knew how to scout—to find where the deer ate, the fox burrowed, the hawk nested. At night he bobbed against piers, one hand on a piling as he watched, invisible, the parties upon porches, someone dressing in a window, teenagers smoking on the beach. A nameless tug, as elusive as the aurora, as shapeless and submerged as algae. For three nights running, he had dreamt of swamp, piss, the reverberation of exploding air.

Now in the heat of the day, he watched the swollen row of houses beyond a screen of mastheads. It was a silly thing to want. Worse than longing for a woman. Besides, sleeping in the sail loft had its advantages, the low whir of the fan muffling the brutal twang of carbines that knocked about his dreams.

Hank leaned out of the office door and yelled, "Phone call for you, Winnapee."

Dropping himself off the side of the boat, Ben figured it would be Honda or his mother. Soon, he would tell them. *Soon I'll be coming to the lake.* In the office, he picked up the phone. "Yeah?"

After a little pause on the other end, a male voice said, "Is this Ben?"

"Yeah?"

"You came to our house the other day?"

Ben turned and faced a chart on Hank's wall. His eyes followed the outline of the shore, the paler lines of submerged topography, the numerical representations of depth. "Yeah?" he said.

"My grandmother wants to meet you."

The room, with its bank of windows, seemed to lurch toward the water. Tables and bureaus were as cluttered as the tables in his mother's cabin, but instead of grasses, bark, and quills, there were photographs, silver boxes, lace. A cross hung on the wall over the bed, and Ben stared at it, unable to move his eyes away from the dabs of red on Christ's hollow hands. The room stank of medicine. Growing up, Ben had seen needles in some of the cabins, the bottles of insulin, whiskey, and cough syrup. There was some of that here. Remedies for the sick, comfort for the dying.

"It's not for sale," said Mrs. March.

Her wheelchair was turned away from him. She stared out the window. Her gray hair was bluntly chopped—not done up or curled—as if she had gotten rid of something unnecessary.

"Ma'am?"

"People think everything's for sale these days," she went on. "Help me up."

He crossed to her as she started coughing, held out his hand. Hers felt as empty as worm-eaten fruit.

"Look," she said, nodding toward the lake when the coughing stopped. A fleet of boats tacked a mile or so out. "Hand me those binoculars."

He found them by her chair.

Clutching the binoculars to her eyes, Mrs. March hissed, "That young Bailey's a fool. His *father* was a fool."

Ben followed her trajectory, could see the waves breaking on the shoal.

"Now, my son . . ." She stopped and looked at Ben, her words drifting off. In her eyes, the clarity of a deer who has seen the bow and knows. "I'm an old woman," she said, shaking her head to clear it. "The light plays tricks."

"About the boat," said Ben. "I don't want to buy it. I just want to fix it up. Didn't your grandson explain?"

Again that gaze. Finally, she roused herself. "I forgot your name." Perhaps she was demented.

"Ben," he said. "I work at the boat shop."

"I'm sorry . . . your face?"

Automatically, his hand drifted to the scar on his cheek. "I was in Vietnam. There was an explosion."

"Ah," she said, nodding as if she knew all about these things. "My son was injured in an explosion."

"His leg?"

Mrs. March looked at him with astonishment, asked him how he knew about her son's leg.

"Because he took me sailing," said Ben, telling her he'd only been nine years old, but it was the best summer of his life.

She leaned forward, her eyes pointed. "And do you have a last name, Ben?"

"Winnapee."

"*Winnapee?*" She swayed, as if the light suddenly bothered her eyes. For a moment, in this room, he wished his name didn't sound so Indian. It seemed crazily out of place. Winston would be better. Or Winfield. She turned away so quickly, he thought she was going to dismiss him, but she raised the binoculars, lowered them.

"It won't cost you a lot of money," he said quickly before she could say no. "If you'd let me sleep on the boat . . ."

"A long time ago, we had girls," Mrs. March said, still gazing out of the window. "From the convent."

Ben ran his hand over the top of his hair. His ponytail seemed too tight.

The old woman roused herself back to the present. "What was your mother's name?"

"Rachel."

She seemed to consider this, then said, "My grandson Rory would rather walk the gangplank than sleep on some flimsy berth. Why would you be interested?"

"I've slept on worse."

Her lips flickered, almost smiled. "Hand me my cane." She gave the wheelchair a little whack. "I hate that thing. So did my son. He learned how to walk again, but I'm afraid it's all downhill for me." She peered at Ben. "So you want to live on the *Blue Heron?*"

"Hank would let me use the hoist. I could do it in my spare time."

"Pretty resourceful, aren't you?" Mrs. March reached over and pressed a buzzer on the wall. "My husband's grandfather was resourceful. He lent money to the Northern army so they could turn around and buy his supplies." She gestured at a sepia photograph on the wall—a gaunt-eyed portrait of a long-dead man. "Pretty resourceful, don't you think?"

Ben didn't know what to say. Everyone in this family seemed to go off on tangents. And now Mrs. March seemed to be sizing him up.

"There's one condition," she said.

Ben's eyes slid to the cross. The look on Jesus' face was dignified and sad.

"If you sail the boat," said Mrs. March, "you have to take my grandson."

CHAPTER TWENTY-TWO

The sails were half rotted from lack of use. Ben stretched them out on the dock until it was shrouded with canvas. Soon the air was filled with bleach and ammonia, the swishing of a hard-bristled brush.

For the fourth day in a row, Rory had set up a beach chair on the dock and covered himself with baby oil, his pale skin turning pink and freckled in the sun. "Really," Rory said, "do you think it's worth saving?"

A thunderhead cast a shadow, then moved on. Ben's eyes trailed up the stays to where the spreader formed a cross. He had found some decent jib sheets in the boat room under the house along with ancient spinnakers and disintegrating life preservers, *Blue Heron* painted on the side. "Doesn't your family ever use this boat?"

Rory shook his head. He seemed to find this effort of Ben's supremely entertaining. In a mock-serious voice, he suggested that they sell the *Blue Heron* for salvage or, better still, sink it. "Who's going to steer?" Rory said as he lit another cigarette.

"The old lady looks like a salt," said Ben.

"You got that right."

"What about you?"

"I'd puke out my guts."

Ben coiled a line and hung it from a cleat. "You don't remember me, do you?"

Rory slicked back his hair. He was the kind of summer kid that Ben and his friends used to ambush in the woods with war whoops. *Give me your money, Kemosabe!* Later, Honda had found out and slammed him against a wall. But his mother's words hit harder than fists. You stay away from those people, she had told him. You think you're tough because you're Indian, but let me tell you . . . those people fight to win.

"I remember," Rory said, but Ben wondered. Did he remember the cool shock of lake water when it sprayed in his face? The feeling of slicing through waves? Had he sat on his father's lap the way Ben had while Mr. March guided his hand on the helm?

Rory adjusted his sunglasses, the mirrored kind that pilots wore. "Tell me, where did my father find you? Were your mother and Hank . . ."

"No." Ben shook his head, irritated. His mother and Hank definitely weren't. As far as he knew, his mother was never with anyone. "We met in the kitchen, remember?"

Rory shrugged. "We weren't allowed in the kitchen much." He got up, stretched. His raised arms were as unformed as a boy's. Useless summer kid, thought Ben.

"Look," Rory said, "don't you want a lemonade or a beer or something?"

"Don't you have anything better to do?"

"Like what?"

"Don't you have any friends?"

"Don't you?"

Ben bit his lips, admitted that he didn't.

Satisfied, Rory picked up his towel, slung it about his neck. "I *loathe* boats," he called over his shoulder as he walked down the dock toward the house.

After a few days, Mrs. March summoned Ben to her room, questioned him closely. How was the boat's keel?

Straight, he told her. But rough. And the lines weren't even safe.

"How about the helm?" Mrs. March asked. "She always had difficulty pointing to starboard."

"If I could replace some of those panels . . ."

"Those are the original sails." She didn't expect the *Blue Heron* to be immaculate, she told him. Just functional. "That boat used to be the gem of the harbor. Twice a week we took out guests." Her eyes glittered as she described what a ferocious yachtsman her husband had been, how he had sailed the shoals to win a race and kept his point even when her son had rope burn so badly his palms bled. "Let me see your hands," she said to Ben.

Ben tried to imagine what it must have been like—the paint on the hull a glossy gray-blue, the brass reflecting the sun.

"Did you grow up around here?" she asked, letting go of his hand. He looked around the room uncomfortably. A vase was filled with purple flowers. Some reading glasses anchored the pages of a book.

"Not far from here."

"Which town?"

"No town, ma'am."

"Did you go to school?"

"You mean college? No."

"Why not?"

"The cost, for one thing. Besides, I went straight into the military."

"I see." She stared at him for a moment. Before she dismissed him, she added, "You can go ahead and fix those sails."

It became a daily ritual. Mrs. March would call him to her room, ask about the *Blue Heron*, then pose a question about something unrelated. Did he have many friends? Did he have a faith?

"Your mother," she said to him. "She brought you up in the church?"

He laughed and shook his head. "No, ma'am. My mother said she'd had it up to here with religion."

"You must believe in something. The Great Spirit?"

"You think all Indians are superstitious?"

"I'm not talking about superstition. I'm talking about faith." She leaned forward in her wheelchair, peered at him. "I see you don't agree."

When he said nothing, Mrs. March began to massage her knotted fingers like beads in a rosary. "I wonder if this house aches as much as these chicken claws. I'd cut them off if I could." Suddenly, she was gripping the sides of her wheelchair, bent over from coughing. When she stopped, she took a tissue from a bag, spit into it. Not meeting his eyes, she said, "If you don't believe in anything, how did you cope in Vietnam?"

"Cope with what?"

"The dying."

He stared at the rug where the yarns had pulled away, leaving the edges threadbare. Half the men in his platoon were gone. His mother used to say there was no point in praying, but still he had prayed. Once, he had laid a stone on a man's chest, as Honda had showed him, to anchor the man's body while his spirit broke free. Once, he had fed a dying man soil.

"My mother says that life goes on." Ben lifted his eyes to Mrs. March, her own eyes dim with sickness. "You think that's true?"

She didn't answer. Instead she pointed to a box on her bedside table. "That's what's left of my son. The man who took you sailing."

Ben looked from the box to the crucifix on the wall. Finally, not knowing what to say, he stared at his hands.

"I'm dying, you know," said Mrs. March. "I'm riddled with cancer. They keep lopping off my body parts and telling me to hope for the best. Well, the best is all I've ever hoped for. And there you have my son." Her eyes fixed again on the box. When she spoke, her voice was tight. "Do you know how my grandson got out of the draft? He said he prefers boys." She looked at Ben. "Do you think *that's* true?"

Ben said he didn't know.

Mrs. March said, "We used to have names for men like that. I suppose it's no different now."

"Rory's okay," said Ben.

But Mrs. March wasn't listening. She was staring again at the box, as if she could will it to be otherwise. "Sometimes, I run my fingers through his ashes and ask myself that very question: Does life go on? Once I found a piece of bone. I thought it might be a vertebra. Or a tooth." Fiddling with her hands, she roused herself. "Tell me," she said, blinking at Ben, "what is it they call women who lose their children?"

Ben stood on the bay-side beach, eyeing the shoals. For a week now, he had been estimating their distance, trying to gauge how a boat could get through. Mrs. March swore it could be done, but he couldn't see how unless the wind was crazy-perfect, and even then . . .

He liked this side of the peninsula. You could see how big the lake was— ocean big, the shores of Wisconsin beyond the curve of the earth. And the beach was isolated. Duney. Not raked into perfection like the harbor beaches where the children played and the ladies sat with lotioned bodies, reading their magazines.

He could see the waves breaking along the line of rocks. In a flatter light, it would look close. But today the sky was pristine, and everything looked sharper.

"Hey!"

The sound startled him into the present. Down the beach someone was standing up, waving him over. Covering his eyes, he made out Elizabeth March. He remembered the first day he had met her, how she had laughed, and how he, too, had felt like laughing. She was stooped in front of a mound of sand. Coming closer, Ben saw it was a sand castle—an elaborate one with turrets and tiny sticks with paper flags glued onto them, ramparts and pebble cannons. "Wow," he said.

"I know." Her voice was gleeful as a child's.

Ben crouched down. There was a moat and a drawbridge and tiny beach stones laid as pavement. "Did you make this?"

"Me?" She laughed. "I have no talent. I found it when I came down for a swim this morning. It's fantastic, don't you think?" She picked up a stone, sent it skipping across the waves. Watching it sink, she pushed her hair back from her face, turned to him suddenly and smiled. "The boat looks great."

He shrugged, inhaling her peculiar combination of perfume and cigarettes.

"No, really," she went on. "It's an artifact, that boat. You should have seen her twenty or so years ago."

He wanted to ask her why she sometimes watched him from the window. He had seen her from the dock. "I'll bet she was pretty," he said.

Her smile reminded him of the jukebox at the Pier Inn, brimming with nostalgia and artificial light. "Yes"—she nodded—"she was." Little lines had formed between her brows.

"I knew your husband," said Ben.

For a moment Elizabeth March looked confused. Then again that dazzling smile. "Really?"

"He took me sailing when I was a kid. If it weren't for him . . ." His voice trailed off.

"If it weren't for him . . . what?"

"I don't know." Ben shrugged. "He kind of changed my life."

Again, she picked up a stone, sent it skipping. This time it hopped twice across the waves, sunk. "He had that effect on people." Before he could ask her what she meant, a boom echoed down the beach. Ben dropped to the sand, covered his head, waited for the blast.

None came. At the edge of the beach, the stand of cedar stood unruffled and serene. Slowly, Ben sat up.

Elizabeth sat down beside him, staring vacantly at the lake. "My husband hated loud noises, too. After the war."

Ben drew his hands across his face. It was only a sonic boom. He knew they flew B-52s on practice runs out of Manistee, but for a moment he had thought the sand was going to explode with artillery.

He looked out to the shoals. Maybe it *was* farther than he thought. A powerboat, surging by, threw up waves that broke first upon the rocks, then again upon the shore. Ben felt the water rush around his legs, saw Elizabeth's face as the walls of the sand castle broke.

In the dim mirror of the *Blue Heron*'s head, Ben examined his face—the thick brows, the skin on one cheek silky, the other splattered, as if by melted wax. Earlier that afternoon, he had gotten word from Mandy that he was to come up to the house for dinner. Now, he slicked his hair into a ponytail, put on the collared shirt he had borrowed from Hank, headed to the house.

At dinner, there were only the four of them. Mrs. March was seated at the head of the table in her wheelchair. Ben, next to Rory, sat across from Elizabeth March in the dim candlelight. His borrowed shirt itched, he felt painfully out of place. Still, he'd been invited, and now all three were staring at him.

"I hope you're hungry," said Mrs. March, pressing the buzzer beneath the table with her foot.

Soon, Mandy was circling them with plates of lamb and new potatoes. "Biscuit?" she said curtly as she held out a basket of steaming rolls.

Ben looked at Lydia March. He had no idea why she had asked him here. She seemed mesmerized by his hands, the way he chewed, the way he played with his silver.

"Tell me," she said, "are you considering a haircut?"

"Ma'am?"

"I can never get used to it," she said, waving her hand behind her head.

He swallowed and said, "It's kind of an Indian thing."

"He could use a new shirt, Gaga," said Rory, poking Ben with his elbow.

Ben shot Rory a look and turned back to Mrs. March. "I'm not a hippie or anything."

"Thank God for *that*," said Elizabeth March, barely suppressing a smile.

Lydia March went on. "My husband was quite a sailor," she said. "The *Blue Heron* was his."

Ben stabbed his lamb. "So you've said. Did he build her?"

She nodded. "Commissioned her back in the twenties. Do you want to see a picture of the christening?"

"Sure," said Ben, his fork in midair.

"You see, *someone's* interested," Mrs. March said pointedly to Rory and Elizabeth, neither of whom seemed inclined to rise. "Give me a hand with this chair." As Ben wheeled her into the living room, she whispered, "They've seen it a million times."

"When I was a kid," Ben said, speaking to Mrs. March's thinning hair, "this was my favorite of all the houses."

"Really?" said Mrs. March, her voice unusually light and happy. "My son once talked about tearing it down. In Europe, you know, there are cathedrals that have stood for centuries." She pointed toward a wall of photographs. "Here we are. 1922. A bottle of Dom Pérignon sacrificed. In those days, we all drank champagne."

Ben, his arms crossed, looked closely at the yellowed photograph of a younger Mrs. March, her cloche hat pulled low, next to a balding man in an ascot.

"She cost ten thousand dollars to build," says Lydia. "A fortune in those days."

But Ben had moved on to some of the other photographs. Old Mr. March with his polo ponies. Woody March and what looked to be his brother, holding tennis rackets. A dim, austere portrait of an elderly man. A young, flashy one of Elizabeth March that made Ben look twice.

"My daughter-in-law and grandson," said Mrs. March, "never look at these pictures anymore."

Pointing at a black-and-white print of Elizabeth and Woody March standing on the dock, Ben said, "This is how I remember him."

"I've never liked that one. He had taken his leg off. Said it itched."

They were both in swimsuits. Elizabeth was wearing pointy sunglasses and mugging for the camera. Woody March leaned upon his cane, staring solemnly into the lens, the left pant leg of his swimsuit dangling emptily.

"When did he lose his leg?"

"The war," said Mrs. March, after a pause. "The war and those dreadful Japanese. We'd already dropped the bomb, you know, and still they flew their planes into our ships. Such a waste. It's why I can't let go."

In the dining room, Mandy was clearing the first course, banging the china. Rory excused himself and left the room.

Mrs. March touched Ben's hand. "You understand, don't you?"

A toilet flushed, then the sound of running water. Ben nodded slowly. He leaned toward the wall of photographs. Together, he and Mrs. March studied the gallery of pictures, each trying to find meaning in the portraits, the fingers of her hand lingering on his.

"You on a vision quest or something?" Rory leaned back in the cockpit, tapped a Marlboro out of its pack, and squinted up at Ben. The morning had crested, faint and colorless, the wind changing from east to west. "You on speed?"

"Crap," said Ben, almost dropping his screwdriver. He had been working long days at the boat shop, fitting the *Blue Heron* in between jobs. After hours, he had towed the boat over to Hank's, using the hoist so he could sand the keel. Now he was back at the Marches' dock, putting the final touches on the spar, making sure the blocks would hold, that the lines would run just right. He had hauled himself in a bosun's chair to straddle the mast, balancing on the spreaders.

"I don't get it," said Rory. He was dressed in shorts and a blue blazer, though it was early, just past dawn. His tie was loose, and even from high up, Ben could see his eyes were red.

"What's to get?"

"I've never seen anyone so taken by a boat," Rory said, exhaling. "Or anything else, for that matter."

Ben lowered himself back onto the deck. Mist hung on the harbor still streaky with the lights of streetlamps.

"Gaga's certainly interested in *you*," Rory said. When Ben didn't answer, Rory added, "I'm crazy, you know. Certified."

"I thought you were in college."

Rory shook his head. "Expelled. From Princeton. Four generations of March men, and *I* get expelled."

"Why?"

"Why indeed," Rory said. "One culture's deviance is another's aspiration. My father's drug addiction? Perfectly acceptable in nineteenth-century Britain."

Ben crossed his arms. "Your father was great."

"Oh, I forgot," said Rory lightly. "You weren't there."

Rory stubbed out his cigarette on the dock. Ben wanted to say, At least you *had* a father, jerk. Instead, he said, "Are *you* a drug addict?"

Rory's eyes locked on Ben's. "It's possible. I would say I have potential."

"Why'd you get expelled?"

Rory sighed. "It's a long story. Sad, but not without a silver lining. My inability to serve, for instance." He nodded at the dog tags Ben still wore.

As they watched the last of the mist evaporate, Ben cleaned a mug with an oil rag, poured some coffee, offered it to Rory.

"You know," Rory said, taking the cup and staring into it, "the thing about staying up all night is that it gives you perspective." He took a sip of his coffee, glanced up at the house. "Like maybe there's hope." He turned back to Ben. "Look, what I said about my father . . ."

"Forget it."

"He *was* a hero, actually." Rory clasped his hands in front of his mouth, made a sound like an explosion. "Or should I say, heroic? Given to dramatic gestures. The leg and all. The boat accident."

Ben remembered what Hank had told him—that some people thought it was an accident, others suicide. Whatever it was, everything had changed after that summer. Honda had come up with the money to buy Horseshoe, and his mother decided to move there for good. She wanted him to know his people, she had said. Learn the forgotten words. Now the inland lake seemed oppressive to him, the language indecipherable.

"You doing anything next Monday?" he asked Rory, who was lying down in the cockpit.

"Next Monday, next Monday." Rory covered his eyes, rolled over to look at Ben. "Why?"

"I've got to teach you how to sail."

Rory looked about the cockpit. Ben could see the distaste in his expression. "Vietnam," Rory said, tossing off the word, "must have been some heavy shit."

Ben thought about the minty green tracers, the crackle of flak. He started to tell Rory about the child, how at first he had thought it was a charred cat. But Rory's was a different form of hopelessness, and Ben couldn't find the words.

The kitchen smelled of bacon and gas and last night's curry. Ben sat across from Mandy at the table, forking scrambled eggs into his mouth.

"When was the last time you ate?" asked Mandy. Her eyes narrowed as she traced down his shoulders to his belly. "That dinner the other night, from the look of you."

Ben smiled and patted his stomach. Mandy had stood on the dock the day before with her hands on her hips till he lowered himself from the mast. "Mrs. March says we got to feed you." Now they were fussing over Ben like he was Jesus after the fast.

"I remember when you was a boy," said Ella Mae. "I'd feed you sweet rolls when you came with your daddy."

"He's not my father," said Ben. "But I remember the sweet rolls."

"Do you now?" Ella Mae looked pleased. She reached out and took one of Ben's hands. "Let me take a look."

For a long moment, she studied his palm till Ben pulled it away and said, "You never seen a hand before?"

Ella Mae looked at him, blew out her cheeks. "I've seen hands," she said. "Some you wouldn't even want to look at, the lines are so knotted. Some are smoothish." She stood up, untied her apron, sat back down with it clumped in her lap. "But I've never seen a hand like yours."

Mandy, spooning some more eggs onto his plate, said, "What's that thing on your face?"

Ben's eyes drifted up, rested on a board of numbers on the wall. "I got burned," he said, wondering what they were for.

"Mmmm, mmmm," said Mandy.

"Hands like that," said Ella Mae, shaking her head.

Someone knocked at the screen door. "Woodman," said Ella Mae, getting up slowly. She peered at Ben. "You say he's not your daddy?"

Honda was standing at the door when Ella Mae opened it. He glanced at Ben. They hadn't seen each other in more than a month, but the first thing Honda said when he walked into the kitchen was, "Someone'd better fix that gas leak before the whole place blows."

"Someone'd better fix a whole *lotta* things around here," said Mandy.

"So," said Honda, looking at Ben, "they said at the boat shop this was where I'd find you. I see that they're feeding you."

Mandy rolled her eyes.

"Can't complain," Ben said.

"People spoil the boy," Honda said to no one in particular. "Always have."

"This boy's special," said Ella Mae.

"That so?" said Honda. He looked at Ben. "How about giving me a hand."

Outside, Honda's truck, brimming with firewood, was idling in the still morning air. A squirrel, digging around for acorns, skipped away as the men came closer.

"Over here," said Honda, handing Ben a pair of canvas gloves and nodding at the stone wall of the kitchen. They set to work unloading the truck and stacking the logs. Neither man spoke but fell into the familiar routine from years before when a boy had helped a man deliver wood to the summer people.

When at last the stack was done, Honda peeled off his gloves, flicked them into the truck. "Your mother's been waiting to hear from you." His hair was graying in the sideburns.

Ben leaned against the stack of logs, watched a dewy-winged butterfly land, take off. "Been busy," he said.

"That busy?"

"I got a lot to do."

"Like eating these people's food?"

Here it comes, thought Ben, about how the summer people had stolen their land in the first place.

"We need you," said Honda. "The powwow's in a few days. If this thing with the government goes through, it could mean a lot to us."

Ben rubbed his sunburned eyes. Yeah, he thought. Like money. But he'd already made plans to take Rory sailing next week. They were going to take out the *Blue Heron* for the first time since she'd been fixed. He'd worked all month for it.

"Did you know," said Honda, jerking his head at the house, "your mother used to work for these people?"

Ben crossed his arms. Honda knew his mother didn't tell him much.

Honda climbed into the truck, leaned out the window. "So what do you think?"

Ben shrugged. "Life goes on."

"True," said Honda as he started up the engine. "But either way, you've got to make a choice."

That night, there was music across the water. Not the drumming Ben was used to or the insistent beat of rock 'n' roll. This was light and airy, insubstantial as small talk, but it moved him anyway, as ancient and foreign as church music.

Ben decided to take a walk on the bay-side beach and think about what Honda had said. He hadn't seen Rory all day. Maybe Rory had slept in till the evening, then risen, brushed off that blue blazer, and headed back into the night. Listening to the music, Ben wondered if youth could be recaptured in the movement of bodies swirling as one. He had once seen a jingle dancer pull the disease out of a man, grow sick herself, only to recover as the other dancers moved in around her. Indians thought salvation lay in the clasping of hands, the shared rhythm of heart and drum.

A ring had formed around the moon. As he made his way down the path to the beach, heat lightning flickered against a stack of clouds. His bare feet sunk into the sand, soothing as his mother's touch. Who could say this was trespassing?

At the water's edge, he began to move, at first to the thin strands of music drifting from the club, then to the cadence in his mind. A steady beat of waves, then drums, the distant hint of chants. He stomped the sand, crouched low to the stone-covered beach. The rat-a-tat in his brain reminded him of gunfire, the screams above the shots. He turned, twisted. Again, the image of something burning. *Hiya-ha-ha, hiya-ha-ha.* He began to spin. The club music had turned to something else, the sound of Spenger's off-key Hendrix. Ben thrust his chest out as Spenger did when he was hit in the back by a spray of bullets, the blood and spit oozing from the corners of his mouth.

What did the cries of a war dance mean? Were they no more than prayers for victory, a plaintive cry that someone else's blood be spilled? Even the Odawa had taken this land through slaughter. Down by the lake, an entire village gone in a frenzy of hatchets.

The lightning pulsed above the horizon. A wave slapped the shore, spilled across his ankles, and still he danced, his calves and arms spattered with sand. A low moan of thunder.

"Ben?"

Elizabeth March was standing on the beach not far from him, her shape faint in the moonlight, her hair pale. With bare arms, she hugged herself, and he assumed it frightened her to see him spin to imaginary drumming. He stopped, ran his fingers through his hair, slicked it behind his shoulders. Catching his breath, he said, "I'm sorry."

"Don't stop." She must have been at the club because she was in a long silver dress that dragged in the sand. He wanted to tell her to watch out for the waves, that they could catch you by surprise, but she was already at the water's edge, her dress wet, and she didn't seem to care.

He half laughed, his hands on his knees, his breathing still hard. "I haven't danced in years."

She was standing up to her calves in water, prom-queen beautiful, even at forty or whatever she was. Probably as old as his mother, but he couldn't take his eyes off the gold of her hair.

She was swaying slightly in the waves as if she, too, was dancing to unheard music. "I used to love to dance," she said, "when I was a girl. Woody would wear his uniform, and we would waltz under those tiny lights till I got so dizzy, I thought I'd fall down."

Another wave struck her, and she seemed to falter. He wondered if she had been drinking. When he took her elbow, she leaned into him, staring at the sky. "All these stars," she said. Her skin was smooth and cold.

"You're freezing."

She wrapped her arms around herself again and shivered. "Dance with me."

"I don't know how."

"I saw you . . ."

He laughed. "What you saw wasn't dancing."

"What, then?"

Anger. Despair. Still holding her, he said, "Praying, maybe."

Elizabeth gave a quick laugh. "My mother-in-law prays all the time."

Ben thought of the useless cells that were multiplying in Mrs. March's body—the embarrassment of riches she had neither wanted nor prayed for. They were killing her, devouring her tissue, pushing up against her organs, haunting her lungs. She had shown Ben the cremated remains of her son, saying, *See? We are nothing but fish bones in the end.*

Elizabeth leaned in closer to him. "She thinks she's immortal. She thinks this whole damn family is." Her eyes grew bright in the starlight. "You've spent time with my son. What kind of odds would you give on his getting married and having children?" It occurred to Ben that she was very drunk. "The things mothers want for their kids."

She leaned into him until he was holding her up. Slowly, Ben began to rock her. Tears were running down her face, and he touched one, licking his fingertip. Perfume, tears, and mascara intermingled as they moved together, the waves pushing in and out. She tasted of sorrow and disappointment, of rigid, stark hope, and Ben felt he knew her the way he had known soil or grass or rain.

He thought about what his mother wanted for him—to go back to the lake and dance with the band. It meant so much to her and so little to him. He'd all but forgotten the steps.

Still rocking, he watched the top of Elizabeth March's head, waiting for a signal, but she moved away and smiled, breaking the spell. "This is some way to end a lousy evening."

Ben shook his head to clear it. Above them, the house glowed in the trees. He liked this house, liked the grand, proud way it claimed the lake, perched like a boulder that had stood there for eons. He should have hated it, everything it stood for—the smug sense of entitlement based on land grants and a too-brief history. His people had pieced together their living from the leftovers of their culture. Moccasins sold in tourist shops. Quill boxes. The lumbering days were over, fur trading barely a memory. The men had gone to the cities, forgotten the forests and the lakes. The women worked in white people's houses, carried their wash, scrubbed their floors.

Elizabeth followed his gaze. A light flicked off in Mrs. March's windows. "Someone should torch this place." Lifting the soggy hem of her dress, she crossed the darkened sand.

I t was early evening. The lake was slate, and the mosquitoes were getting thick. Along the beach, a temporary village had gone up. Dozens of people—maybe more—had camped around the lake in trailers and cars, in tepees, tents, or blankets laid across the ground. Someone had a radio on in one of the cabins—Old Jedda, probably—listening to a ball game out of Detroit. Rachel could hear the distant static of the announcer calling plays, the crescendo of cheers, someone swearing in response.

"Taw," said Minnie. "That man's got a mouth."

"There's mouths and there's mouths," said Ada, who had come with Bliss to watch the powwow.

The day had ended badly when one of the girls had stabbed her hand with an awl. Teaching these girls to quill was an art, and not for the first time, Rachel wondered how her grandmother had put up with her.

"I have better things to do," the girl had said as Ada stitched up her hand.

"So did I," muttered Rachel.

The quill lesson had been a disaster. Patiently, she had shown the girl how to use the awl to puncture the bark. *Think of the pattern,* she had said to the girl. *Think of how the quills will lie.* But the girl had been fidgety, and now she was down at the water, throwing stones with her friends, flirting with some boys who had come down from Escanaba. Rachel was sitting on her porch alongside Ada, Bliss, and Minnie in hand-me-down rockers—broken pieces of furniture Honda had mended after scavenging them from dumps or from summer people who'd offered him their refuse when he'd come to deliver wood.

"These girls," said Rachel.

"And were you so different?" said Minnie.

Ada laughed and said she remembered the way Rachel had taken it upon herself to walk to the lake in winter. "About ten months pregnant, and we could barely see her head above the snowbanks."

"Even so," said Rachel, "you followed me."

Ada pressed her lips together and glanced at Bliss. In the past few years, Bliss's vision had grown dim, and her right eye was beginning to wander. Still, she smiled at the memory. "What would we have said to the nuns?"

Rachel raised an eyebrow. "Ada would have lied." She flicked away a mosquito. "Like always."

"Ha!" said Ada.

"Tsss," said Minnie. "Who are *you* to talk about lying?"

Rachel avoided her eyes. If she lied, it was because it was for the best. To what end should Ben know that his father's family had abandoned him, paid her off, or worse, that she had asked them to? Blackmail money, she had explained to Honda, stolen from the Marches. Honda had laughed and said, *Good for you,* but Rachel made him promise to say it was his. Better that it came from Honda than from her. Better that no one should add up the pieces. *And what do you want me to tell them?* Honda had asked. *That I found it on the street?* Tell them you won it in a crapshoot, Rachel told him. Tell them anything you want.

And so he did. But no one believed it. The stories went from dull to wild, died down eventually, flared up when someone got mad at Honda, then fizzled out altogether. From time to time, someone dragged out the ancient admonition that "you can't trust a Jackson," but no one listened. It didn't matter where the money came from. All that mattered was the land.

In the beginning, only a few families had moved back—the remnants of those who had lived here and gone. More came later. Everyone said they belonged to the tribe, but Rachel wondered if all of them really were Indian, much less Odawa. _Blond_ Indians? But anything was possible, Honda had reminded her. A lot of these people had the blood, even though it was only a half, a quarter, an eighth. _Look at you,_ Honda had said, adding, _Look at Ben._

But Ben wasn't here. And Ada, Bliss, and Minnie kept asking when he was coming until Rachel finally snapped, "Who knows? He hasn't been here in months."

The powwow would be starting the next day. Ben had been one of the best dancers, and though Honda wouldn't admit it, Rachel knew he was proud. Why did he pretend not to care? Now Honda, winner of crapshoots, was _ogema_—a leader of the band. He had negotiated for years with the Northern Michigan Odawa Association, had worked with them to fight for what the treaties hadn't provided. There was money at stake. The band was up for review, pleading their case to gain recognition. The Horseshoe Band. If they drew attention, anything was possible. Rumor had it, the federal government was coming around. Anyone who was a member of the NMOA was qualified, but they had to be accepted first, and there were standards.

"Honda," said Minnie as if she had read Rachel's mind, "is working too hard lately."

Bliss nodded slowly. "Someone should take care of that man."

All three women looked at her, but Rachel pretended not to notice. Honda was practically her brother. Besides, he had other women. Hadn't they seen the tattoos on his arms?

"Speaking of working too hard," Rachel said, "you two aren't getting any younger. You should take those people up on their offer."

Bliss's eye drifted slowly south, making her look even older. For forty years, Ada had lived with her on the farm. Their two sets of hands were knotted from labor, their faces sagged and lined from hard weather and helping girls give birth. Now all the land around the farm was being bought up by developers, subdivided for housing—three-bedroom ranch houses, A-frames, and split-levels. *Like weeds,* Ada said.

"Tsss," said Bliss, her eye focusing on Rachel. "And where would we live?"

Rachel shrugged. "Why not here?"

"Sure," said Minnie, slapping Ada on the arm, perhaps a bit too hard. "We'll make you honoraries."

"Some honor," said Ada, rubbing her arm.

"We're family," Rachel said. "At least, that's what you two used to tell me. Besides"—she patted Bliss's callused hand—"you like it here."

Bliss's good eye traveled upward. Rachel knew what she was thinking. The farm had been in her family for generations. It was their *home.* But Rachel knew they couldn't keep it up. The place was growing over, falling down.

Down by the lake, the teenagers clustered, silently sharing a cigarette. Someone threw a stone at the water, making rings that disturbed the rushes. They said a *matchi-manitou* lived at the bottom of Horseshoe Lake, that he used to lure young girls when they stood at the water's edge. On nights like these, when the air was still and filmy, the drowned maidens were sometimes spotted dancing on the water.

"What the hell was that?" said Ada.

A loud, plaintive screech wailed across the water.

"Loon," said Rachel. *"Mong."*

"You're getting better," said Minnie, surprised that Rachel knew the word. "When you first came back, you were a know-nothing."

"You couldn't even *find* it," said Ada.

"I hardly remembered the place." Rachel nodded.

More than a hundred years before, the federal government had bilked them out of their treaty and tried to move them to Kansas. The Odawa refused to move. Instead, they had packed their canoes, moved to Manitoulin Island until, someday, they could buy back their land.

"But now . . . ," said Minnie.

"Now it's ours," Rachel said, picking up her awl and a piece of bark, suddenly feeling as rooted here as the two midwives did to their farm. "It will always be ours."

It was dark when Rachel crept down to the lake—the noiseless predawn hour when everything slept. Peeling off her nightshirt, she waded into the water, her toes sinking into the oatmeal softness of clay and decayed leaves. The water was urine warm and boggy. No breeze moved the pines. Sometimes, while she swam, she imagined the fishy incarnations of the *manitou, au-sa-way* and *naw-me-gon,* ghoul-eyed and watching. She imagined Woody, his spirit choked in sea grass.

But not this morning. This morning, as she swam with the unhurried strokes of someone born to water, she was thinking about the jingle dress she was finishing for the niece of a friend—a seventeen-year-old who went by the name of Jolene, though her mother called her Laughing Brook. Three hundred and sixty-five jingles on that dress, one for each day of the year. Rachel had zigzagged the rows to show off the girl's figure. If Ben showed up for the powwow, maybe he would notice this Jolene/Laughing Brook.

Rachel's own dress was made of buckskin and beads. Each passing year, she had added to it, sewing into it some of the glass bits that Woody had given her, attaching a Petoskey stone at the eye of a sunburst, its fossilized surface pricked with tiny stars. The rest of Woody's gifts she kept in a box along with the braids she'd cut off after Ben's birth. Someday she would sew all of those odds and ends into that dress—the rusted toy train, the pages torn from books—weave them into a design only she could understand.

Steam rose from her body as she came out of the water. Dawn had made gray out of blackness, and in the first light, she could make out shapes, but no colors. The bent chimney pipe of a cabin. A rock on the beach. And at the edges of the woods, the tepees and trailers set up for the powwow.

"Rachel."

Honda was standing on the beach. She hadn't noticed him at first. She picked up her nightshirt, covered herself. Her hair, the wild souvenir from some nameless French ancestor, curled down her back.

"Do you smell it?" she said.

"The fires?"

She shook her head. "Rain." And even though the dawn sky was cloudless, all the signs were there. The smell of water, the way her hair stood on end.

"You always had a better sense of smell," said Honda.

"It's Ben who has the sense."

The low glow of a propane lantern leaked from one of the cabins. Honda seemed to be waiting, watching her. Rachel had never felt self-conscious around Honda. But now, she hurriedly put on her nightshirt and started up the beach.

He followed her. "I tracked him down. That boat shop where he works? They told me where to find him."

"And where's that?" She held up her hand and said bitterly, "No, don't tell me. Anywhere but here."

"He's not ready, Rachel."

"Did I ask you?"

"In so many words."

Rachel stopped and turned to him. "Why are you telling me this?"

Honda's arms were crossed. He looked as big and stubborn as an old beech tree. "So you can stop all this waiting and hoping. Men should leave their mothers."

"And do what? Work on boats?"

"He likes them well enough."

"*This* is his land."

"Is it?"

Honda touched her shoulder. Rachel shuddered. For so many years, she had lived like a nun, wrapping her mourning about her like a shawl. How happy it would have made Sister Marie to know that her little heathen had lived a convent life after all.

"You're late," she said abruptly. "You have to set up the ring."

For a moment, his hand tightened on her shoulder. He seemed about to say something, then he pushed himself away. She watched Honda as he walked toward the cabins. For a moment, her hands ached with the prospect of sewing jingles. She sniffed the air. Truly, she thought, it is going to rain.

By 10 A.M., the grass on the meadow beyond the village was flattened out, the arbor built in the middle with leafy branches and plywood. Honda had organized it so that anyone could set up a stand for food or drink or crafts or books—anything that might bring in money from the tourists who would come to watch. A band from Escanaba was selling beads and leather. Another from Manistee had been out west that spring, returning with cheap turquoise and fancy new steps.

The air was filled with the smell of fry bread, coffee brewing, the low chatter of Indians. Rachel walked around, from campfire to campfire, catching snatches of conversation and gossip—who'd gotten married, divorced, who'd had a baby, what was happening with the NMOA and the government, the fishing treaties, some talk of bingo, land rights. A teenager wearing a Mickey

Mouse shirt war-whooped around a group of girls, trying to get their attention. Laughing, they turned away.

Ben should be here, Rachel thought. He should be dancing with the other men. A boy in fierce face paint reminded her of that time they had danced on a lake near Ponshewaing. She had set up a booth with her quill boxes, had sold them all to summer people from Moss Village and Chibawassee who'd told her about the times they'd been to Arizona and New Mexico, about the beadwork and the weavings they'd seen. Nothing as fine as this, they'd say. And even though she hadn't admitted it, Rachel had flushed with pride.

This sand-filled soil. The tall grasses clotted with Indian paintbrush, wild yarrow, thistle. Down by the far end of the lake where the brooks flowed, birch trees had given their skins. From that tamarack came medicine to stop arthritis and to clot the blood. All these trees. So many cut for lumber, and still they grew back so that they might be cut again, used for shade, boards, and firewood.

Soon it would be time. Everyone would come together in the prayer-celebration of dance. The bands had had their differences in the past, but now their cause was the same. Fishing rights. Land. Representation. They huddled as they had a hundred years before on Mackinaw when the white men had taken their children to teach them another language, another way to be.

A sudden squawk of the microphone, and everyone looked up as Honda Jack tapped it, saying, "Testing, testing." He still seemed amazed that they had electricity, although he had put in the lines himself. Everyone was invited to join in the processional, Honda said. Contestants. Guests. Everyone.

Minnie fanned herself under the shelter of the elders' arbor. "Well," she said to Rachel, "turnout's good."

Soon the ring was clogged with dancers in costumes of Grass and Traditional, Jingle and Fancy, their colors blurring as if they were already swirling together in one great dance. Rachel fingered a jay feather knotted into her braid.

"Go on," said Minnie.

"You, too."

Minnie shook her head. "I'm too old. The sun."

Falling in line with the other dancers, Rachel started into the ring, eyes forward, face solemn, a feather clutched in her hand like a fan. At the head of the procession, Old Jedda, currently forgiven by Minnie, carried a staff decorated with fur and feathers. The tinkle of ankle bells moved in rhythm with the drums, and sometimes a dancer darted out, spinning, before moving quickly back into line. Rachel scanned the faces of the crowd, hoping to catch sight of Ben, but the faces were those of strangers.

The grass beneath her feet was matted and dry. Dancers who had come from as far away as Battle Creek and the Brule River fell silent in the ring. Two drumbeats and Honda began to speak about how their lands had been taken, but still they came together as family. In fields, in parking lots, in stadiums, they would come. Rachel looked around at strangers' faces. Were these people on the sidelines family? She looked at Honda, his eyes closed, rocking a little. Under the shade of the arbor, Minnie, her red face next to the pale ones of Ada and Bliss. Two kids poked each other and tried not to laugh. An old woman was selling trinkets. The drums started beating softly, then harder. Rachel thought of her grandmother's hands. She thought of Woody. Who was her family now? A young man on the other side of the rope was standing at attention, his hair pulled into a ponytail, his eyes hidden behind dark glasses. Rachel watched him as he leaned down and pinched a bit of soil, tasted it. She mouthed his name. The drums stopped.

The soil still tasted of clay, the grit of his ancestors and something even older. Ben looked around the ring. Honda hadn't exaggerated—there must have been more than a hundred people, mostly strangers. His mother might be at the cook tent with Minnie or under the shade, shooing the children away from the folding chairs so that the elders might have a seat. She could be selling her quill boxes in a booth next to someone selling moccasins or beaded bookmarks or corny Native poetry painted on plaques. He scanned the crowd for her.

In the ring, the Men's Traditional had started. It had been one of Ben's dances, but not his best. The double-hop of leather-clad feet, head low, arms dangling free at the side. Later, the Fancy Dance would start, and the pretend warriors would come out crouched, leading with the head, birdlike and predatory.

Ben scraped his foot in the dirt. The summer people watching the show looked as if they'd just come in off the lake, their hair beaten back and lightened by the sun, eyes red, skin tanned. He supposed he looked like one of them.

He tapped his fingers to the sound of the drums and chants, but his body felt rigid. Old Jedda had taken the mike, adjusting it down to his height.

"Ceremonial," Jedda said, and began to talk about the honor of tribes, about how their people had fought to defend borders they never wanted in the first place. "Still," said Jedda, "we fought." Now it was time to give back, to take their place among the honored. Many of them had fought valiantly, given their lives for the lives of others, given their limbs, their minds.

"Me, for instance," said Jedda, craning up to speak in the mike. "I fought in the First World War. I was lucky, though."

The shrill squeal of the microphone interrupted the rest of the story. When it was quiet again, Jedda continued. "Will Stan Geeshegaw come up?" he said. "World War One. Son of Josiah Geeshegaw, who fought under Grant. Will Merle Olway come up? Also World War One. And Len Tucker. And the Kiosha brothers."

The names went on. Ben shifted his weight, tongued the grit in his mouth as

Jedda called up the World War II vets and those who had served in Korea. "Honda Jack, would you please come up?"

Honda, taller than the rest, broke from the crowd. He was wearing a traditional costume today, a beaded breastplate, a headband with feathers. Ben wondered if his mother had made it. He watched as Honda went forward and whispered something in Jedda's ear. Jedda nodded.

"And Vietnam," said Jedda, leaning into the microphone. "Will William Wemegwase come up?"

Soon the men had formed a half circle along the edge of the ring. The old ones from the earlier wars, and some Ben's age, their eyes with that same wounded and wary look. He sensed that Spenger was with him now.

"Excuse me?"

Ben turned.

"Aren't you Rachel Winnapee's son?"

The girl was young and wearing a jingle dress, her hair pulled tight into a basket of braids. Girls like this made him nervous—pretty girls who knew they were, their light, quick happiness foreign and false to his ears.

"She made my dress," the girl said.

Her voice was high and singsongy, like the girls in the Delta. Brave girls who thought they had to dance and giggle to get a GI to buy them drinks.

"It's nice," said Ben.

"Listen." The girl hopped up and down, but it was Jedda's voice, not the sleighbell tinkle of the girl's dress, that caught his attention.

"Today," the microphone boomed, "we have another returning son, one who we want to represent all those we honor for serving their country in Vietnam."

A vague buzzing in Ben's ears. He wanted to say, _It was the soil that saved me._ But they were calling his name, and Honda was looking at him, and somewhere his mother was, too, and Ben, hesitating at first, rubbed his cheek against his shoulder and ducked under the rope, coming forward until he was face-to-face with his teacher. Honda took his hand, put an eagle feather in it, clasped his palm around it. Before Ben could say anything, the singers started crying out a song of honor and celebration, of grief for those who had fallen, and Ben and Honda were at the front of the procession, Jedda explaining to the audience that this procession is open to anyone who fought, that they were all braves and must be included.

"Anyone," he said.

Ben clenched the feather, thinking it was not for him. He was representing Spenger, the private from Mississippi, and all the others whose spirits had rushed home. He turned and said as much to Honda, but Honda shook his head.

"You're here. That's what matters," Honda said. "Take it."

Rachel knew he hadn't seen her. She had become invisible, blending into the crowd like a tree in the woods. Not for the first time, she could see Woody in her son. She watched as he staggered forward, unsure as to which side of the rope he belonged. As he led the procession, she wanted to go to him, but like the rest of the women, she could only join in at the end.

The ranks swelled as men of all ages fell in behind one another, shuffling or striding, some heads bent, some high, some Indian, some not. Soon the families followed Rachel, became part of the line that curved in upon itself until it was a spiral of those who had fought and those who loved them, circling even tighter until they were three abreast. A boy in Levi's in front of her, an American flag stitched to the rear pocket. Women held their children. The sun bore down, and Rachel flinched in the glare, thinking she saw someone—a soldier, gaunt and limping—turning toward her, and her heart leapt. She could have sworn—those eyes! And why wouldn't Woody be walking here, in this helix of warriors, closing ranks in their solidarity and sacrifice? There could be thousands of them, hundreds of thousands, a river of heroes, but before she could run to him, before she could say his name, the tide closed in, the image vanished, and there toward the front of the line, next to the boy who would never be his son, Rachel saw Honda, the cold snows of Korea melting down his face.

Down the beach, the campfires were growing dim. The dancing had gone on till past ten. Rachel sat on the rocker Honda had repaired, Ben on the porch beside her. Down the beach in Minnie's cabin, Ada and Bliss were sleeping.

"So," she said.

Already, her son looked better, the hair grown in, the scar less angry. How many months since she'd seen him? He was tan, filled out, stronger than she remembered. She had always thought of him as having a pencil-thin body with a too-big head, a child who was into everything. She could have sworn that last time she'd seen him he had been younger by a half. But what was memory? Sunbeams on the water.

"Boats," she said. "It's not surprising."

When they found each other after the ceremonial, their embrace had been awkward. Even as a teenager, he had been easy with her, pulling her toward him, calling her "mama," taking her arm in his. But now.

"You used to love to dance," she said. "You were like the wind."

The rain had started. The campfires sizzled and grew smoky. You should stay here tonight, she told Ben, but he shook his head.

"Do you remember," he asked, "the boat we sailed on that summer?"

Rachel shivered as if the wind had kicked up, although the rain was falling soft and straight. Ah, Rachel thought. He knows, just as he knows the story of rocks by the taste of them.

"I remember," she said.

Ben was stroking his scar with the eagle's feather, gazing ahead as if he could read something in the rain-splattered lake. At least it's ours, Rachel thought.

"That pale-haired boy," she said.

"Rory? He's a painter. An artist. Not that it makes his grandmother happy."

No, thought Rachel, almost smiling. It wouldn't. The rain smelled dense and green. It fell thickly from the roof, the trees. A baptismal rain that seemed to wash over her, tamping down the dust, cleansing the air. It's time, she thought. "I have something to show you."

Rising, she went inside. The screen door thumped behind her. It had been so many years since Ben had asked about his father. But seeing Woody in the procession, she knew it was a sign.

Returning with the shoe box she had kept beneath her bed, she held it out to her son. "Open it."

Drawing back the lid, Ben pulled out the tiny rusted toy train.

"I found that," Rachel said, "in the bottom of a bowl of soup."

Ben turned it around in his palm like the fragile carcass of a bird that had flown into a window. He set it aside and took out a Petoskey stone. That, Rachel told him, she found in a laundry hamper. As he pulled out each item, she described where she had found it, as if she were remembering a piece of land she had once owned and lost. The crab claw in her pocket, beach glass in a crumpled napkin. A rock the size of a human heart. Ben took out the maps, yellowed and fragile with age, opened them slowly.

"Those are charts of the Philippines." He traced his fingers across the longitudes and latitudes, the islands of Mindanao, Samar, Luzon.

The next item was a piece of tissue, folded into a bundle. He unfolded the flap, took out the pinch of hair trimmings, lighter than Rachel's own. The rain fell hard now, the air smelling as damp and woolly as the dewy brow of a child.

"Hair cuttings," said Rachel. "I found them in a book he gave me."

"Who?"

"Your father."

Ben ran the bit of hair beneath his thumb and forefinger, smelled it, licked it, ran it down his cheek. With both hands, he held the bit of hair to his lips—a wafer blessed by a priest.

Then he took the photograph, its edges much-fingered and curled. A young man sitting on a dock, splashing the water with his legs. She had stolen it, Rachel told him, when she was just a girl.

"Woody March?" said Ben.

She met his eyes. Reaching for the box, she pulled out one of her braids, held it in her palm. "When I had you, I cut them off."

CHAPTER TWENTY-FOUR

B en's brain was pushing against his skull, and someone was calling his name.

"Winnapee?"

He was curled up at the base of a boat mast. The sun, already high above the trees, seared the side of his face. Slowly, Ben opened his eyes, squinted at Rory standing on the dock with three people he didn't know.

"What time is it?"

"This is a first," Rory said, lifting an eyebrow. He was dressed in shorts, one foot raised on an enormous ice chest.

"What day is it?" asked Ben. He had the vague recollection of running down the road from Horseshoe Lake and, later, sitting in the seat of someone's truck. And then he was at the Pier Inn, his hand curved around a sweating bottle of beer. It must have been two in the morning when they finally kicked him out. This is it, he remembered, Monday: the day he'd promised Mrs. March—his *grandmother*—to take Rory out on the boat.

"I've procured some friends. Are you going to take us sailing or not? Because if you're not, I'd be perfectly happy to have bloodies on the porch."

"Right," said Ben.

Rory pointed at the ice chest. "Sandwiches," he said. "And beer. Ella Mae packed them for me this morning."

"I thought you weren't allowed in the kitchen."

"Things change," Rory said before turning to his friends. He said each of their names as if they were new and fresh and he was saying them for the first time. Hewett. Bailey. Kitty something. He beamed at Ben as if he had brought about a minor miracle by assembling a crew. "Kitty," said Rory, indicating the girl, "has been asking about you."

The girl rolled her eyes, strode past Ben and onto the boat. One of the guys—either Hewett or Bailey—slapped a stay and looked around.

"See you've pulled the old girl together," he said. "I would have had her junked by now."

"I think it's a beautiful boat," said Kitty. "So old-fashioned."

The breeze had already kicked up from the west. It would be a good day for sailing, even hungover. Why had he gone to the bar? Then it came to him, what he had said, and what his mother had said in return.

Why didn't you ever tell me?

I promised Lydia March.

Ben dragged himself into the cockpit, put on the blower, twisted the key to the engine. Diesel belched and water steamed from the stern as Ben gave everyone instructions for stowing the beer, setting out bumpers.

"Help me with the sail cover," he said to Rory.

As the two of them rolled back the canvas, Ben stared at Rory's soft, white hands.

"So, bro' . . . ," Rory said.

"*Bro'?*" said Hewett, his voice mocking. He raised his eyebrows at Rory.

"It's a term, asshole," said Rory. "It generally implies fondness or camaraderie. An allegiance of brethren transcending race." He shrugged at Ben. "Wouldn't you agree . . . bro'?"

As they pulled away from the dock, Ben moved back and forth from the helm to the rail to shove off. The wind gusted, and Ben turned the bow into it, shouting at Hewett or Bailey to haul up the main, then the jib. As the boat came off the wind, the sails filled with a jerk, and they were sailing.

"Oh, God," Rory groaned as they came out of the harbor, escaping the lee of the point, rounded up, the boat heeling. "I hate this."

But not Ben. He had been waiting for this all summer. The tension of the wheel, the torque of trimmed sails. Now he considered sailing toward the horizon, sailing until he could sail no more. That, or run the hull against the rocks. He adjusted the jib sheet and got two degrees higher. Kitty's yellow hair was blowing, and she kept shaking her head, while Bailey and Hewett tossed back beers, talked to each other, ignoring Rory, who looked even paler than usual.

Six or seven miles to Chibawassee, and then they could cut up that shore or reach back and dance down the edge of Beck's Point. Bits of flotsam mixed in with the deep, dark blue of a lake that seemed as boundless as the sky.

My father *sailed on this lake.*

Ben could almost feel the delicious crack of splintering wood. Rory laid his head in his hands. Hewett (or was it Bailey?) glanced at him with amusement, then looked at Ben. "Hey, Winnapee, how much is Aunt Lydia paying you to drive this Caddy around?"

"She should be paying *me*," said Rory.

My ancestors paddled their way up the shore.

Ben decided to tack the boat, telling everyone to duck as they came around. They eased off and headed toward the Beck's Point shore.

Hewett tossed a beer bottle off the stern of the boat, took bets on how long it would take to sink. "You a betting man, Ben?"

"Depends."

They were close to the beach now. The Marches' house stood stalwart toward the tip.

What had she been thinking? She—who had wanted Ben to learn Indian ways. They had *paid* her.

You lied.

Could Lydia March see them from her window? She had taken to her bed the last few days, but it might rouse her if she knew they were sailing. If she looked out, she could see her gem of the harbor again under sail. Questions surged and ebbed like tossing surf. *Watch this,* Ben wanted to say, dashing the bow against the shoals. The slightest shift in the wind, and its whole course could be different. Even now, the wind had skewed toward the north. An anomalous wind that wouldn't last, would either turn toward the east and bring in weather, or ease back into a tranquil, constant westerly.

"I'll make you a bet," said Ben.

He had brought the *Blue Heron* tight up again, pointing her as high as he could into the wind. "You see those shoals?" he said, pointing off the starboard bow.

"You're getting too close," said Rory.

"How far do you think it is between them and the shore?"

"Billy Bailey runs his ski boat through there all the time," said Kitty, who had been examining her toe polish. She jerked her head toward Bailey. "Tell him, Billy."

Bailey leaned against a winch and shrugged. "Kid's stuff."

"How about sailing through it? In this boat?" said Ben.

Bailey laughed, shook his head. His slow grin and messed-up eyes reminded Ben of Spenger. "No way, man. This boat's a tub."

"She's done it before."

"Ancient history."

"So," said Ben, pointing the helm higher, making the sails luff, "are you going to take the bet?"

For a moment, no one spoke. Then the other one—Hewett—said, "And if you run it aground?"

Ben looked from face to face. They were with him now, colluding among friends, each making their wager but in the end wanting to see it through. He'd done it with his platoon before an advance.

What are our chances?

Zero.

What'll you give me if we live?

"I'll put on a coat and a tie and come down to that club of yours."

"That I'd like to see," said Rory.

"And if you win?" Bailey said, his loopy, Spenger smile betraying his amusement.

"I'll buy you a beer at the Pier Inn," said Ben. "Maybe give you some grass-dancing lessons."

"Dancing lessons?" said Kitty, perking up.

Picturing her in a jingle dress, Ben tried not to smile.

"Let's do it!" said Bailey, and even Rory was looking interested.

Choosing his words carefully, Ben described the maneuvers through the shoals as if they were navigating a minefield. "You do what I tell you," he said. "Don't hesitate, even for a second."

He glanced up at the Marches' house. The windows were like blind eyes reflecting the lake, but for some reason, he was sure Lydia March was watching.

The wind was perfect. Ten degrees to the north, just enough to get the lift that could keep them parallel to the beach instead of drifting into the shoals.

"Hewett," he said, "you're on jib. When I say tack, grab the sheets and bring her across. Don't wait for the wind to do it. Rory, you and Bailey are on mainsail. If I say ease, ease. If I say come about, crank her in as tight as you can till we're off the wind. Bailey, you take the winch. Rory, you tail."

"What about me?" said Kitty hopefully.

"I need you on the bow. You're my eyes. You lie on your belly and watch the bottom like a hawk. If you see a rock, yell and point. Got it?"

Kitty nodded and bounded forward.

They tacked onto starboard. For a second the wind knocked them down. Unless the shift in the wind came, they'd have to tack again to make the thin opening between the shoals and the shore. Ben could feel the wheel tugging him to drop. "Trim the jib!" he yelled up to Hewett. He could feel the point improving, but it still wasn't enough. Just five more degrees. At the last minute, they would have to come about and get enough momentum to tack again. He wasn't sure they'd have room. "Tighter!" he shouted.

It wasn't going to work. If he came up more into the wind, the boat would stall. "Okay," he said, "we're tacking."

The boat flopped. Hewett wrestled the jib across.

"Crank it in!" screamed Ben.

For a moment, the *Blue Heron* drifted like a stunned bird, unsure of her bearings. "Go," said Ben under his breath, waiting for the sails to take the wind. It had been a sloppy tack, and they would pay for it.

Slowly, the sails filled, and the *Blue Heron* overcame the inertia and started to move. They had twenty feet to go before he'd need to fall off and start again. By then, the wind could have shifted east or west. Either way, they would lose their chance.

Ben watched the sails. The belly of the main had filled, the curve of its draft just right. The tip of Beck's Point was just ahead of them. Even now the water was changing from sapphire to jade as they headed toward the shallows. He closed his eyes, could feel the keel, the rudder, the hull respond.

"Okay," he said. "This time, let the main out a little after we tack. Keep it easy. Let the sails find the wind."

Everyone took his position, and once again Ben spun the helm, bringing the boat around. Bailey and Rory eased the main.

"Back the jib a little," Ben yelled up to Hewett, telling him to forget the sheets and pull the canvas by hand so that the wind could power it faster. He could feel her moving like a dancer finding her steps. Soon she would be in the rhythm of the dance, moving as she should move, with the grace of wind and water.

"Okay," said Ben. "Okay."

They were making the entrance to the shoals now. On their left, the water suddenly became shallow, the talus of the glacier peaking above the waves. Beck's Point was to the right, the crooked finger. The wind should come down the shore just so, then bend along its edge the way a river bent at a turn in the bank.

Ben felt the boat edge higher. They were moving above the shoals. Off starboard, there was plenty of deep, bottomless blue. Forty feet, and they would be clear. There wasn't room to tack.

"Ben!" said Kitty. "A rock! Over there!" She pointed a few degrees off starboard.

Ben yelled back, asking how close.

"You need to scootch to the left."

"Damn." Ben eased the helm to port.

And then the wind gusted hard. It was as if a huge, invisible hand had slapped them. The rails dipped, the deck took on water. Kitty squealed, and Hewett grabbed an air vent. The boat was heeling almost on its ear, and Ben was losing control as they began to slip sideways.

"Let it out!" he screamed at Bailey and Rory. "Let it out! Let it out! Let it out!"

Bailey released his hold on the winch handle, but Rory was still holding fast. The sheet started to run. Ben could see Rory fighting the line, the look of pain and terror on his face as the line ripped his palms.

Swearing, Ben jumped forward, pushed Bailey out of the way. As the boat came up into the wind, easing the tension on the line, Ben grabbed it, wrestled two loops around the winch to take off the pressure.

"Rory," he shouted, "the helm! You've got to steer!"

Rory, staring at his wounded hands, didn't seem to hear. Then he looked at Ben bracing himself against the side of the cockpit, straining against the line. He grabbed the helm.

"Drop her down!" Ben yelled.

The boat was bucking in the waves that had broken on the rocks. If Rory overcorrected, they would be sucked into the shoals.

But Rory didn't overcorrect. He held the wheel almost tenderly, then looked at Ben for instructions. "Watch your point," said Ben, nodding up at the sails, telling Rory to drop her down. He glanced off the port edge. Straight ahead was the opening. Any shift in the wind, and they would ram.

"Steady," said Ben. He looked at Rory's stricken face, his pale hair blowing straight back, and wondered if Woody March had ever shown his son how to take the helm the way he once showed Ben.

From the bow, Kitty yelled that they were too close. Ben held his breath, counted the seconds as they slipped toward the end of the wave-whipped shoals. "Yes!" he cried as the water widened and calmed.

He looked at Rory. Their eyes met. And they were through.

CHAPTER TWENTY-FIVE

The truck jounced down the road. It was Honda's truck, and Rachel had never gotten the hang of it. Even now her shifting of the gears, her pressing of the gas and brakes sent the truck lurching and hopping as she headed toward Moss Village.

She hadn't slept. The dress she wore was the dress she had worn the day before—Women's Traditional—brightly colored and threaded with feathers and beads. Her hair, unbraided, curled crazily down her back, and she looked like an exotic, feral bird as she pulled up to the gates of Beck's Point.

"Chet?" she said to the guard who peered out of his shack. "Remember me?" She reminded him how she used to work at the Marches', how her son was working there now. She held her breath until he waved her through, relieved she didn't have to tell him it was Mrs. March she wanted to see, Mrs. March who had to be told that Rachel had broken the treaty. She had told Ben, and now he knew that these people were his people, and that she had lied and covered up and whispered the truth to no one. *I'll take an oath,* she had told Lydia March, given her Woody's letter and taken the money in return. They had made a treaty, but what were treaties, after all? Broken promises, corruptible as flesh.

Yesterday everything had changed in the spiral of dancers—perhaps it was the heat—she had seen it, hadn't she? The eyes of her beloved. Or was it her own eyes, dazzled, tearing up with the glare and the fact of her son that had conjured the vision from nothing?

Either way, she had told Ben. And later, when the screen door banged and she was alone, some hoot owl was keening in the woods as Rachel was keening, the detritus of her life strewn about her when Honda came in. She was holding the yellowed photograph of Woody sitting on a dock. *I told him,* she had said, and Honda reached for her, his hands not soft, his eyes not blue. A man with eyes like burnt molasses—not someone she had thought of as a lover—not Woody March, but this man.

He had taken her in his big arms—not a brother now. He told her with his tongue, with lips, with hands, that it would be all right, that Ben would be better off knowing. Rachel hadn't realized that caresses like these could come from such a large, blunt man whose body was tattooed with the names of other women. Then she was kissing him back—madly. Years without food. Years without water. Only the soil on her tongue.

Now she was pulling up in front of the Marches' house. There it stood, as it had always stood, like some eternal, fortified lump. Except for the *Blue Heron,* the dock was barren of boats. A beach towel hanging from the rail of the porch was the only sign of life. What if no one was home? What if Ben had returned and embraced Lydia March? Would Rachel find the carcasses of stripped beds, the family gone on a train?

She shook her head to clear it. It was just a typical afternoon on Beck's Point when everyone was napping or had gone off to play bridge. Soon they would be returning for cocktails on the porch. Down the stairs, she banged on the kitchen door. Through the screen she could see the antiseptic coolness of fluorescent light. "Ella Mae?"

There was no response. In a louder voice, she called out again. But it was Mandy who came to the door, an older Mandy who looked like her mother, huge and black, her many braids gone now and twisted into a bun.

"May I help you?" she said elaborately.

Rachel sighed with impatience. "It's me," she said. "Rachel Winnapee. I've come to see Mrs. March."

Mandy stared at her from the other side of the screen. Rachel could hear a chair push back in the kitchen and someone calling out, "Who is it, child?"

"Rachel Winnapee," Rachel said again, loud enough for Ella Mae to hear.

Mandy opened the door. "Well," she said, turning to her mother, "she's come back again. Every ten years or so like the plague."

Ella Mae was gray now. Thinner. The glasses she wore looked like hand-me-downs, something from the 1950s. "Come here, girl, so I can see you."

Rachel drew a deep breath. The kitchen smelled of gas more than ever. It closed around her, made her want to retch. Ella Mae was eyeing her up and down the way she had twenty-five years ago, checking to see if she was dirty, peering into her eyes, motioning for her to turn around. Rachel realized she looked ridiculous in this costume, her hair unruly, the smell of lovemaking still on her skin.

"Let me see your hands," said Ella Mae.

Rachel held them out, and the old woman took them. Her fingernails were torn, and her palms were rough. Ella Mae ran her thumb across the leathery lines, nodded, and let them go. She looked at Rachel.

"Well," she said. "After all these years."

Rachel felt that same weakening she had years before whenever Ella Mae spoke kindly. It was a subtle blade, this kindness, designed to throw her off her path.

"I need to see her," Rachel said.

"You need to know something," said Ella Mae.

"So does she."

"She's sick, child. She's got the cancer."

Rachel bit her lip. She wanted to say, She *is* a cancer, but she knew if she spoke recklessly, Ella Mae would never let her up those stairs. Not that Ella Mae could stop her. Rachel would push by both these women if it came to that.

Ella Mae laid her hand on Rachel's arm. Again, that kindness. "The boy's like his father."

"What boy?" said Mandy, looking from Rachel to her mother. "Who's she talking about?"

"Yes," said Rachel without thinking. She stopped herself and looked into Ella Mae's eyes. Dark as treacle, those eyes. Darker than her own. "You knew."

Ella Mae drew her hands together, pressed her lips against their points. "A little like his uncle, though. Fearless. Lord, that boy could sail."

Rachel tapped her foot. "I'm not here to talk about genealogy." But it was exactly why she was here, and Ella Mae knew it and was making her reckon for it now.

"Funny how these things pop up," said Ella Mae. "I had a nephew once looked just like my cousin on my mother's side."

"Ella Mae!" said Rachel.

"You'd think Elizabeth March would have seen it."

"Seen what?" said Mandy.

"Then again," Ella Mae went on, "maybe she does."

"It was you who took that letter he left me, wasn't it?"

Ella Mae nodded her head slowly, her cloudy eyes staring into some far-off place. "He propped it up on the bureau the day they left. He must have known someone besides you could find it. I showed it to Mrs. March. I thought it would change her mind. He did love you, you know. But Mrs. March—she couldn't accept it."

Ella Mae jerked her head toward the stairs, her eyes not leaving Rachel's.

The stairs creaked in the same places. Twenty-five years, and Rachel remembered which ones. She crossed through the dining room, past the gallery of pictures, the heavy mahogany, its gleam duller than she recalled. There was a smell of urine and medicine as she climbed the next set of stairs.

At the top was the large landing, the many doors of rooms. To the right was Woody's old room with its children's books, it nautical bedspreads. Beyond that, the guest rooms. Rachel started toward Mrs. March's bedroom when one of the doors banged open.

Elizabeth March, in a robe, stood in her doorway. It was late in the afternoon, and she looked as if she had just come from the beach or the shower. She tottered for a second, then said, "I know you."

Rachel froze as if a bear had tumbled out of the forest into her path. Elizabeth March looked different. The hair, still blond, seemed limp. Her lips were pale.

"You're the one," Elizabeth March said, and Rachel stiffened. "You're the one who makes the quill boxes."

Rachel was stunned. She hadn't seen the woman in years—not since she first came to the store—but Elizabeth March seemed neither surprised nor alarmed to find her here.

"Say," Elizabeth March went on, suddenly brightening. "Would you show me how you do it?"

"Sorry?"

"C'mon," she said, pulling Rachel into her room.

A cigarette smoked and sputtered in an ashtray. The room itself was a faded photograph, the flowers of the fabric yellowed and pale. Neglect clung to the dust ruffles. An unmade bed. The stench of loss.

"See?" said Elizabeth March. She gestured toward her bureau on which a dozen or more quill boxes were clustered. Rachel recognized some of her best. The head of a coyote. An eagle's wing. "They're yours, aren't they?"

For years Honda had been selling her boxes to a collector, but he had never told her it was Elizabeth March. Rachel stood mute. She didn't want to talk about her quill boxes or spend another minute with the woman Woody March had married. It was the other Mrs. March she needed to see. Abruptly, Rachel said, "Most of them."

Elizabeth March picked up a glass from her bedside table, sipped and swallowed hard. Putting it down, she said, "It's my hands. I need something to do with them. I refuse to knit, and everyone needlepoints. I thought maybe you could teach me."

"You want to . . . ?"

"Give it a shot. You never know."

Rachel almost laughed. "You don't remember me, do you? The summer the war ended? I brought you tea."

Trying to focus her eyes, Elizabeth March shook her head. "It was so long ago." She pulled her robe tighter, pushed back her hair, looking both tough and vulnerable.

Compassion crept in like an uninvited guest, and Rachel said, "It's not your fault. I was just a girl."

Rachel looked about the room, remembering the strewn clothes, the magnificent harbor, Miss Elizabeth running up from the beach. More than twenty years ago. Where was that sunny girl holding the trophy now?

"Give me your hands," Rachel said.

Slowly, Elizabeth March held them out. The bitten nails were no longer polished. Rachel took them in hers, ran her fingers across the palms. No calluses here, but they were lined with misery. "Your hands are so tender," Rachel said, releasing her. She picked up one of the boxes, its lid patterned with an eagle's wing.

He bleeds for me.

"Honda Jack said you could help me," said Elizabeth March, her voice suddenly small and pleading. "He said you teach girls how to do it."

Rachel touched her temple. Honda and his big ideas. She heard a faint buzzing, perhaps an outboard motor on the harbor. "Look," she said. Again Rachel took the other woman's hand. She tried to imagine working with Elizabeth March the way her grandmother had worked with her, teaching her how to puncture the bark, showing her how lives stitch together, how fingers sometimes bleed. She pressed her palm to Miss Elizabeth's.

"I can't help you," Rachel said. "You need tough hands like so."

"Are you saying no?"

Feeling that old urge to touch that yellow hair, to take in her scent, Rachel hesitated.

"Miss Elizabeth," she said, "I have something to tell you."

There was no view of the bay that afternoon. The shades were drawn, the curtains closed, the casement brittle as memory. If Elizabeth March's room smelled of loss, Lydia March's smelled of illness and disappointment. Rachel knew the smell, had known it since her childhood. Even the insidious odor of perfume failed to mask it completely.

A moan. Rachel's eyes adjusted to see the body in the bed. In a childish voice, Mrs. March said, "Ella Mae?"

"No, Mrs. March. It's not Ella Mae."

Mrs. March barely opened her eyes. She leaned back against the pillows in a ruffled bed jacket.

"My medicine?" Fingers played at the edges of a blanket cover, lips muttered. Where was her damn rosary? Where was the girl?

Rachel moved in close. "It's me. Rachel Winnapee."

"Ah," said Mrs. March. Her hair had thinned to a silver fuzz, her skin was sallow as moonlight. "So you've come."

It was August, and summer was in its death throes. Soon they would be packing up. From the look of her, it would be the last time for Mrs. March. The air was stifling, lightless. Rachel wanted to push back the curtains and say, See the bay? This lake? This is where your son drowned. And now you're taking mine.

"Do you remember me?"

Mrs. March licked her lips. "The girl."

The girl. Not a person. Just hands for folding sheets and picking up and ironing and giving the shots and comfort. Rachel pulled up a chair next to the bed and sat. "I've told Ben about Woody."

She expected Mrs. March to protest, to rail against what she believed to be untrue and unworthy. But the old woman merely said, "My sons are dead, and my house is rotting."

"I'll pay you," said Rachel. "I'll return the money." She wasn't sure how, but over time, she would. And if the government came through for the Odawa, they'd have quite a bit. Enough to pay off this debt and really own the land.

"I was going to tell him myself," said Mrs. March, waving her hand and beckoning Rachel closer. Rachel leaned until Mrs. March's lips nearly touched her ear. "Have you ever prayed for a miracle?"

Rachel didn't know what to say. Had that been praying so many years before when she pleaded to *Nanabozhoo* and the *Gitchi-manitou* as her belly swelled with child?

Mrs. March's eyes grew shiny. "Tell me," she said, her voice lucid and sharp. "This lake you bought. Are there children living there?"

We will fill the pond with fish, the house with laughter. It was all Mrs. March had wanted. Even now, drawn by sickness, the old woman's face was eager as if she needed to know that something had worked out after all.

"You arranged it, didn't you?" Rachel said. "The two women in the farm-house where I went to have the baby?"

Mrs. March sighed and shrugged. "It's so dark. Would you mind letting in some light?"

"You took the letters I wrote to Woody?"

Mrs. March fingered her rosary. "He had become a drug addict. And I couldn't forgive you."

So it was true. Rachel went to the windows, threw open the curtains, opened the sashes. The whole room seemed to breathe. When she looked at Mrs. March, she saw the old woman staring back at her, and for the first time Rachel noticed that Mrs. March's eyes were as blue as Ben's and Woody's were blue— a feature in the landscape she was noticing for the first time. After a moment, she went and sat again by Mrs. March in companionable silence, forgetting for the moment that they were from different tribes.

Mixed among the crystal bottles of perfumes and toiletries were boxes of cottons, cough syrups, syringes. Rachel thought of all the letters she had written Woody during that long, cold winter. Were they sitting in the bottom of one of Mrs. March's drawers? Or had those words of longing, hope, despair long ago been turned to ash?

"Are you in pain?" Rachel asked the old woman.

A deep, rattling sigh. Mrs. March tried to sit up. "I've been wrong about many things," she said as Rachel leaned forward to help her. She pointed to the box on her bedside table. "Open it."

The box was the size of a brick, its top carved with the silhouettes of pine trees. Rachel lifted off the lid to find a grim patch of beach.

Mrs. March nodded at the gritty ash. "I never buried him, you know. Father Tom said it was wrong to cremate, but were my children ever really Catholic? Ashes to ashes, I told him." She ran her fingers through the sandy remains. "At least this way, I got to keep him home."

It occurred to Rachel that Mrs. March probably touched Woody more in death than when he was living. Repelled, fascinated, she resisted the urge to run her own fingers through the silty remains of her lover. Ella Mae had told her that the first thing to wash up on the shore was Woody's leg, and for a moment she had the crazy notion to ask Mrs. March if they had cremated that as well. Glancing at the crucifix standing guard as always over Mrs. March, Rachel said, "I never buried him either."

Suddenly, a sob spasmed through her—a deep, welling shudder as if her own spirit was leaving. Next to her, Mrs. March was wheezing slightly. A gurgle in her lungs like waves pulling back from a stony beach.

"Please," said Mrs. March, "can you help me?"

Rachel fixed her gaze on the old woman. What did Mrs. March want of her now? To tend to her the way she once had tended Woody? Mrs. March may accuse her of having given him too much morphine, but Woody March had grown strong, walked. What else could Rachel do?

"In my drawer," said Mrs. March.

Still queasy from the sight of Woody's ashes, Rachel reached for the knob. As the drawer slid open, the past seemed to fold in on her as she stared at the cluster of gleaming vials. Wasn't it only yesterday that she had stacked sheets in the linen press, listened for the sound of Woody's voice?

God divines all of our purposes, Rachel.

Mrs. March's eyes had drifted away, as if she was recalling days when the family was together. Holding out her arm, she barely seemed to notice Rachel. The old woman's skin was bruised. Her bed jacket fell away revealing a slim, satin strap. Rachel could see the sharp bones of her clavicle. For years, Rachel had worn her own necklace of pain. Now Mrs. March's lips were pulled back in a grimace.

The night before, Ben had told Rachel that Mrs. March's grandson was a painter, that Elizabeth March was *kwa-notchi-way* and *we-saw-gun*—beautiful and bitter—and that Mrs. March wasn't as fierce as she seemed, that her pride grew out of fear.

You don't know these people, Rachel had said.

No, you don't, Ben had answered before he slammed out the door.

"I understand your grandson is a painter," Rachel said, waiting for the grunt of contempt. Through the window stretched the bay, end to end as if someone had smeared a line of blue across canvas.

"I have *two* grandsons."

Rachel watched a flock of seagulls swoop down and land on the shoals, the waves rippling around them. Deep layers of blue clashed with lines of shallower green. Somewhere out there, secrets, drowned and waterlogged, clung to the sandy bottom.

No longer invisible, Rachel turned toward Mrs. March. She lifted the carved box of Woody's ashes, ran her fingers through it, tried to recall his voice. She took a pinch of what was left—the flinty granules of bone or teeth. For the first time in more than twenty years, Rachel crossed herself, then seized the woman's jaw and squeezed. "Open your mouth."

Mrs. March let out a dry rasp of protest. Rachel could see her already darkened tongue beyond the yellow teeth.

"Taste it."

Mrs. March wheezed and struggled.

"Taste it." Then, more tenderly, Rachel said, "It will take you home."

Mrs. March's eyes filled with tears, then with comprehension and, finally, grief for her son. Obedient as a postulant, she swallowed, and in a voice as parched as the bit of ash that clung to her lip, said, "Forgive me."

It was a simple request, and Rachel, looking again at the crucifix, wondered if she would do the same for Ben. Would she, like Lydia March, procure a girl to appease his demons? Would she bind him so closely to the land she felt was theirs that he could walk, dance, but never stand?

She laid her hand on Mrs. March's forehead, then filled the syringe as she had for Woody, held the old woman's stick of an arm, pressed the needle home. Mrs. March gasped at the prick, then succumbed. Rachel knew that look. She had longed for it once, waiting for the pain to vanish from Woody's face. Now she could see Woody in Mrs. March—those same crests around the cheeks, the prominent nose, those eyes.

"More," said Mrs. March in a voice so faint Rachel strained to hear it.

Horrified, Rachel thought, *I can't*. It's an abomination, not a mercy. Silently, patiently, Christ stared down. *You!* thought Rachel. *What would you know about this? No better than Woody who went and left the rest of us behind. You call that mercy? You call that faith?*

A dull, weary ache crested between her throat and her chest. She stared at Mrs. March's face, saw the pain and knew it. Remembering how Ada had once leaned into her when her own body was so racked she could not breathe or think, Rachel refilled the needle.

The room seemed to thicken after that. As the light ebbed, the churning of stones in Mrs. March's lungs quieted. Rachel rose and moved about the room, searching until she found a rock on the bureau, fossilized with a pattern of tiny suns. Returning to the bed, she set it on the old woman's chest where her breasts had been, then counted the breaths, listened as they slowed, watched as Mrs. March's hands became rocks, faintly blue. Soon there were no more breaths.

Rachel closed her eyes, fingered the contours of Mrs. March's face, of Woody's, found pieces of her son. Already the old woman was growing cold, the room silent except for the lapping of waves.

Ben was on the beach when his mother found him. He had come down after they folded and stowed the sails. The boat was tied up, Rory and his friends gone for an early cocktail at the club to brag about sailing through the shoals. That was hours ago. The setting sun was farther south, boding shorter days. Soon the summer people would leave, the houses would be boarded up, the boats put into dry dock.

He picked up a rock and threw it. He would go to Mrs. March and tell her that he had cleared the shoals like she'd dared him. He would tell her that Rory had helped, and what would she say to that? Her grandson whom she had dismissed as a mama's boy, a sissy. *He'll probably never marry*, she had confided in Ben, who was her boat hand—no, her grandson.

He tossed another stone. It skipped twice, rippling the surface with aftershocks. Come autumn, he wasn't sure what he was going to do. Help Hank in the boatyard. Help Honda deliver wood. It was too late to apply to school, but maybe next year. Mrs. March had asked him if he knew about the GI Bill. He could go to her and say, What about it, then? He was her grandson, after all.

"Ben."

He turned and saw his mother, her hair a bird's nest, her dress from yesterday looking like a cheap trinket here on this beach. The Marches' house looming behind her, she looked small and dark and out of place, and he wondered if she had walked on this beach with his father, or if her duties and couplings had been confined to the house. Too bitter to ask, he turned away.

Her bare feet sunk into the sand. The waves slurped around her ankles and calves, begging her to come in. I know you, she thought to the water. You do not fool me anymore. You have taken what I loved and drowned it.

She had found him on the sand, not far from the dune where she and Woody had met, her back pressing into the sand, ants crawling up her legs. Had Ben been conceived in that dune? Or by the lake at night when her knees had bled, the water swishing about her thighs? It could have been in the boat room, surrounded by ghostly piles of canvas. A guest room. A hall.

Here, she decided. By the water.

"I used to come to this place," she said, "with him."

"Don't," Ben said, holding his hand up quickly. "They're your memories, not mine."

Somewhere, the luxurious smoke of someone's fire—warmth in an evening that was not yet cool. In the dusky light, the dunes glowed like the ghostly curves of thighs. A blackness of forest beyond them, some bird crying out.

"You lied," said Ben.

"Yes," she said. "I lied. I told you he was a brave man, a sailor. He wasn't brave. Not really."

Ben's nostrils flared almost imperceptibly. For a moment, Rachel wanted to take back her words. It is impossible to resurrect a hero, she thought. Yet here on this beach, standing before her, was proof to the contrary. "Forgive me," she said. "I was wrong."

The hot coals behind his eyes sizzled, sputtered, expired. She saw his hand was shaking, wanted to touch his scar and say, *It's like this.*

He pointed toward the shoal. "We sailed between those rocks and the shore today. How far do you think that is?"

Years ago she would have said, Not far. But now she knew her estimates were off, that distance was impossible to measure and could change from near to vast, depending. A happy distance to swim with your lover. A yawning chasm that swallowed men.

She drew in a long, full breath. "I used to swim to those rocks when everything seemed closer. I never realized how far it was until Woody didn't make it." She wanted to tell him how the stars had domed, about the haunting of a man so beaten down by the aftershock of war that nothing could free his spirit. Instead, she showed him her hands. Hands for stitching quills, ironing sheets, tilling soil. Holding children. Holding him.

Ben said nothing. And Rachel, suddenly peaceful, thought of Honda, of the taste of him. She couldn't explain why until now there had been no one after

Woody. Perhaps it had been her own deep dread that someone else would be taken from her. Perhaps it had been her rage, delicious as stones. But now her heart was open and placid as the lake, while Lydia March's was forever still. The air smelled of hope, the smoke hinting at reddening trees, and soon the summer people would be gone.

Ben looked at her. "Did you come here to tell me all this?"

"I came to tell Lydia March."

The smell of smoldering cedar. They would be building their own campfires soon to summon the autumn fish.

"And now she's dead."

Ben's face drained of color. Behind her, suddenly, the sound of breaking glass and firecrackers. She wanted to tell him that it was all right, that Lydia March had confessed her sin, that she no longer denied him, but Ben was looking up toward the house. Turning, Rachel saw what he saw, and together, they ran.

By the time Rory showed up, slightly drunk, dazzled by the heat and the obscenity of popping windows, Ben was wrestling a hose, watering down the steps and porch. In the ghastly light, Rory's eyes were wide. He held up his bandaged hands, raw from the rope, started to move his mouth, but nothing came out.

"Stay here," shouted Ben. "I'll get her." Handing the hose to Rory, he started for the house.

Ella Mae and Mandy were standing on the lawn amid a growing crowd. Mandy screamed at him that both Mrs. Marches were still inside, but Ben knew only one mattered now. Inside, he struggled to breathe, and every bit of instinct told him to turn and run. The flames, the smoke, the memory of a jungle ignited. Glass exploded from the heat. Why were there so many windows?

He groped his way to the stairs, thought he heard a voice, but it was only the hissing of steam as the pipes broke loose in a bathroom. The fire didn't seem to be coming from anywhere in particular. It was as if the whole house had spontaneously burst into flames.

He found her in her bedroom, standing by the window, tossing quill boxes onto the lawn three stories down. Intoxicated by the smoke, she looked as if she had lost all sense. She threw box after box, and for a moment, he thought she was going to pitch herself after them. Grabbing a towel to hold over her face, Ben picked up Elizabeth March and carried her like a bride over the threshold, down the stairs, through choking rooms, and out of the burning house.

When he came out, Rachel knew it was safe to breathe. She had stood, immovable as a boulder, watching the house succumb to fire. Even as the firemen tore at it with axes, she knew it was too late. The wood was old and full of rot.

In the vast wallow of time, she could hear bits of words. That ancient, leaky oven, someone said. But then, everyone knew Elizabeth March was a drunk. She probably lit a cigarette and passed out.

"Lord," someone added, "I thought that house would be around forever. Look at it now. Kindling doesn't burn that fast."

Ben had set Elizabeth March down on the lawn and was crouched beside her, his head in his arms. Rachel started toward him, but stopped herself. Wait it out, Honda had told her when Ben had curled up in the corner that winter, making himself as small as possible against whatever it was he'd seen. Fear comes out in bits at first, then gushes like an open vein.

How did Honda know these things? A brave man like him? Suddenly, Rachel could hear Bliss's voice—or was it Ada's? *A patient man, too.*

One of the firemen had come out of the house and was shaking his head. The crowd thickened, and through the glowing silhouettes Rachel could see

Ben was no longer with Elizabeth March. She craned her neck, her eyes darting from face to face until she made out a dark head close to a pale one, Ben's arm around Rory's shoulder, the sirens moaning plaintively. The whole town seemed to have arrived to watch the spectacle. Certainly, all of Beck's Point had gathered. Kitchen servants huddled with men in dinner jackets, women in jewels. Mothers called to their children, held them close. Elizabeth March was hugging herself, rocking, saying over and over that she hadn't meant to, she hadn't.

Rachel's face burned, and someone screamed as the roof collapsed. So much, she thought, to tell my son. Room after room combusted until the house was a writhing skeleton, exuding the faintest smell of burning flesh as something rose and sped into the sky.

Go, Rachel thought as Lydia March's spirit went in fire. Leave this place. We're alike, you and me. We cleave to our land. We're afraid we can't hold it, but we believe we must. Ours. Ours. What a ridiculous notion. Not even our children are ours.

Abandoning the house, the men fought to keep the fire from spreading. Already it had jumped the walk and charred one side of the Hewetts'. Some of the treetops were aflame. The harbor shone red in the reflection; the sky an angry, septic yellow. Finally, the sirens stopped, and everyone stood in stunned, reverential silence as the flames died down.

Rachel forced herself to look at the once grand house. Incinerated wicker, the windows like put-out eyes. Inside, water would be soaking the blackened furniture, the damask gone, the silver melted, and all of the photographs vanished. In the dripping, smoking mess, Rachel could see it all. Her boy had returned from war. He had become a man. On this land where spirits dwelled, some other family would build a house, shinier and bigger still. The trees that blocked the view would be cleared away, and long after the March name was linked with this place, someone passing by would say, *There was a family here once, but like the glaciers, they came and went.*

Another joist collapsed, and everyone screamed. Someone was wailing, most likely Mandy, but that, too, was replaced by the stillness of absolution. In air grown thick with grief and shock, a sooty rain of ash fell, gentle as feathers, and Rachel, turning her head toward the sky, opened her mouth, welcomed it with her tongue.